UNSUITABLE MEN

THE 'COMMITMENT' SERIES BOOK 2

NIA FORRESTER

This is a work of fiction. Names, characters, places, and incidents are the product of the author's imagination or are used fictitiously. Any resemblance to actual events or persons, living or dead, is entirely coincidental.

ISBN: 9798569736423

2nd Edition

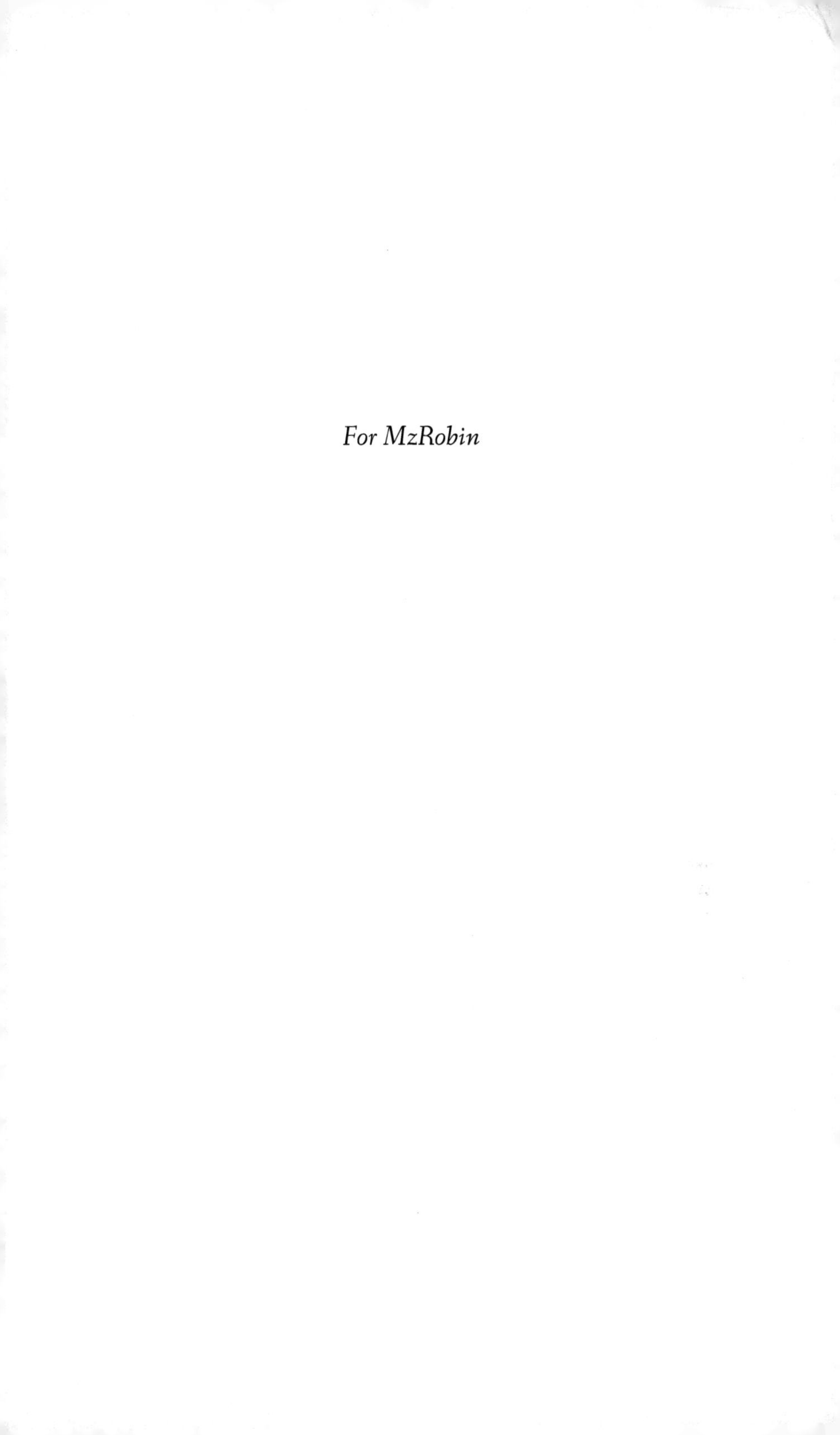

For MzRobin

ONE

"THERE'S NO POINT," TRACY SAID, BALANCING THE PHONE in the crook of her neck, surveying her fresh pedicure.

"Does everything have to have a *point*?" Riley asked. "Just come because it's Saturday and you have nothing to do. And because I'm asking you to. Please."

"And there won't be any weirdness?"

"That's completely up to you. He seems to really like this one. He may even be serious about her."

Tracy tried to ignore the immediate ping she felt just beneath her breastbone on the left side of her chest.

"Serious?"

"Well, he's mentioned her a few times and this is the third time he's brought her over and that's never happened before," Riley said. "So ..."

Brendan, serious about someone? Tracy blinked. It didn't seem likely. But stranger things had happened. Like Riley and Shawn being happily married, for instance. Of all the skeptics out there—and there had been many—no one was more skeptical than Tracy when her best friend, a progressive political writer had a whirlwind romance with and married one of the planet's biggest hip-hop stars, Shawn Gardner, also known by the absurd handle, 'K Smooth.'

After the first year of marriage from hell which no one thought they would survive—least of all Tracy—they seemed as happy as any couple she had ever known. Now they were closing in on year four and Riley, pregnant with their first child, was placid and happy as a cow in a country meadow. Not that she would have appreciated the comparison.

The coming of the baby led to them buying a house in New Jersey which Tracy helped find. It was a beautiful old five-bedroom Tudor with turrets, ivy-covered walls and an English garden and pool out back. After one of their frequent battles of wills, this time about where to raise their family, Shawn and Riley compromised by buying the house without getting rid of their Central Park condo.

Riley loved living in Manhattan and wanted to spend most of her time there while Shawn for some reason suddenly decided that even on Central Park West, there was danger around every corner for his wife and unborn child. So now they were in Jersey just about every weekend, and as often as possible, Riley roped her friends into coming out for barbecues, pool parties or brunch. And because she wasn't the kind of woman to have anything as cutesy as a "baby shower" had preemptively invited a few friends over for a cook-out now that she was one month away from her due date.

"Okay, I'll come," Tracy said finally.

So she was curious. So what? How could she *not* want to see this person that Brendan was supposedly 'serious' about? After all, one of the hallmarks of Brendan's personality was his complete and utter lack of seriousness.

"What's her name?" she asked, keeping her voice casual.

"Meghan," Riley said. "She's not at all like the other women I've seen him with."

"So she's not a model, or hoping to break into Broadway as a dancer?" Tracy asked, trying and failing to keep the sarcasm out of her voice.

"Nope. I think she's an accountant or something. In fact, under different circumstances, I could see you two being friends."

Tracy bit back the knee-jerk response that rose to her lips, which was something along the lines of, 'no way in hell'. After all, why should she care who Brendan was dating?

"I'm sure I'll like her just fine."

"Good," Riley said. "And if you could come a little early that would be great. You can make yourself useful by, I don't know, helping me out of chairs and stuff. I feel like such a whale."

Tracy laughed. "That's what husbands are for."

"When Shawn's around I try to pretend like I can do everything I've always done," Riley said. "He's been pressuring me to take my maternity leave, so I don't need to give him any more ammunition."

"Ah, I see," Tracy said.

She was only half-listening. She couldn't get out of her head the idea of Brendan with an actual girlfriend. And someone of substance at that. The bimbos were no competition —not that she was competing—but someone with an actual career ...

"So get here around noon. You can help me get out of the tub," Riley said, only half-joking.

As soon as she hung up, Tracy was already planning what she would wear. If Brendan was bringing a woman, she would have to look amazing. The thought embarrassed her because she had spent the last three and a half years telling herself she wasn't at all interested in him, reminding herself that they were just friends. *So what on earth did it matter how she looked when she met his girlfriend?*

But, Tracy reasoned, she also hadn't seen Brendan in about four months. Not since he had become COO for So Def Records, Shawn's label. Now that he was no longer Shawn's manager, he traveled less but it had the opposite effect from what she expected.

While their best friends were going through their relationship drama, Tracy and Brendan had been thrown together quite a bit, and over time became good friends themselves, but things had changed. His being local and not traveling as much hadn't made any difference—she never saw him now. Perhaps even less than she had when he was globetrotting with Shawn.

It shouldn't have surprised her. Men didn't like being put in the friendship column, especially when they made their interest you in more than that abundantly clear, as Brendan had done with Tracy. Still, there was no way around it then and there was no way around it now. Brendan did not fit into her life plan.

True, he was almost perfect for her physically—tall, lean and with angular good looks—but in almost all other respects he was wholly unsuitable and over the years when he occasionally made a move, she made sure he understood that. Even before she saw what Riley went through trying to adjust to becoming the wife of a rap star, she was sure that no one who lived in that world could be the right person for her. Though Brendan wasn't performing onstage, his life was pretty interchangeable with Shawn's. The incessant travel, the nightclubs, the women and all the hallmarks of a subculture that produced what Tracy considered, at the end of the day, crude music.

Nope, she knew what she wanted and Brendan was not it.

Still, that was no reason she couldn't look good when she saw him and met his new girlfriend.

TRACY COULD NOT RECALL a time in her life when she had not commanded attention. From she was a little girl, she remembered people telling her mother how beautiful she was, so that by the time she was twelve and had begun to get male attention, she saw it as her due. When she walked into a room, heads turned. Her hazel eyes were large and arresting and her unusual coloring—burnt sienna hair and skin tone the color of a honeycomb—something that set her apart. And though her family tended toward tall but hippy women, she made sure she didn't suffer that fate by scrupulously adhering to a low-carb diet, doing cardio five days a week and yoga on weekends to make sure her long legs remained lithe and lean.

Still, her looks came with one drawback: women tended to hate her on sight, or reach the conclusion that she was likely to be hateful herself. She noticed it first in high school when friends and acquaintances alike pushed her away after a very short period of time, deciding that they didn't like her any longer for very vague and sometimes nonexistent infractions. But Tracy thought it more likely that they couldn't stand the competition.

That her friends' boyfriends sometimes became besotted with her was not her fault, but she was invariably blamed. She coped by developing aloofness to mask the hurt of being rejected. And later, she learned how to make the most out of being so often alone. When she had no girlfriends with whom to spend her time, she studied. And all that studying on Friday nights paid off when she graduated at the top of her class.

By the time she got to Gilchrist College, she was prepared

for a repeat of her high school experience and had developed a resilience that most college freshmen probably didn't have. This time she fully expected *not* to have all-nighters with a best friend, braiding hair and doing each other's manicures. She assumed she would date, but expected to spend much of her remaining free time alone.

She hadn't been prepared for her freshman year roommate, an artsy, quirky girl who wore clothes that looked like they were from Goodwill or the seventies, and had a head full of crazy unkempt curls. Her name was Riley Terry, and she was sitting on a pile of boxes when Tracy entered their dorm room for the first time. Riley looked up and did a literal double-take.

Holy crap, she said, *you're stunning!*

It was the first time in Tracy's memory that another girl had told her she was pretty without having an envious or resentful edge to their voice. It was disarming.

From that moment on, Riley slowly chipped away at the walls Tracy had spent her entire adolescence fortifying and by the middle of freshman year, they were inseparable; and had been ever since. Today, Tracy could think of no one, not even among people to whom she was related by blood, who was as important to her as Riley.

But there was still part of her that wondered how it was that her best friend had so easily wandered into the love of her life while she—the so-called beautiful one—had been so luckless. Not that Riley didn't deserve it, but she had never been preoccupied with finding Mr. Right. Heck, even when she did, Riley was ambivalent about getting married and only did it because he would accept nothing less.

Tracy walked into her large closet and looked through her considerable collection, wondering what would be most suitable to the task of looking sexy-without-trying-too-hard at a poolside brunch. She finally settled on an orange knit maxi-dress with a crocheted racer-back. It complemented her complexion perfectly, looked great with gold accessories and made her toned arms and shoulders look amazing. She would wear it with her brown wedges and put her hair up in a sloppy ponytail that would belie the thought and effort she put into her appearance.

THE DRIVE OUT to Jersey only took about forty-five minutes. Tracy enjoyed those occasions when she could take her Range Rover out for a real spin, not just the stops and starts that typified life in Park Slope, Brooklyn. If it wasn't for alternate side of the street parking, there would be entire weeks when she didn't have reason to start the engine, so maybe this brunch would serve a purpose after all.

When she bought the SUV, Riley warned her that she would regret it, and truthfully, it was an unnecessary extravagance. But she'd made so much in bonuses the last couple of years that the growing bank balances had only heightened her sense of having no core purpose, and no person with whom to share her success. Getting rid of the money by buying things like an expensive SUV and pricey designer clothes made her feel better. And it wasn't as though she was irresponsible about it. Besides, as a hedge fund manager, the bonuses seemed to keep rolling right on in.

When she was five minutes away from Riley's Tracy checked her face in the rearview mirror to make sure her lipstick held up and taking out her phone, dialed Riley's number.

Shawn answered. Great.

"Hey Tracy," he said.

His voice was flat. Shawn and she had never completely

warmed to each other and it was only partly because she had given him a hard time about Riley when she thought they were all wrong for each other. She also knew for a fact he thought she had strung Brendan along. So *he* at least had to be happy about this Meghan person.

"Hey Shawn, is she around?" Tracy asked, keeping her voice cheerful.

"Getting dressed. What's up?"

"Just letting her know I'm almost there, that's all. Anyone else there yet?"

"Yeah," he said.

Tracy waited, but he didn't say who. And of all the people she didn't want to ask about Brendan, Shawn would be at the top of the list.

"Okay, so tell Riley I'll see her in a few," she said.

"Yup. See you soon."

He hung up and Tracy rolled her eyes at the phone. That man sure knew how to hold a grudge. Granted they would never be best friends, but you would think he could manage to be a little nicer to his first kid's godmother.

By the time she pulled up to the security post, Tracy was feeling a lot more confident. She punched in the security code and waited for the wrought iron gates to open, honking the horn as she pulled up the long gravel driveway. Still, as she parked next to the white BMW roadster, which was she was quite sure was not Shawn's or Riley's, she could feel some apprehension returning.

Aside from Riley, Brendan was one of her best friends, or at least he had been until he fell off the edge of the earth. It would be awkward figuring out how to greet him after all this time had passed, and when he had a woman with him who he was involved with. Perhaps coming had been a bad idea, she decided. But it was too late now.

As the enormous front door swung open, Tracy could not help but smile at the sight of her friend coming toward her. Riley was at the end of her pregnancy but still looked like someone who had maybe swallowed a watermelon whole. She was all belly, with very few of the unattractive elements of pregnancy, lucky heifer. Her arms and legs seemed to have remained pretty close to the same size though her boobs were bigger and her face slightly fuller. Her hair had grown fuller and thicker as well. She now wore it out more often than not, in a mass of messy curls down past her shoulder blades.

Today, like Tracy she was wearing a maxi-dress though hers was white with spaghetti straps and on her feet she wore brown sandals.

"You're waddling," Tracy lied as she got out of the truck, reaching for the bottle of wine she brought along for the occasion.

Riley laughed. "Shut up. I can't wait for you to experience the pressure of an infant's head against your cervix."

"Ugh. Spare me the details," Tracy said, hugging her.

"Come on in," Riley said looping her arm through hers. "Don't worry he's not here yet. It's just Chris."

"Oh." Tracy relaxed. "Are you sure he's coming?"

"I'm not sure if you're hoping he will, or hoping he won't," Riley said glancing at her as they entered the foyer.

"I'm not sure myself," Tracy admitted.

The house was beautiful, worthy of a write-up in a design magazine. Riley had gotten over her aversion to being wealthy at least for as long as it took to get this decorating job done, probably because she was pregnant and too exhausted to do it herself. She had even gone so far as to hire one of the most famous celebrity designers in New York to complete the task. The result was a warm, homey interior filled with craftsman pieces and clean Shaker lines. Like their Central Park condo, they had chosen earth tones but with the occasional burst or orange and red hues.

Riley led Tracy out to the back where under the loggia, Shawn and his friend Chris Scaife were sitting, each with a beer in hand. They looked up as she and Riley entered.

"Hey Tracy," Chris said. "Long time no see."

"Chris."

As with Shawn, there was no love lost between Tracy and Chris Scaife. As one of the biggest rap moguls in the world, he was a walking, talking breathing symbol of what ailed Black America as far as Tracy was concerned. I mean, as rich as he was, would it kill the man to pull his pants up to the waist? But other than that, she bore him no personal ill will. He was just one of those men who, if he wasn't sleeping with you or planning to, or you weren't unavailable to him for some other reason (like Riley was), he really had no inclination to give you the time of day.

"You want something to drink?" Shawn asked, standing.

"Sure," Tracy said amiably. "A sauvignon?"

Shawn headed for the bar at one corner of the loggia and Tracy took a seat where she could watch the sunlight reflecting off the pool and admire the splendor of the pink tea roses in bloom nearby. She turned and watched as Riley joined her husband at the bar and he handed her a glass of what looked like cranberry juice.

Riley took it from him and tilted her head back to look up at him, a slight smile on her face. He gazed back at her and one corner of his mouth turned upward. He reached out and playfully tugged a lock of Riley's hair. Tracy looked away, feeling like an intruder.

Say would she might about Shawn, he definitely adored Riley. Not just loved, but *adored*. There was almost nothing about his life that had remained unchanged since she had come into it. Despite his fame, money and his considerable physical attractiveness—that even Tracy had to grudgingly acknowledge—he seemed not to see anyone else.

Unable to help herself, Tracy glanced in their direction yet again, just in time to see Riley reach out and place Shawn's hand on the swell of her pregnant belly while sipping her cranberry juice and him smiling, probably feeling the baby kick.

"So what have you been up to, Chris?" she asked, tearing her gaze away from them again.

"The usual," he said, taking a gulp of his beer. "Defending America against bullshit pop music."

In spite of herself, Tracy smiled. "Yeah well it's a dirty job ..."

"But someone had to do it," Chris finished for her.

"Well, then I'm glad the task is in your capable hands," she said.

"Don't listen to him," Riley called from the bar. "I saw a Lisa P CD in his car a couple weeks ago," she said naming the latest pop princess to saturate the airwaves.

"Well, you have to know the enemy," Chris said unfazed.

Shawn returned with her wine and Tracy took it gratefully.

She needed a drink, fast. If she was beginning to enjoy Chris Scaife's humor, she must be lonelier and more desperate for male companionship than she thought.

"You guys want to get that grill started?" Riley suggested. "We're only expecting a few other people."

"How few?" Tracy asked.

If it was only Brendan and his girlfriend, she was going to kill Riley. If she had known it was going to be such a small party, she would have brought a date. Either that or she would be stuck with Chris Scaife all afternoon.

"Just another six or so," Riley said. "Want to come help me get these steaks and stuff together?"

"Still no household help?" Tracy asked, her voice disapproving. Riley and her arbitrary austerity measures.

"Nope," Shawn said. "No household help. I think she's hoping that going up and down the stairs will bring on an early labor."

Clearly Tracy had stumbled across one of his pet peeves.

"At this point, if I go into labor it's hardly *early*," Riley said. "I'm well within the range."

"Not for a first kid," Shawn said.

"Okay Shawn. Whatever. C'mon Tracy ..."

"Bickering over meaningless crap?" a voice said from the entrance to the house. "I know I'm in the right place now."

Everyone looked around. Brendan was standing at the door. He was wearing a white polo, chinos with brown loafers and looked like someone who had just come from a cruise; relaxed and at ease. Maybe it was because he was in the presence of old friends, but Tracy feared that it might be something else. Like maybe the young woman at his side.

She had a fashionable tousled pixie-cut and the perfectly-even oval-shaped face ideal to pull it off; she was pretty and petite, and wore a denim summer dress and bright white tennis shoes. Tracy expected her to be attractive and she was, though that was not what shook her.

What she wasn't able to process, couldn't even bring herself to look directly at, was the unpleasant fact that Brendan was holding her hand.

TWO

He never held women's hands. On the very few occasions when Brendan had brought women around, Tracy was relegated to guessing whether they were dates or not. Most of the time, it was the women who staked their claim, touching him in some way to demonstrate that he was with them. But this time, he seemed not to intend to let go of this woman's hand, even when he realized Tracy was there.

Riley was right. It *was* serious.

"Tracy," he said, his face breaking out into a smile. "Stranger!"

Tracy stood and returned his smile, maintaining it even when he brought Meghan along as he came toward her. At least he let the girl go long enough to hug her. Meghan was probably only about five-foot four, which to Tracy's mind made her a ridiculous match for Brendan who was somewhere in the neighborhood of an imposing six-five.

"It's been a while," he said. "At least well before Rae turned into a beach ball."

"Hey!" Riley said, laughing.

Riley and Brendan were very close, bonded in part by the fact that they were the closest people in the world to Shawn and one of a small handful of people he let in. Only Brendan called Riley by the nickname 'Rae', and only occasionally did he use it.

"It was a few months ago," Tracy acknowledged, nodding.

"I missed you, Trace," he said.

Tracy's smile faltered. "You too," she mumbled.

"Did you?" Brendan grinned at her. "Miss me I mean?"

Tracy felt her face grow hot with her blush.

"So," she said briskly, looking at Meghan. "I'm Tracy ..."

"Tracy's been Riley's friend since college," Brendan explained.

"Yes," Tracy said pointedly, stung by the implication that she was *only* Riley's friend and not his. "A friend of Riley's."

She took Meghan's hand and shook it briefly.

"Nice to meet you," Meghan said, smiling. "I think I've heard Riley mention you a few times."

Tracy resented the implication that Meghan and Riley, Brendan and Shawn had socialized together in her absence. But clearly that had been the case. And it wasn't as though Tracy had her own plus-one to bring to these little gatherings. Great, so now Meghan was moving in on her best friend as well as her ... as well as Brendan. She had slightly crooked bottom teeth, Tracy noted with pleasure, and her lips were a little too thin. She was pretty, but nothing to write home about, for sure.

"Meghan, can I get you something to drink?" Riley asked from behind them.

"If you've got a red that would be great. Thanks," Meghan said.

"Sure. Merlot? Malbec? What's your preference?"

"Why don't I come see what you have?" Meghan suggested.

She followed Riley over to the bar so that Tracy and Brendan were left alone for the moment. Tracy sipped her wine and looked again out to the pool. She should have brought a swimsuit. She had a brand new white one that made her breasts look amazing.

"So what's been up with you?"

Brendan reached out and ran a hand down her arm to get her attention. Tracy instinctively jerked away from his touch and his smile faltered for a second. For a moment she felt badly for making him think she didn't like it when he touched her. Problem was, as she recalled, she liked it too much.

"I should be the one asking that," Tracy said. She cursed herself for sounding like she was accusing him of something.

"Well you know I transitioned at work, right? So now I'm back in NYC. Getting used to being stationary is an adjustment."

"You seem to be making out just fine," she said, drinking more of her wine.

Brendan leaned in, his eyes searching hers. "What's with the attitude?" he asked softly.

Tracy sighed.

She didn't mean to give him attitude. She meant to be as cool as a cucumber. But she was still a little thrown by the hand-holding. Not that she was jealous or anything, it was just ... unexpected was all.

And Brendan was supposed to be her friend as well. How was it that he never mentioned that he was serious about someone? How was it that he had *gotten* serious with someone and hadn't bothered to try to see her these past few months? Not so much as a phone call to invite her for drinks. Or just the phone call, for that matter.

They used to talk on the phone all the time. It was something she had looked forward to, especially with Riley newly married and all. She missed him. And evidently while she was doing that, he was dating Little Meghan.

"No attitude intended," she said looking up at him. "And I am happy to see you, Brendan. Even if I ..."

"*Whew*," Meghan returned with a glass of red wine in hand. "It's a scorcher today, isn't it?"

"Hellish," Tracy agreed, before Riley came to collect her to help in the kitchen.

For the first few minutes, Riley didn't say anything, so Tracy was beginning to think she had escaped the inquisition. But of course not. That would have been too much to expect.

"So how did you feel?" Riley asked, cutting to the chase. "Seeing him with her?"

"Fine," Tracy said breezily. "Why would I feel anything other than fine? Brendan and I have only been ..."

"Friends, yes. I know," Riley said, busying herself with pulling a tray out of the enormous Viking refrigerator. It was laden with rib eyes marinating in what looked like a garlic balsamic emulsion. "Except for, you know. The one time."

The one time. Yes. There was that.

Tracy took the tray from Riley and put it on the center island, turning to await further instructions. Riley's eyes were searching hers, clearly trying to read her true emotions, as only she was capable of doing. Finding nothing, or more likely deciding to pretend she hadn't, Riley turned once again to the refrigerator, this time pulling out a bowl of what looked like spinach salad.

"You're like Little Suzy Homemaker," Tracy commented. "Making salads, marinating meats ..."

"Yeah," Riley said, sounding in awe of herself. "I'm telling you, there is something to that whole nesting thing. I wake up in the middle of the night with an uncontrollable urge to start cleaning the bathroom. It's the craziest thing." Tracy looked at her and Riley laughed. "I'm serious!"

"And do you do it?" Tracy asked. "Get up and clean the bathroom?"

"No. That would be giving in to the crazy. And no matter what, you can't give in to the crazy."

"Well at least you'd be joining Shawn."

"He's actually calmed down quite a bit since we spend so much time out here. I even managed to talk him out of that stupid bodyguard idea."

"Well, *that* idea actually wasn't that stupid," Tracy said, taking the salad from Riley and putting it next to the tray of steaks. "People are still really curious about you two. And I bet a lot of women hate your guts because you're carrying Shawn's baby."

"If you feed into it, the next thing you know, you won't be able to go to Target without a small army," Riley said shaking her head. "If I ignore them, people pretty much take their picture and go away."

"Anything I can help with in here?"

Tracy and Riley looked around as Meghan came sauntering in, wineglass in hand.

"You could take these out," Riley indicated the steaks and smiled at her. "Thank you."

Meghan put her wineglass aside and took the tray. Tracy watched her as she left, sizing up her figure, and her walk, assessing her general attractiveness quotient. Brendan usually liked his women taller, around five-nine at least, and more overtly beautiful. This understatedly pretty girl was a change for him. So obviously his attraction to her went beyond the skin-deep.

"You're going to have to stop looking at her like that," Riley said, her voice quiet.

"How am I looking at her?"

"Like you want to scratch her eyes out."

"You only see that because you know me so well."

"Ah, so you do want to scratch her eyes out," Riley said, raising an eyebrow.

"The thought did cross my mind," Tracy admitted.

"Well banish it," Riley said firmly. "Right now."

They both laughed and Tracy nudged her friend in the shoulder.

By the time the festivities got underway, they had been joined by two other couples, the closest neighbors of Shawn and Riley's and a young attorney who had once represented Shawn and become a friend along with her husband. By default, Tracy was thrown together with Chris who, though he was pretty amusing company, did not adequately distract her from Brendan and Meghan sitting apart from everyone else, near the pool talking and eating from the same plate.

Riley and Shawn intermittently mingled with their guests and sat on a chaise together, Shawn's legs wide apart, Riley reclining against his chest. Watching them together Tracy was reminded that men could change. If they loved you enough, and you were willing to hang in there through the growing pains, they could become the man of your dreams. Rarely, but it did happen. And the Lord knew, few if any came ready-made.

Shawn certainly hadn't. Though he was the one who pushed the whole marriage agenda, it would be fair to say that he had been dragged kicking and screaming into the whole monogamy thing. But now that he was there, even Tracy would stake her life that he never even looked at other women in the way he now looked at his wife. Like she was the only one of her kind in the history of womanhood. Because for him, she probably was.

As the sun set, everyone gathered under the loggia for a good-natured argument about politics. Riley was always the instigator of these discussions. She had started a new publication a couple years back that was quickly building a reputation as the African American community's version of *The New Yorker*. While Tracy was proud of her, it was all a little too intellectually high-brow for her. She liked to think of herself as having exhausted her brain cells for only as long as it took to graduate from college and get a high-paying career. Riley on the other hand liked to think about things because she, well, *liked* to think about things.

Tracy stayed at the edge of the conversation, not quite a part of it, sipping her fourth glass of wine, feeling a mellow sleepiness begin to overtake her. It was almost nine o'clock and she didn't much relish the idea of driving back to Brooklyn. She could probably crash in one of Riley's spare rooms and head out early in the morning if it came to that, or maybe she could say her goodbyes now. She looked up, trying to make eye-contact with Riley, hoping to signal how tired she was when she instead met Brendan's gaze.

Tracy gave him a half-smile which he returned. Next to him, Meghan was leaning in, engrossed in the conversation, listening to Chris talk about some campaign Riley had roped him into joining to include get out the vote messages on all his artists' new CD jackets.

"C'mon walk with me," Brendan said to her. "Let's get a drink."

Tracy stood and followed him as he went over to the bar, going behind it to look through Shawn's considerable array of alcohol. Tracy leaned forward, watching him as he did. Brendan held up a bottle of tequila, his eyes questioning.

"No thanks," Tracy laughed. "As it is, I'm not sure I'm going to be able to make the drive home."

"Then don't," Brendan said. "From the looks of Riley she could go into labor any second and Shawn might need you to bring him hot water and towels."

"Hmm. I'm pretty sure all he'll need is someone to call 911 since he's going to be a nervous wreck."

"Yup," Brendan agreed, laughing. He glanced over at where Shawn was walking around the pool, sipping on a beer. "I don't think he's figured out yet that this means he's actually coming back from the hospital with a kid. But that's Shawn, all heart but no head when it comes to Riley."

Brendan poured them each a shot and slid one across the bar to Tracy. She looked at it for only a moment before lifting it. He knocked his glass briefly against hers before tossing back the clear liquid in one quick gulp. Tracy followed suit, enjoying the heat on the back of her throat.

After going clean-shaven for awhile, Brendan had grown a goatee once again she noted. Impeccably-shaped, and smooth to the touch as silk. Unbidden, a memory returned to her, of the scratch of his facial hair against the sensitive skin of her inner thighs and the pleasant burn as it brushed against ...

"Don't fall asleep on me," Brendan was saying. "Damn, I didn't know you'd pass out from a single shot, Trace."

She smiled. "I'm not. I was just thinking."

"About?"

She knew she shouldn't; and that it was unfair. But she said it anyway.

"I was thinking about that night," she said, looking him directly in the eye.

That night. Their code for ten reckless hours spent together over two years ago. Ten hours that Tracy, despite her best efforts, had been unable to get out of her mind. Brendan looked at her now, his eyes hooded. She couldn't tell whether he was remembering it as fondly as she was, or was just annoyed that she brought it up at all with Meghan a few feet away.

"I'm sorry," she said quickly, before he could respond. "That was tacky, with your girlfriend sitting just over there."

"Not my girlfriend." He shook his head.

"Really? I thought you didn't do repeats," Tracy said. "Riley said you've brought her over before."

Brendan smiled. He had the best smile. His eyes practically disappeared when he smiled. It wasn't all lips and teeth. His entire face smiled.

"Didn't know you cared," he said.

"I wish I didn't," she said. Maybe it was all the alcohol, but she seemed unable to censor herself.

"Tracy, I know you," Brendan said. "Fifty percent of why you care is competition. I don't recall you blowing up my phone these last few months, even though you knew I was around. So I show up with someone else and all of a sudden, you've been thinking about me?"

"I didn't say I *had* been thinking about you. I said I *am* thinking about you right now."

"Is anything different?" Brendan asked, suddenly serious.

Tracy swallowed. "Excuse me?" she asked. But she was stalling. She knew precisely what he meant.

"Since the last time we had this conversation. Is anything different? Does the fact that I have a desk job now make a difference? Is that what this is?"

There was an edge to his voice, a tone that suggested he was a little bit angry with her, or at a minimum, frustrated. And why wouldn't he be?

"I wasn't thinking about any of that," she admitted. "I was just thinking about ... how it was. It was good. Wasn't it, that night?"

"Yeah. It was," he said almost resentfully. "Better than good."

Brendan poured himself another shot and offered her one as well, but Tracy shook her head. When he looked up at her again, there was unmistakable annoyance etched on his face.

Tracy turned away from him and headed back to the circle where everyone else seemed to be preparing to leave. Putting a hand on Riley's shoulder, she pulled her aside and let her know she probably wouldn't be driving back.

"No problem," Riley said. "You know where everything is. Are you going up now?"

"Yeah," Tracy nodded. "I think between the heat and the wine, I'm done. I'll help with clean-up in the morning if ..."

"No, no worries. Go get some sleep." Riley's glance shifted momentarily to the bar where Brendan was just tossing back his third shot. She squeezed Tracy's arm before rejoining her guests.

Upstairs, Tracy took a shower in the guest suite and changed into a t-shirt she pilfered from the master bedroom. She could hear the activity downstairs; it sounded like the party was breaking up after all. Turning off all the lights in the suite, she crawled under the covers of the immense bed and hugged one of the pillows. She was tired, but unable to sleep, thinking about Brendan's words: *fifty percent of why you care is competition*, he'd said.

It was true that she felt competitive toward Meghan, but that wasn't because she didn't value him, it was because she did. But that didn't change the fact that Brendan was the walking, talking epitome of what her mother had always told her could end in her ruin: a good-looking, fast-talking, fast-living, charming rascal. A man who seemed so easy and affable that he reeled you in, stole your heart and eventually, finally, left you in shreds because he never had, and never could see you as anything more than a playmate.

Not that Brendan would ever be at all mean about it; in fact, he was probably quite the opposite. He was the guy who would treat women like queens, whispered sweet nothings in their ear, all the while leading them out the front door, never to call again. He hadn't done that to her because she avoided letting it get that far. There had only been the one time. And the only thing that complicated it was that she had to go on seeing him after that, and that they were friends. And that he was so damn *sweet* to her.

Tracy shook her head as though hoping to shake out all thoughts of him and turned over, pulling the pillow closer. But he'd looked so good tonight. Smelled so good. And that smile.

Who was he to smile at her like that? Asshole.

IT WAS THE *GRAMMYS*. How could anyone avoid getting excited about the Grammys?

When Riley mentioned it, Tracy jumped at the chance. Not because she was a music fan necessarily, but she did enjoy glitz, glamour and any excuse to get dressed to the nines and hang out. The ceremony was only part of it. Shawn and Riley got A-lister seats and would be visible during the primetime broadcast, while Tracy sat with Brendan a couple of rows back. She didn't care. She was within reach of the guys from OutKast, and could smell Keri Hilson's perfume from where she sat.

All through the show, Brendan leaned in, telling her funny inside stories about some of the performers: like who had terrible B.O. after each performance, who kept vodka in their water bottle as he danced and sang his way his way half-intoxicated through every performance, and who made it a habit of sleeping with her dancers while banning her husband from her tour.

Halfway through the show—which was way longer than one might think if they'd only ever watched it on television—Brendan leaned back in his seat and stretched his long legs in front of him, resting an arm across the back of Tracy's chair as he stretched. And suddenly she was hyper-aware of him; his scent, his masculinity, the size of his hand resting on his thigh.

During the second half of the show, it was obvious he was growing restless, as was she. The speeches had all begun to blend one into the other, and soon she didn't care who won. She couldn't even have said if Shawn's category had gone by. Brendan seemed to sense this and without warning, he gripped her hand and pulled her up from her seat, leading her out through the back of the auditorium.

Outside it had only just begun to get dark and they weren't the only ones making a break for it. Some of the performers were getting into their cars, waving at fans as they did, probably off to prepare for the much more important post-Grammy parties.

Tracy was surprised how many times Brendan got stopped, how many high-profile artists knew him by name and seemed to want to talk to him. He laughed and joked with them, carried on relaxed conversations and introduced her to everyone. With each person who stopped him, he leaned somewhat away from them and in her direction, signaling with his body language that he didn't have much time to chat, that he was on his way someplace else.

Finally, he pulled out his phone and made a call, and moments later, grabbed her hand again, pulling her into a limo—one of a long line of identical vehicles—that eventually made its way to the curb in front of them. Inside, the air was cool, offering welcome relief from the muggy Los Angeles evening, and better yet, there was a bar.

Brendan had immediately gone for it, holding up a bottle of chilled champagne for her approval.

"God, yes," she sighed and he laughed out loud.

They had watched some of the show on television from the cool confines of the limo, eating the snacks and chocolate-covered strawberries from the mini-refrigerator.

"I think I like the Grammys better on TV," Tracy admitted.

"This is probably the first time in over ten years I've watched it on television," Brendan said.

Tracy looked at him then, noticing for the first time that he looked a little tired. This was his work, she recalled. Not something he did for fun, which made her wonder what he *did* do for fun. So much of their growing friendship centered on what was happening with Shawn and Riley, she sometimes forgot to think of him as a whole and separate being from his famous best friend and client. Even her anger at Shawn she had taken out on him on occasion.

"What would Shawn do if he came out of the auditorium and you were gone?" she asked.

Brendan thought about it for a moment. "He would call me. And if I didn't answer, he'd leave it alone."

"He wouldn't be pissed?" Tracy asked.

Brendan laughed. "Nah. He'd be relieved. He'd probably skip out on all the parties—which I would never let him do—and go back to the hotel to spend some quiet time with Riley."

"So let's let him do that," Tracy said.

Brendan opened his mouth to resist her suggestion but after a moment closed it again.

"What would we do instead?" he asked.

But it wasn't a suggestive question, it was asked as though

he had never considered for a moment what he might do with his time if he wasn't spending it managing Shawn's career.

"Anything you want," Tracy said. "But my inclination? I say we go back and change into jeans, sit around eating pizza and watch pay-per-view."

It wasn't the evening she had in mind when she planned her trip to the Grammys for sure. And if she stuck to Shawn and Riley there was no telling how many high-profile not-to-be-missed insider parties she would get to go to. But at that moment when she saw the look of boyish exhilaration on Brendan's face, there was nothing else she could imagine she would rather do than sit in a hotel room with him and eat fattening food while watching bad action movies.

TRACY LISTENED as Shawn and Riley ascended the stairs and heard their tread on the wood floors as they passed her door on the way to the master suite. Then there was the sound of footsteps stopping and turning back. She shut her eyes just in time as Riley opened the door, peeking in to check on her. She didn't feel like talking and rehashing the evening. Her emotions were all in a jumble and she was preoccupied by the thought of Brendan heading home with his not-girlfriend Meghan.

On nights like this one, it seemed so foolish to stick to these rules she made for herself about men, weeding them out, the suitable from the unsuitable. She had put Brendan firmly in the unsuitable column and had done so a long time ago, so why was she obsessing like this? Because she was alone, for one thing. Riley had seized love with Shawn with both hands, damn the torpedoes, and now look at her.

Despite the bumps along the way, she was better off. And while Tracy wasn't all-out crazy about Brendan, or even a little in love with him, she liked spending time with him. *Why shouldn't she just embrace that?* Maybe if she did, she wouldn't be alone almost every night hugging pillows.

Right now, there was no doubt Brendan was hugging a lot more than that. Probably screwing Little Meghan's brains out. She would be a high-pitched screamer, Tracy was certain. And Brendan knew how to make a girl scream, that was for damn sure.

Around one a.m. when Tracy was sure she would never get to sleep, she slipped out of bed and headed down to the kitchen to nibble on leftovers. Riley and Shawn had a pretty elaborate alarm system but Riley told her they never armed the motion sensors inside the house. Shawn had a habit of getting out of bed in the middle of the night and wandering into his studio downstairs just beyond the living room to listen to and mix music. And Riley herself liked to do some writing in her office pretty early as well, so they never used the internal alarms for fear of tripping one accidentally.

Tracy sat in the kitchen eating cold steak and salad and poured herself a glass of red wine, knowing that its narcotic effect, along with the full stomach would have her drifting off to sleep in no time once she made her way back to the bedroom. She would have to double her workout tomorrow to make up for the late-night meal. In front of her, on the kitchen counter was a card which she idly opened while taking her last swallow of wine. It was from Meghan, wishing Shawn and Riley "all the happiness and joy in the world" when they welcomed their "little one." How cute.

As she made her way back up the stairs, Tracy hesitated at the sound of a voice. Wondering whether Shawn and Riley were still up, she paused, standing still for a moment. There it was again, the voice, but not speaking. Not intelligibly anyhow.

Tracy rolled her eyes. *Seriously?*

It was the sound of her best friend, eight months pregnant but *still* getting some. Were pregnant people that huge supposed to do that? What could you even *do* with all that belly?

She gave a shudder and quickly returned to the guest suite and shut the door, climbing back into bed without bothering to brush her teeth again, and putting the pillow over her head, preferring not to fall asleep to the sound of someone else's clearly satisfying lovemaking.

THREE

WHEN SHE AWOKE JUST AFTER SIX, TRACY FULLY expected that no one else would be up, but when she got to the kitchen, Shawn was already there, standing shirtless and wearing only boxer briefs at the open refrigerator, drinking directly from a carton of orange juice. Remembering the sounds that emanated from the master suite the previous evening, she considered slipping back out of the kitchen before she was detected, but he turned as she entered.

Tracy noted his arresting physique—v-shaped torso, narrow waist and enviable abs. She discreetly averted her eyes and turned to find coffee.

"Hey," he said. "Forgot you were here."

Clearly, Tracy thought. *If the racket you and Riley made last night is any indication.*

"Yup. Still here. But I'll be out of your hair as soon as I get some coffee," she said, looking through the cabinets.

The coffee was just out of her reach. Shawn came over and reached above her, setting it down on the counter.

"Thanks," she murmured. "Riley awake?"

"Nope. She sleeps later these days. It's hard for her to get comfortable at night so she stays up a lot later."

Tracy moved about the kitchen, grabbing things for her coffee. It had been a while since she had awoken to anything other than solitude. She wouldn't have minded sitting out on the loggia and having breakfast with someone, making leisurely, comfortable conversation. But Shawn probably wasn't her best bet for that kind of morning. Over the years they had many conversations, and none of them that she recalled could be characterized as "comfortable."

"She say anything to you about when she might take off work?" he asked.

This was as close as Shawn would ever come to enlisting her help with anything. She knew he wanted Riley on bed-rest or at the very least staying home, and she also knew that Riley was resisting. For him to have mentioned it to her was his oblique way of finding out whether she might join his team.

"Yes, she told me she plans to take off when she goes into labor," Tracy said, her tone flippant.

A muscle at Shawn's jaw twitched.

She couldn't help it; she still enjoyed goading him. Part of it was a throwback from the days when she was certain he was the worst idea in the world for her best friend, but the other part, the part she rarely acknowledged even to herself, was that it rankled her that he never seemed to be in the least bit attracted to her. Not even a little bit. Few men found her as uninteresting as Shawn did.

Shawn seemed to see through her somehow. He understood what others didn't—that beauty didn't mean anything and the only purpose it served was to mask a multitude of sins. Being so beautiful himself had likely taught him that lesson. The difference between them was that while she was only too willing to exploit her good looks to her advantage, Shawn seemed to find the extra attention tiresome. It satisfied Tracy to remember that it hadn't always been that way.

There had been a time when they were two of a kind—somewhat selfish, spoiled, and impatient. Tracy had always suspected that he didn't like her at least partly because she was so important to Riley, and he wanted that position all to himself. The turmoil he had gone through in his marriage and with his career a couple years back had changed him though, and now he was a more mature man, a more patient husband, and to Brendan, a better friend.

According to Riley, he had actually *fired* Brendan as his manager, telling him that he needed to settle some place and get an actual life; an act of selfless friendship that didn't make one iota of business sense since Brendan was the manager who had ushered him to the highest pinnacle of his career. So, while Shawn had changed, she remained very much the same. It was unfair of him to judge her, she thought, when he understood perhaps as no one else did, what it was like to be catered to, indulged, deferred to. With him, it was in large measure because of his fame as well as his looks, with her it was entirely because she was beautiful in a way most women wished they were.

"Did she tell you about her last doctor's appointment?" Shawn asked from behind her as she watched her coffee brew.

Tracy shut her eyes and inhaled the welcome scent of the roasted beans. "Uh uh. Nope."

"Her blood pressure's higher than it should be," Shawn said. He sounded almost accusatory. "And her amniotic fluid levels were low."

Tracy's eyes popped open and she turned to face Shawn again, feeling chastened. She assumed he wanted Riley to quit working because of his usual overprotective BS, which sometimes looked an awful lot like control to Tracy. But apparently she was wrong.

Shawn was leaning against the kitchen counter across from her, his arms folded. Tracy could see that there was real worry in his eyes even though he was masking it with irritation.

"Well," she said quietly. "It's not as though it's life-threatening, right? If she agrees to take it easy and maybe cut back on …"

"I know you couldn't possibly be talking about me behind my back," Riley said.

She had clearly just woken up because her hair was pulled back messily and she was wearing only a thin tank nightdress that stopped mid-thigh, made shorter by her burgeoning belly.

God, Tracy thought. Her boobs were *huge*. She was pretty sure she wanted kids someday but the bodily changes freaked her out a little. Especially the idea of voluntarily allowing herself to gain weight.

Riley headed in Shawn's direction and he instinctively, almost absentmindedly opened his arms for her. She pressed her face into his chest, eyes closed, and moaned.

"One cup, baby," she said. "Just one cup. I'll be a much better wife to you today if I can just have *one* cup of coffee."

Tracy turned to grab herself a mug and pour her own cup while Riley conducted her negotiation.

"What do you think caffeine does to high blood pressure?" he asked, his voice level.

"Negligible effect," Riley said. "I Googled it."

"Funny, because I did too and it said something very different," Shawn said.

Tracy noted that he managed to look annoyed, but not *at* Riley. How he did that, she would never know. She mixed creamer into her coffee and took a deep swallow. *Perfect.*

For a moment, anticipating the first sip of coffee had distracted her from her other mission, but now she refocused.

"So when were you going to tell me about the doctor's appointment?" Tracy asked casually. "About the fluid levels and all that?"

"I wasn't aware I had to report back to you about my OB appointments," Riley said, her voice light.

She pulled away from Shawn's embrace and opened the fridge, taking out the same carton of orange juice he had, and like him, drank directly from it.

Tracy wondered idly whether that was the kitchen etiquette they would teach their kid.

"You don't. But I think it's pretty telling that you failed to mention something so important. I feel kind of hurt, to be honest," Tracy lied.

That got Riley's attention. Riley did not like hurting people, however inadvertently. Her friend was such a pushover in that way. She turned to look at Tracy, her eyes wide.

"I didn't mention it because it wasn't the end of the world, Tracy. Women get elevations in blood pressure during pregnancy all the time. And as for the fluid levels ..."

"So what if something happened to the baby?" Tracy demanded. She knew just how much pressure to exert and exactly where to exert it. And with Riley you had to be just short of brutal, remembering that she was a pretty strong-willed woman after all.

Riley put a protective hand on her stomach and rubbed it, her brows furrowing. "I don't think it would hurt the ..."

"So I guess the doctor just checks stuff like that for shits and giggles," Tracy said taking another sip of coffee. "Fine. Take care of your little literary journal. I mean, after all, what could be more important than that?"

Tracy watched as Riley's eyes filled with tears.

Hormones, she thought, unaffected.

Shawn noticed the tears as well and made a move toward his wife but Tracy shot him a look. *Did he want his pregnant wife to stop working or not?* If he did, he was going to have to man up and not let a few tears get to him.

"Nothing is more important than this baby, than my family," Riley said, her voice trembling. "*Nothing*."

"Hmm," Tracy said coldly. She took her last gulp of coffee. "Really? Then if so, I suggest you start acting like it." She put her coffee mug in the sink and then headed for the door. "Call me later if you're still talking to me."

As she left, she caught a glimpse of Shawn's face, on it just the shadow of a grateful smile and a hint of something he had never had much of for her before: *respect*.

FUCK HER.

The thing about women like Tracy was that they were all game. After months of complete silence, all of a sudden she was thinking about that night in L.A.? Right. More likely she took one look at Meghan and decided she needed to make sure no one was stepping in to take him off her stand-by list. Well, the hell with that.

Brendan slammed his car door then winced, regretting it immediately. He loved his car, his beautiful midnight blue, Aston Martin V12 Zagato. It was reliable, did what he asked it to do, and didn't change shit up from one moment to the next. Unlike women. Unlike Tracy.

Because of her, he had messed up a perfectly good evening with Meghan. Coming back from the brunch at Shawn and Riley's he had been too drunk to drive so she had to, which made her mad.

Meghan was not typical of the women he had been with in the past. She didn't tolerate that kind of ghetto shit; going out with a man who at the end of the night was in no shape to drive her home. So he had to spend the night at her place, which he may have done anyway, but the circumstances made her freeze him out of the bedroom.

"I *like* Riley and Shawn," she'd said. "They're your friends and I want them to like *me*. If you get too drunk to even drive me home, they get the message you don't respect me. And if you don't respect me, Brendan, why should they?"

She had a point there, he had to admit. But he had spent most of the brunch trying to avoid Tracy, trying not to look at her. Trying not to get roped in all over again. Drinking seemed like his only recourse. And then to make matters worse, she had to go remind him of that time at the Grammys, which was practically an act of aggression as far as he was concerned.

Brendan laughed as he let himself into his apartment. *Right*. Like he'd been able to forget that night to begin with. But even more than the night itself—when he had what was easily one of the most memorable sexual experiences of his life—he remembered the morning after, when they met up with Shawn and Riley again for breakfast and Tracy had looked at him coolly across the table like he was a fucking stranger. And worse, later on when he cornered her alone to ask what was up, she had tugged her hand from his and pushed gently on his chest to get some distance between them.

Brendan, she said. *C'mon. We know what that was. Let's not fool ourselves into thinking it could be anything more.*

Kicked. His. *Ass*.

As a matter of fact he hadn't known what it was. He thought it was the beginning of something. He wasn't sure what, but *something*. Instead she had given him the Cold Tracy Stare and popped that bubble. And to add insult to injury, wanted to pick up where they left off like they should be phone buddies again; sidekicks to the main event that was the Shawn and Riley Show.

Nah. That wasn't happening. The difference between him and Tracy was that while she might be happy to live vicariously through her best friend, Brendan was not. To be as beautiful as she was, he had never once seen Tracy with a man.

Sure, he worked his ass off for Shawn and the label, but he had a life. A whole and full life that he intended to live. And for now, Meghan was a pretty damn good part of that life until Tracy had to show up in that figure-hugging long orange dress that had the perverse effect of reminding him that he knew perfectly well what was underneath it, telling him she was thinking about him.

Well fuck her. He had been on that carnival ride, thank you very much. No way was he going back.

Still, as he lay on Meghan's couch last night, sleeping off the six shots of Patrón, he was grateful that she kicked him out of bed. If he had sex with her last night there was no telling whose face he would see. And he didn't want to do that to Meghan. She was good for him, and more than that, just fundamentally a good woman. Almost as good as Riley, even.

And Tracy? She was many things, but she was not good.

Tracy was the kind of woman who wore her beauty like a sword, walking around just slaying motherfuckers. He had watched her do it countless times; she would notice a man's appreciation for her and meet his gaze, looking back at him with complete and utter contempt. How *dare* your dick get hard? How dare you think you could even look at a woman like *me*?

That might intimidate the average man, but Brendan had never let that faze him. He had cracked on her pretty much routinely when they first met, sometimes half-heartedly, but never honestly believing that it would pay off one day. Not that he didn't have confidence in his skills, it was just that he chalked Tracy up as an ice princess.

His world was full of women and there were generally three types. Hoochies, homegirls, and the ones who were frigid, pretty and bitchy. Tracy wasn't in their world, but she had many of the same characteristics as women in the last category. Beautiful but untouchable, cold as ice, and if they ever "let you" have sex with them, they never really let go of their inhibitions, never called out your name, never had a loud-ass, holler-at-the-moon type orgasm. They were just too pretty for all that.

At least, that's what Brendan thought Tracy was. At the Grammys she proved him wrong.

Brendan shed his clothes and tossed them across his bed, heading straight in for a shower. He hadn't showered at Meghan's this morning, slipping out before she was even awake. First time he had ever done that. And all Tracy's fault.

His bathroom, like the rest of his apartment, was sleek, ultra-modern lacquered bachelor cool. Women might visit him here, but they never slept over. Never, no one, not *ever*. This was his sanctuary, made for one person only; it had a huge bedroom suite and enormous living space, and open loft-style rec room and adjoining kitchen overlooking it.

The kitchen being in the loft, adjacent to the rec room, and the bedroom downstairs was a feature that his realtor said pretty much guaranteed that he'd never sell the place unless the buyer wanted to gut and remodel it but Brendan didn't care. He had no intention of conforming to anyone else's standards of what an apartment should be like, not when he could afford to do whatever he wanted.

He stepped into the shower and turned on the jets. He had an eleven-thirty appointment to go over the final details for the opening of the Lounge Two-Twelve. Two-Twelve was his and

Shawn's newest venture. They had long planned, and now were finally opening a chain of nightclubs in all the happening cities around the country, beginning with the flagship in Manhattan. A week from today the doors would open to what they expected to be the flyest joint in the tri-state area.

Probably because of Riley's influence, Shawn was now all about taking charge of his own wealth, not patronizing places like Xander's where the owner had no compunction about taking your money as a patron but wouldn't want you living next-door to him in a million years. So Two-Twelve was their nod to keeping Black wealth in the Black community.

Between them, he and Shawn knew dozens of young Black millionaires who were spending like there was no tomorrow, but hardly ever at Black-owned businesses. Two-Twelve (named after the Manhattan area code) would hopefully begin to shift their loyalties back to their own community in the nightlife arena and later, Shawn and Brendan's plan was to work on more substantive things, like music management and ownership. It was crazy how many artists didn't realize that they didn't even own their music.

Thinking about business, and about music was a welcome distraction for a moment, but soon Brendan's mind wandered back to Tracy. He looked down. Yeah, he was thinking about her alright.

And the Grammys. Always back to the Grammys.

BRENDAN DIDN'T BELIEVE his ears at first. She wanted to skip the parties? Tracy. *Skip the celebrity parties*. But more confounding was that she would skip them just to sit in a room with him watching movies. He agreed to it almost just to call her bluff.

But once they were in her suite, him in jeans and a t-shirt and Tracy in a pink flannel PJ bottom and tank top, he saw that he had underestimated her. She wasn't just one thing. She could do the laid-back night at home thing just as well as the going out being fabulous thing.

For the first hour or so they watched broadcast television then decided to pick a movie and argued good-naturedly over what to watch. Finally they picked a Colin Farrell cop movie because Tracy claimed the last time she was in L.A. she saw him and he winked at her.

"Sure he did," Brendan laughed.

"Why?" she asked with a pout. "You don't think I'm cute enough for Colin Farrell to wink at?"

Brendan let his eyes run over her body quickly, taking in the pert breasts, nipples hard because of the chill in the room, and finally settling at the peek of caramel-candy brown flesh between the tight tank top and the PJ bottoms. He wanted nothing more than to lift that tank top and lower his head to ...

"Yeah, you're cute enough," he finally admitted.

They watched the first fifteen minutes of the movie and ordered dinner, two garlic chicken pizzas and two bottles of wine. And for good measure, a six-pack of beer because Brendan wasn't much of a wine drinker. Before their food arrived and when Tracy was in the bathroom for a minute, her cell phone started buzzing on the bedside table. Shooting a look toward the closed bathroom door, Brendan glanced at the console, and seeing that it was Riley, reached over and shut it off in case Tracy heard it and felt compelled to answer. Then for good measure, he shut his phone off as well.

This was the first time he could remember being *this* alone with her. They had shared a couple of car rides together alone, eaten a couple of meals alone, but had never been alone together in an enclosed space. This, he thought, might be his very best chance. If he wanted to get up in that, this was his time.

And then Tracy had come out of the bathroom and there was a look in her eyes, and a smile on her face. Her expression was almost predatory, but he kind of liked it. She advanced toward where he was half-reclining, half-sitting on the bed and before he could even begin to wonder what she was up to, straddled him. She pressed her pelvis against him in a way that left no doubt that it was intentional.

"Before we get the wine and the beer and get so drunk that you wonder whether it's okay to even make a move, I just want to assure you; it's okay to make a move."

Those words and her closeness were all he needed to get him from half-mast to standing at full attention. Her scent was clean, like that of freshly-washed cotton. And of course, that was when the food arrived.

Tracy went to the door to let them in, tipping the servers and even making friendly banter with them before showing them out. And while she sounded cool as a cucumber, he sat on the bed, trying to wrap his mind around what had just transpired, wondering whether it had happened at all.

They ate their pizzas and watched the movie, had some wine and laughed and talked. They were just about to find a second movie and Tracy realized the time. It was dark out, and she wondered aloud why Riley hadn't called her.

"She must have been trying to get rid of me all along," she complained, heading for her phone.

Brendan dived across the bed to grab it and stave her off, but they both reached it at the same time, which led to some breathless wrestling, and gratuitous mutual grabbing. Finally, Tracy got the phone from him, but only because he let her. They were both still on the bed, Tracy on her back and

Brendan next to her on his side. She looked at the dark console of her phone and then turned to him.

"You turned it off?" she demanded.

Brendan shrugged.

"Why?"

"Why do you think?"

They were so close; he could see how beautiful her eyes were. Flecks of brown and green mixed in with the predominantly golden hue. And her mouth, perfectly-shaped and full. He wondered idly how many men had made fools of themselves hoping for a chance to press their lips against that mouth. Before he had even formed a conscious intention to do it, he was kissing her. And she was kissing him back. And not just kissing him back either, but diving into the kiss, her tongue actively, enthusiastically, wholeheartedly tussling with his, her teeth nipping his lower lip.

She actually pushed him back and tried to get on top of him, but he wasn't having that. Letting her get on top first set the wrong tone for what they were about to do here, and about who would be in charge. He pushed back until he was on top her, his legs straddling hers, his weight on his forearms. She tasted like garlic, but it was okay because he knew he did too and because underneath the garlic she was so, so sweet.

"Did you need to get drunk to do this?" he asked her, his mouth on her neck.

"Yes," she said surprising him. "But not because I didn't want to do it when I was sober. That's what I was saying earlier. Just needed some liquid courage, that's all."

He kissed her, purposely avoiding contact between her pelvis and his increasingly uncomfortable erection, because he knew she was curious. Women always were because of his height. He couldn't speak for any other man's assets, but he was pretty damn confident about what he brought to the game. He concentrated on her lips and neck, behind her ears and along her collarbone until she was raising her hips, trying to press against him.

By then Brendan was pretty sure she was making a little wet spot in her PJs but he forced himself not to check, moving instead to another area of curiosity. He slowly raised her tank, which she willingly facilitated, and took her in.

She was fucking beautiful.

Her nipples were a dark plum color and looked ripe, he played with them, torturing her and himself, hearing her loud breathing echo throughout the room, feeling good that he was making her feel good. She was the one who finally removed the top altogether and then she was reaching for his shirt, practically ripping it. He had to rear back a little to pull it off and noted with satisfaction that her eyes fell to his groin.

She reached for the fly of his jeans but he grabbed her wrist and stopped her. If she touched him he would embarrass himself.

So he pushed her back against the bed again. Then he did something he never did the first time he was with a woman. He moved south, kissing her along her breastbone, over her perfectly flat stomach, teasing and sucking and licking her there for a while until once again Tracy moved things along by shoving her pajama bottoms over her hips and shuffling them down.

Brendan finished the job, and looked at her in astonishment. Not only was she wearing nothing underneath but Tracy had recently had a very, *very* thorough and complete Brazilian bikini wax. He tried to swallow but his tongue seemed to have lodged in his throat. Never had he wanted to taste a woman so bad. So much that he was almost afraid that he wasn't up to the task.

Tracy was propping herself up on her elbows now, looking

down at him between her legs. Her lips looked almost bruised, because they'd been kissing for a long time, sometimes really hard. When Brendan's eyes fell once again to the juncture between her thighs, he saw just one pearl of moisture, peeking out between those smooth, hairless ...

And that it was it, he was done. He went in for the kill.

Never had he gotten as much pleasure out of going down on a woman as he did then. He didn't just want to taste her, he wanted to climb *inside* her and just fucking live there. When she squirmed and moaned and raised her hips, pressing herself against his thrashing tongue, grinding into it, he grabbed her thighs and used his forearms to press them apart. Brendan almost didn't even register the sensation of her pulling on his ears until she just yanked those suckers like she wanted to rip them off. He lifted his head, almost annoyed at being interrupted.

"*What?*" he demanded.

Tracy was breathing heavily, like she was having trouble catching a breath and he realized for the first time that she must have reached her climax.

"Get up here," she said. "Get up here and *fuck me right now.*"

Yeah. *Tracy*. Said the words 'fuck me right now'. She didn't need to ask him twice. His jeans were off in half a second and in two, he was buried deep inside her. As he pressed into her, it felt like she had the sun between her legs, like he was enveloped in something impossibly hot but in no danger of being burned. No, not the sun, because she was wet too, perfectly hot, perfectly wet.

Neither of them had even talked about it, but he was all the way in her, totally raw. Another first. He had done that so seldom that he had almost forgotten how damn good it was. But with Tracy, it was even better, and he didn't want to say anything that might make common sense prevail. He didn't want to say anything that might mean he would have to stop.

Tracy was a talker. And she liked it hard. She pressed her mouth against his ear, telling him what she liked, how she liked it, making him go faster, slower, harder ... Brendan didn't mind the direction because nine times out of ten, she was spot on. It was all good. And when he thought he might come, she felt the tension in his thighs and sensed the change in his movement and wrenched free of him, so he slid partway out of her and his impending orgasm stopped dead in its tracks.

"*No!* You'd better not!" she hissed.

That was pretty hot.

But when he finally did get off, he thought his head would explode. Behind his tightly shut eyes, he saw fireworks, all the synapses in his brain shutting down for a second and then re-firing in an instant. Then Tracy was getting off the bed and going into the bathroom and Brendan was too spent to even raise his head to investigate what she was doing. He heard running water and thought she might be getting ready to shower, but the next thing he felt was a warm washcloth as she cleaned him off, gently, almost tenderly.

He raised his head then and she smiled up at him, a sweet, un-Tracy-like smile.

"Thank you," she said. "That was amazing."

Thank you?

He was only just beginning to consider how fucked up that made him feel when she tossed the washrag aside and smiling one more time, took him in her mouth. And then he didn't think it was so fucked up any more.

FOUR

"When did you know you wanted this?" he asked her.

It was much later and they were both naked, sprawled across the bed. The only light was from the television and Brendan was having a hard time keeping his eyes off her perfect-in-every-way ass. Her head was at the foot of the bed, and he was at the opposite end so he had a great view.

As he spoke, he ran a hand up her inner thigh. Without looking back at him and without hesitation, she opened her legs to him. After all they had done in the past five hours, he shouldn't have been surprised that she was so responsive but he was. He was exhausted, but still couldn't help himself, he had to touch her.

"I wanted you from the moment we met," she said. She squirmed against his fingers and emitted a sound that was part moan, part sigh.

That answer he hadn't expected. He stilled the motion of his fingers inside her, thinking that over. That caused her to look back.

"What the hell are you doing?" she said. "Don't stop."

So he resumed his manipulations, amazed that after the marathon session they just had, she still wanted more.

"You're lying," he said. "From the moment we met?"

"Uh huh." She pushed herself back and forth gripping the sheets.

"Then how come whenever I tried ..."

"Brendan, for god's sake, shut *up*." She flipped over and before he could blink, she was astride him.

He laughed at her expression, the naked lust in her eyes. *Was this even happening?* She wanted him right now more than he was physically capable of responding to.

"You're kidding, right?" he said.

Tracy smiled back at him then leaned forward to kiss his neck. It felt so damn good, he almost couldn't stand it. After two orgasms of his own and however many she had, he felt like one massive raw nerve ending. Anywhere she touched him felt like she was pressing a lit match against his skin.

Could you die from too much sex? he wondered idly, as she moved to his chest.

"Tracy," he said, his voice firm. "Stop. I want to know. If you wanted me from the moment we met, how come you always said no when I tried to get you to go out with me?"

Tracy heaved a defeated sigh, seeing that he wouldn't be distracted and sat up. Brendan could feel her pressed open against his stomach but even that—hot as it was—he was too spent to respond to.

"Because I was seeing what Riley was going through with Shawn," she said. "His crazy life is *your* crazy life, Brendan. And I have no interest in living a crazy life."

"That simple, huh?"

"That simple," she confirmed.

"But you don't know anything about me," Brendan said.

"Oh, I know your type," Tracy said in a tone that pissed him off.

"What do you know about my type?"

"Brendan," Tracy sighed. "You're wrecking our flow."

He couldn't help himself. He laughed. "Wrecking your flow? What's that? Your approximation of how people in the music business talk?"

"Isn't it?" she asked. "I saw that rap movie. You know the one with Taye Diggs and Sanaa Lathan."

Brendan laughed. "You stupid, man."

"I'm not a man," Tracy said.

Brendan reached out and pressed a thumb right at the juncture of her thighs, watching her eyes close in pleasure.

"Oh no," he said. "You most definitely are not."

HE WAS AWAKENED in the early hours of the morning by Tracy on top of him. Thinking she was about to jump him again, he hesitated, but Tracy instead kissed him, slowly sweetly, which he kind of liked. Then she kissed him on the shoulder one last time.

"I think it's probably best that you not wake up here," she whispered against his neck. "Riley has a way of stopping by unexpectedly."

He blinked in the dark and tried to clear his head. Normally, he never would have fallen asleep in the first place and was actually grateful that she woke him up. That awkward morning-after scene had never been his thing. So he dressed in the dark and straggled back to his own suite where he fell asleep almost immediately without bothering to undress again.

Later that morning, when he still felt like he'd been hit by a

Mack truck he was so damn tired, he met Shawn, Riley and Tracy for breakfast. Shawn and Riley were suspiciously silent about the fact that he and Tracy had been AWOL halfway through the Grammys and for the rest of the evening so he knew someone had either figured it out, or someone else had spilled the beans.

When he met Tracy's gaze, she smiled at him blandly as though she hadn't spent a good portion of the last evening spread-eagled beneath him. He ate his eggs and waffles and listened to Riley rhapsodizing about someone's Grammy win, wondering what approach to take with Tracy when they were alone.

But they were never alone. In fact, she seemed to make sure of it. They all spent the entire day together just hanging out but whenever he tried to create chances for them to speak privately, she rebuffed them. Finally, late in the day, he lost his patience and dragged her off with him on a bullshit errand to grab smoothies for everyone.

"So what's up?" he asked her.

She looked at him blankly, coldly he thought. "What's up with what?"

"I'm trying to figure out what we're doing here. Is this on the DL? Did you ..?"

"Is what on the DL?" she asked, her expression blank.

"Tracy," he said. "Last night ..."

"Was wonderful. Th ..."

"If you say thank you, I'ma flip out," he warned her.

She shook her head and looked at him through veiled eyes and Brendan knew immediately that the old, guarded, distant Tracy was back.

Whoever she'd been in that room last night, the girl who laughed so hard beer came out of her nose, who insisted with a perfectly serious expression that she was one of only ten Black women in America who genuinely enjoyed fellatio, who was so insatiable he was literally sore, whoever she had been then, she sure wasn't that person now. And for sure the woman he was looking at right now definitely would not utter the words "fuck me".

That was when she said it: *Brendan. We know what that was. Let's not fool ourselves into thinking it could be anything more.*

And it all came back to him, what she told him; she wanted him the *moment* she met him. Until her common sense clicked in. The same common sense that clicked in for him right then. Tracy was basically telling him that he wasn't good enough. For a phone pal, maybe. Someone to hang out with when they were thrown together by her best friend and her husband, sure. And as a one-night-only fuck buddy, yup. Beyond that? Not good enough.

And in principle, he had nothing against being a one-night stand. Brendan had definitely had a few of those in his day, but never had anyone dismissed him as he was being dismissed by Tracy in that moment. And what's more, he had never dismissed a woman like this either.

But okay. That was the way she wanted to play it? Fine. He was a big boy and could move on, even if his toes curled just thinking about some of the things they'd done.

Since then, Brendan had been careful to treat Tracy exactly as he had before they spent the night together, with one key exception. He wasn't as accessible to her as he made himself before. No more impromptu phone chats to shoot the breeze just because she was bored. She was a friend, but not a friend. Now, he told himself, she was more like a woman he once screwed.

Running into her at Shawn and Riley's shouldn't have surprised him. It was actually more surprising that it hadn't happened sooner. But hell, it was no big deal. It had thrown him for a little bit, but now, Brendan thought as he got out of the shower, he had a sense of perspective. Tracy looked good to him at the brunch because Tracy always *looked* good. But he had to remind himself that not only wasn't she good, more importantly, she wasn't good for him.

TRACY SLAMMED her hand against the emergency stop button of her treadmill and jumped off, bending at the waist and catching her breath, feeling her heartbeat begin to slow. Her trainer had warned her that sudden stops like that weren't good, that she should gradually reduce speed and allow her heart rate to return to its resting state over about ten minutes. But she preferred the abrupt ending because it helped her go hard with her workout until she couldn't push herself for one more second, until she felt like her legs were going to give out.

Over the last week she had lost three pounds, all in preparation for tonight, Lounge Two-Twelve's grand opening, which she was attending with Shawn. Riley was finally taking it a little easier because of Tracy's shaming technique and Shawn called her—imagine the shock—to ask if she wanted to go with him. She knew he would never verbally thank her, but this was pretty darn close, so how could she refuse?

She of course called Riley to make sure she knew, and it turned out it was her idea. But, Riley was quick out point out, she'd suggested this before for events she couldn't make that she knew Tracy would enjoy, and every single time Shawn had been quick to shoot it down. This time he shrugged and said 'fine'. So that was something anyway.

Tracy was reluctant to admit it, but she didn't like it that her best friend's husband didn't much like her. Especially since he managed to be gracious to just about every other person on the planet, including pesky fans who accosted him and Riley everywhere they went these days wanting to rub her pregnant belly. Tracy had watched him fight a battle with himself, obviously wanting to smack the tar out of these people with no sense of boundaries, but restraining himself, heeding the look Riley invariably gave him.

The looks that passed between those two were something to behold, wordless communication that Tracy swore was as close to mind-reading as she'd ever seen. If Riley looked at him and he felt that she was okay, then he would be okay, and vice versa. It made Tracy sick, sick, *sick* with envy every time she watched it happen. *Why the hell couldn't she find that?*

In any event, she was walking the red carpet with Shawn tonight, and was sure he would be at pains to explain that she was his pregnant wife's best friend. Ever since that little episode a few years back, he was constantly plagued by cheating rumors. If he was so much as photographed with a semi-attractive woman within ten feet, there was unwelcome speculation.

Tonight Tracy was more than happy to keep her distance both on the red carpet and when they were in the club. Her only mission was to have a great time and maybe meet someone interesting. And of course to keep an eye out for the women who were sure to make a play for Shawn since his wife wasn't in attendance. If there looked to be any of those predators around, she would swoop in and stick to him like glue. Not her idea of a good time so she hoped to god it didn't happen, but what were friends for?

She was wearing a silver metallic scalloped micro minidress tonight, so it was important that her legs look long and toned. Playing dress-up was one of her favorite things to do, particularly if she was going someplace where she got maximum attention and exposure. She never got tired of being admired. It gave her a little flutter in the pit of her stomach to have men look at her with such frank desire, their girlfriends next to them fuming.

But even she had to admit that the thrill was fleeting and hollow, and sometimes made her despise those very same men shortly afterwards. The problem was that once they noticed her looks, they could think of nothing else. If and when they had the chance to have an actual conversation with her, they never paid attention to what she said, were never interested in going beyond the surface. She was to them nothing more than a pretty little bauble.

Tracy had once made the mistake of sharing this complaint with a co-worker who she thought was somewhat of a friend.

Oh cry me a river, she said, her voice dripping in bitterness. *I wish I had* your *problems.*

Well, it was true, very few people could relate. Riley sympathized at least when she told her about the encounter with the co-worker. Riley got it because it was in her nature to want to be known and understood on a deep level; and to want to know and understand the people she loved. Still, the look of almost pity on her face had been pretty hard to stomach as well.

Given the double-edged sword that was male admiration, Tracy sometimes wondered why she went to such pains to emphasize her beauty, but preferred not to dwell on it. Uncomfortable questions almost always yielded uncomfortable answers.

SHAWN SENT a car to pick her up. One in which he—unsurprisingly—was not himself riding. So Tracy rode alone in the back of a Lincoln Town Car to Lounge Two-Twelve. Outside, a step-and-repeat was set up and a small crowd had already gathered. As the driver pulled up and got out to open her door, Tracy smoothed her mini-dress down over her knees and practiced her smile. The door opened, she extended a leg, paused for a beat and climbed out.

As the driver helped her exit, Shawn stepped forward and waited for her. He was wearing a dark suit with a white shirt underneath and no tie. As always, he was clean-shaven and looked flawlessly masculine. Over the last couple of years, he stopped wearing street-wear altogether and adopted a more mature look. Ever since Riley's mother, a university professor at her and Riley's alma mater had arranged a speaking series for him on gender, rap and his experiences in the industry, he had developed a new gravitas and thoughtfulness about him. People took him more seriously and as a result, he considered more carefully what his image was and how he wanted it projected. Baggy jeans and oversize shirts were no longer a part of his wardrobe. Some tabloids had taken to calling him "The Dapper Rapper", a label that Riley said made him roll his eyes.

"How're you doing?" he asked her now as they walked the carpet, flashbulbs going wild around them.

"Good. Thanks for the invite."

"No problem. But I might leave a little early," he warned her. "Riley's alone at the condo tonight, so ..."

Tracy said nothing. The condo was literally five minutes away, so there was no earthly reason for him to leave early. If Riley called to say her water broke, Shawn could make it there before a drop of moisture hit the damn floor. But Tracy knew that the truth was he just didn't enjoy this kind of thing as much as he used to. Not unless his wife was with him.

As she waited for him to pose solo for pictures in front of the lounge's logo, Tracy wondered whether it would be poor form for her to stay after he took off. She hadn't starved herself into a size two and worked this hard on her appearance to duck out only after an hour.

Just as she was mulling that over, Shawn was joined on the step-and-repeat by Brendan. As the two main partners in the venture, photographers wanted several shots of them together. And then there was the parade of celebrities, national and New York-based who wanted to pose with them both.

Brendan, unlike Shawn, was dressed more casually, in an ecru shirt with dark brown slacks. He smiled as he hugged a popular television actress against him and Tracy pursed her lips, uncomfortable with how watching him embrace the woman made her feel. Fidgeting with her bracelet she looked around, hoping they would be done soon.

Finally, Shawn held out a hand to her and called her over. She hesitated for only a moment and went to join him and Brendan, smiling in the general direction of all the flashes, trying not to squint. Predictably, questions came shooting out of the crowd. No one except friends called Shawn by his name. They all knew him as K Smooth.

"K, who's the girl?" someone yelled.

"Where's your wife, K?"

At that, Shawn's smile visibly faltered and Brendan stepped in, wrapping an arm about Tracy's waist.

"She's with me," he lied, doing so jokingly because of course everyone had seen Tracy walk the carpet with Shawn.

Really, what he was saying without saying was that he had no intention of telling them something that Shawn pointedly had not.

"What's her name?" someone else yelled as the flashbulbs exploded with renewed vigor, capturing the embrace.

"Wouldn't *you* like to know?" Brendan called back.

He laughed with them and the photographers ate it up, swayed by his charm, as most people were. In the meantime,

Shawn had discreetly stepped away and was safely entering the club.

Brendan kept his arm about Tracy's shoulder and led her away from the photographers and they walked in together. Inside, Tracy took a breath.

The lounge was beautiful. Elegantly designed in white and silver, it had just the right amount of "bling" to appeal to the target demographic of people in the entertainment business, without being off-putting to your average upscale patrons. Each seating area was tented by gauze-like nets that could be pulled back or closed for semi-privacy, and all the seating was upholstered in white leather, whether it was the benches with plush curved backs in the private sitting areas, or the barstools. The bar itself was all silver covered with tiny disco-ball mirrors.

Tracy turned to look at Brendan who was taking in her reaction.

"What do you think?" he asked.

"*Amazing* job," she told him, nodding. "You guys hit it out of the park."

"Well, if you like it, then I know it's tasteful," he said. "Shawn was worried it might be a little too over the top."

Tracy studied his face, flattered at his compliment on her taste. "No, it's not over the top at all," she said. "Just *amazing*, Brendan. Really."

"Let's get you a drink," he said, putting his hand on her back and leading her over to the bar. "In a moment there'll be a crush of people in here."

"Thank you, I'd love a drink." Tracy looked around for a moment, wondering where Shawn had gotten off to.

"Probably in the back office calling Riley for the first of a hundred calls he'll make tonight," Brendan said, noticing her search.

"He won't have to," Tracy said following Brendan over to the bar. "He already told me he's not staying long."

Brendan shrugged. "No shock there. Sometimes I think he fired me just so I wouldn't keep him from running home every five minutes."

"Well, I think it's sweet," Tracy said leaning against the bar.

A bartender dressed in all-white, wearing silver lipstick and eye-shadow approached and smiled at Brendan.

"Mr. Cole? What can I get for you and your guest?"

"Give us a couple of the signature martinis," Brendan said. "Thank you." Then he turned back to Tracy. "I want you to tell me what you think about this drink."

"Sure," she said, flattered again that he cared what she thought.

"So back to Shawn and Riley. Yeah, I agree, it is cool that they're that into each other. But a man's got to make a living, right? Can't sit around staring into your wife's eyes all day."

"Now you're exaggerating," Tracy said laughing. "He still spends at least one week a month on the road. And she *is* pregnant. So I'm thinking there's a little haterism in your commentary."

Brendan grabbed his chest, as though she'd shot him in the heart. "Haterism? *Me*?"

"Yessir. I can hear it. And I recognize it, because I have occasional bouts of the same affliction myself."

Brendan grinned at her. "Do you? You *want* that? All that crazy-out-of-your-mind type love?"

Tracy nodded slowly.

Brendan looked at her, his smile disappearing for a moment. "I don't know if I want that," he said quietly. "I mean, I want a partner and someday a family, but that shit they have? It's ... disruptive."

Tracy burst out into surprised laughter. "I've never heard true love described in *quite* that way."

"You know what I mean," Brendan said. "You were there. You remember all that? I know there was a time there when I thought my boy had straight-up lost his mind. I mean, *everything* was about Riley."

"She helped him grow up though, Brendan," Tracy said. "He's the man he was supposed to be, now."

At that, Brendan leaned in closer as though studying her. "Damn," he said. "Am I mistaken or do you actually *admire* who Shawn is today?"

Tracy shrugged. "He's a good man who's all about his woman. How can you not admire that?"

Brendan nodded. "True story."

The bartender returned with their drinks in frosted martini glasses and Brendan held up his glass. Tracy followed suit.

"Let's toast to the opening of Lounge Two-Twelve," she said.

"And to you finding a good man who's all about his woman," Brendan added.

Tracy forced a smile at that last addition but drank to it anyway.

THE CLUB WAS STUFFED to maximum capacity, everyone was enjoying it, and the launch was an undeniable success. Brendan circulated through the crowd, shaking hands, accepting congratulations and pretending to himself he wasn't looking for Tracy again. When Shawn slipped out just after midnight, he made sure to let Brendan know he was leaving and asked him to tell Tracy and make sure she got home okay. So he had gone in search of her and found her.

She was sitting in one of the alcoves with some dude who was leaning in close, ostensibly so she could hear him over the crowd and music. Brendan swallowed the flash of annoyance he felt and interrupted their conversation to deliver Shawn's message.

She looked up at him, her gaze as impassive as though he was a waiter coming to refresh her water glass, and took the news of Shawn's departure with a nod and a shrug, smiling in assent when Brendan offered her a car home whenever she was ready. Then she looked at him with dismissal and returned her attention to her companion.

When she turned back to dude, there was something in her eyes, something he'd only seen before when they were in L.A. in that hotel room. He walked away shaking his head. She was planning to fuck that guy. He just knew it. He would bet everything he owned that she was going to wait a reasonable interval, probably come find him to say she didn't need a car after all and then she was going to go fuck that guy. Not that it affected him either way, of course.

But damn. It was like *that*?

That was two and a half hours ago, and he hadn't seen her since. Brendan spent one of those hours in Meghan's company, walking her through the club, showing her his office in the back and giving her the VIP treatment. She had a working weekend planned, so hadn't been able to come earlier, nor to stick around, and Brendan was surprised how promptly after she left he became preoccupied once again with Tracy's whereabouts.

Maybe it was because of how good she looked in that damn dress, and when she sat, you could see the length and shape of her caramel-toned legs. The dude she was sitting with hadn't been able to keep his eyes on her face for more than five seconds before they would fall once again to her legs. And Brendan couldn't say he blamed him. That damn dress was genius, really. It had a high collared neckline but plunged low at the arms, offering a tantalizing and fleeting peek at the sides and curve of her breasts. Enough of a peek to make you want to lean in closer, if you weren't also distracted by how short the damn thing was.

Brendan shook his head and made his way towards the bar. What the hell was he doing, thinking about her breasts and legs anyway? Been there, done that. He had seen them, and he knew they were spectacular. There was no reason to *obsess* about it. There were probably dozens of women here tonight who could give her a run for her money. Not that he had seen any of them.

And another thing; the dude she was sitting with? No way could ol' boy hang the way he had that night. Five times minimum he had Tracy screaming her brains out. So if she wanted to go screw some okie-doke motherfucker in an off-the-rack suit, then that was her prerogative. Just as long as she was prepared to be mightily disappointed.

When none of the bartenders acknowledged him immediately Brendan raised his hands above his head—which made him impossible to miss—and clapped until the young woman who'd served him and Tracy earlier looked his way. When she came over with a smile, he leaned in so she could hear him loud and clear.

"When I step to the bar," he said, "you better damn well stop what you're doing and serve me first. You feel me?"

She pulled back and blinked in surprise at his tone and then nodded. "Yes sir, Mr. Cole."

"Get me a scotch and soda."

When she turned away to get it, Brendan shoved aside the fleeting embarrassment that he let his temper get the best of him like that. He never spoke to his staff that way; and he hated people who did. He would leave her a sizeable tip by way of apology. And what the hell was he so agitated about anyway? When she returned with his scotch and soda he slid her a fifty and she glanced at it in surprise before pocketing it and smiled briefly before returning to her other customers.

At just past two-thirty a.m., it was probably optimistic of him to expect that things would be winding down, but he was beginning to wish for a shower and his bed. That was how it started; soon enough he would be like Shawn, yearning only to get home, rub his wife's pregnant belly and fall asleep in her embrace. But he had only just turned thirty-three and it seemed a little early in his estimation to throw in the towel on his free-wheeling lifestyle. There were still too many women yet to meet and bed.

That was the problem he was having now with Meghan. She never pushed or pressured, but he could tell she was looking for a commitment. Not an engagement, necessarily, but at least some indication that he *could* head in that direction, and the truth was, he just wasn't sure. She wanted him to be a proper "boyfriend" who pledged monogamy and if things went well, the ring, the wedding and the whole nine. She was just past thirty herself and told him that while she had come close a couple of times, she never wanted to marry anyone she dated.

The undeniable implication behind her words was that he might be different. Thinking about that shit made Brendan's head ache. Maybe in a couple months, he would revisit where he was with her. The monogamy thing would be a pill, but he could swallow it for the right woman. The question was whether Meghan was that woman.

Just then, as if conjured up by the Devil himself, Tracy walked by. She was scanning the room, searching the crowd. Leaning as he was on the bar, Brendan doubted she would spot him in the crowd, so he stood and headed toward her.

Catching sight of him, she smiled.

"Hey," she said, putting a hand on his arm. "I won't be needing that car after all."

Of course she wouldn't.

Brendan looked at her coolly for a moment. "Yeah?" he said. "Why not?"

Tracy hesitated for a moment.

He knew it! She really *was* going home with that corny-looking, Men's Wearhouse-suit-wearing, short-ass, grinning motherfucker. And here he thought she had some semblance of taste.

"I'm all set," she said.

"I believe that's what they call a non-responsive answer," Brendan said.

Tracy folded her arms. "Actually, it's very much responsive. You asked why I didn't need the ride and I said I was all set."

"Who with?" Brendan asked.

"That's none of your business, Brendan," she snapped.

"No need to turn into a raging bitch with me, Tracy. I told Shawn I'd see you safely home and that's all I'm trying to do."

And to his surprise, she bought his little righteous indignation act because she looked a little humbled and swallowed hard.

"Okay, well, you can tell Shawn I ran into an old friend. And anyway, I'll probably talk to Riley tomorrow morning so he'll get all the assurance he needs that I didn't wind up in a ditch somewhere."

Brendan smirked. Old friend his ass. A *new* friend was more like it.

"Okay, Tracy. Thanks for coming out. See you around."

He turned his back on her and headed to the bar. Though he couldn't see her, he sensed that it took her a moment to walk away.

FIVE

SHE ALMOST SCALDED HERSELF GETTING INTO THE DAMN shower. Tracy cursed under her breath and grabbed her loofah, working up a strong lather and scrubbing her skin until it burned. She let the water course through her hair even though it ruined the expensive salon job she'd gotten for the club opening. It took her a long time to feel clean again.

At least he was getting dressed and would be gone by now, and she could sleep. Bringing him back to her house had been a lapse in judgment, but one she intended never to repeat. She wasn't even sure what brought the whole thing on.

Who was she kidding? *Brendan.* That's what brought it on.

He was so ... nice to her and so utterly uninterested in her all of a sudden. Sure, he walked her in, got her a drink and chatted with her a little. And then he toasted to her future husband and walked away to go survey his little party, not giving her a second thought. A little later on she had seen him standing across the room with his arm about someone's waist and when she squinted and looked closer, she realized it was Meghan.

Not his girlfriend? Sure. Right.

From where she stood, Tracy thought they looked like a very cozy little couple. Meghan was wearing a perfectly ordinary black cocktail dress and yet Brendan's eyes as he looked at her couldn't have been more bright and admiring had she been Miss Universe. Oh, but that was Brendan's particular talent; he knew how to make a girl feel special.

She grew even more bitter when she recalled that she shouldn't still be thinking about him when he had never meant more to her than just a friend. And more than that, she had allowed herself to bring home some guy she might never otherwise consider, just to salve her wounded ego. The moment when she unclothed herself to a new man was always the best moment—that instant when their eyes opened wide because they couldn't believe their good fortune that a woman like her could want to be naked with them. Even the great-looking men reacted that way.

The problem was that it was almost always downhill from there. They went quickly from feeling lucky to having a lewd look on their faces, as though thinking about all the really nasty things they wanted to do to her. That was about where she generally lost interest in the proceedings. They touched her and she would drift off someplace far away in her mind, moving through the motions, moaning on cue, sometimes faking orgasm to get it over with.

A few men were skilled lovers and brought her back to the present and she participated actively, because at the end of the day, she really, truly did enjoy sex. If it was good sex. But those occasions were few and far between. Most of the time, sex made her feel empty unless she took total charge of it as she had done tonight. But even forcing all her favorite positions hadn't worked this time, because she was preoccupied.

Brendan, the one night they'd been together, hadn't made

her feel empty; and not only because he filled her up with his considerable, er ... girth. He treated her body not as a playground, the way most men did, but as a temple at which he wanted to worship. He looked at her and touched her face a lot, and sometimes when they kissed, she felt his smile against her lips. Charming, even in the middle of the act of lovemaking. And he'd done what none of the men ever had, no matter how awed they seemed by her. He told her she was beautiful. And not only when he was looking at her, but when he was inside her, so it felt like he meant more than her physical appearance, like maybe he was referring to her very essence.

But what the hell was she thinking about that for?

It had just been one night and there was a good chance she was idealizing it. Besides, now he clearly had no interest in her whatsoever.

Tracy stepped out of the shower and toweled dry, pulling on the sweats and t-shirt hanging on the back of her bathroom door, and using a tie for her wet hair. She sighed, feeling a vague soreness between her legs. She hadn't been ready when he entered her the first time but he didn't care. He was half-drunk himself and clearly could not have cared less about her pleasure, which was probably fair since she didn't give much of a shit about his. Not that he hadn't gotten any. He seemed to enjoy himself just fine and she was the one left wanting and feeling like a human trash receptacle afterward.

She pushed open the bathroom door and stopped dead in her tracks when she saw the form spread across her bed. He was only partially dressed, wearing his undershirt, dress pants and socks, and looked to have fallen asleep. Tracy's shoulders sagged.

Oh hell no. She was not having this joker sleep in her bed. As it was, it was past four a.m. and if she let this go on, she would have to face him in the light of day. No. Way. In. Hell.

Tracy approached the bed and reached out, nudging him on the shoulder. He turned in his sleep and grunted but did not wake up, so she nudged harder. This time he opened his eyes, slowly, lazily.

"What?" His tone was immediately resentful.

"You were getting dressed," she said. "I guess you drifted off."

"I'll be gone in a minute," he said belligerently. And then he shut his eyes again.

"Hey!" she said sharply. "You *cannot* sleep here."

This time his eyes stayed open. He looked her over with naked hostility, but said nothing. Tracy felt pinpricks of alarm at the back of her neck, considering for the first time that this was a man she did not really know, that she was alone with him in her locked townhouse, and that there was some pretty significant sound-proofing between her walls and those of her neighbors.

"I'm expecting a friend for brunch," she lied, trying to keep her voice light. "I really need to get some rest."

As she spoke, she walked over to her closet, she hoped casually, and slid her feet into her Keds. In her mind's eye, she recalled that her keys were downstairs in the foyer.

"If you need to get some rest, why're you putting your shoes on?" he challenged.

"I have to grab some things at the store," she said.

Her voice sounded less steady now, less confident. She was afraid to look directly at him, apprehensive about what she might see.

"At this hour?"

He was standing now, sliding his own feet into his loafers. Tracy watched him out of her peripheral vision.

"The bakery opens in less than an hour."

"Lying bitches, man," he said, his voice cold.

Tracy froze. The fact that he said *bitches*, plural, somehow made it much creepier. She wasn't even an individual to him, just a *type* of woman; a type he did not like very much, though he was willing enough to fuck that *type* of woman.

Thinking about his relentless charm at the lounge, it was apparent that his animus only reared its head once he was done with you in bed. It didn't take a degree in psychology to know that men who equated sex with anger were not exactly poster-children for good mental health.

A chill traveled down the Tracy's spine.

"Look, Kevin ..."

"*Kelvin*!" he snapped.

"Kelvin," she said. "I just need to ..."

He shrugged on his shirt and brushed by her and out of the bedroom. Then seeming to think of a better idea, he stopped, turned and grabbed her face in his hand, squeezing her cheeks painfully.

"You're a fucking whore," he said between his teeth, his face inches away from hers. And then perversely, he planted one last, kiss on her lips, his sour tongue pressing into her mouth.

Tracy's eyes were shut, and when he released her, she froze in place waiting for what might come next. Hearing him descend the wood stairs, she opened her eyes and turned to make sure that when he opened the inner and outer doors, he actually walked down the steps and into the street. When she was sure he had, she ran downstairs and bolted the doors with trembling fingers, wiping her mouth with the back of her hand.

Damn it! She couldn't seem to stop shaking!

Her first impulse was to call Riley, but it wasn't even morning. She would be asleep and if Shawn answered he would be beyond angry that she called and woke his pregnant wife up. And she didn't want to admit what had happened, not to him and maybe not even to Riley who she had promised she wasn't doing this anymore. The near-anonymous pick-ups and hook-ups had stopped, she promised her months ago.

And they had, for awhile. Until tonight.

And when Riley expressed concern about what—and who—she might be exposing herself to, Tracy insisted, *I'm safe; of course I'm safe. I make sure of that.* But she was lying. What she was referring to was using condoms—which she always did—when she knew that Riley meant much more than that. She wanted to know that Tracy was *physically* safe, and this little episode proved once and for all that as far as that was concerned, she was becoming somewhat reckless.

Tracy walked through her living and dining rooms, checking windows, drawing blinds. A man, whom she had let into her home, into her *body*, had called her a *fucking whore.*

She crouched on the floor near her sofa as though hiding, but she couldn't hide from herself. She *was* a fucking whore. She had done this before, many more times than she cared to admit; picked up men who she didn't care about, who she knew didn't care about her, just to help her feel something, *anything* for a few hours. Except she never did feel anything. Just emptier than before.

And now, thanks to Kelvin, she felt empty *and* dirty.

The only reason she knew the sobbing must be her was because there was no one else here. She was alone. That realization was both painful and a relief. Kelvin was gone, but she was alone.

She pulled herself up from the floor, talking to herself, telling herself she was being melodramatic, and that this was no big deal. Some men turned aggressive when they were rejected, every woman knew that. She had chosen poorly, that was all. Kelvin was a fluke. One bad apple ...

But it didn't work. She was still shaking uncontrollably

even though her rational mind told her there was no danger. And she couldn't face the idea of going back upstairs to her room and even looking at, let alone, sleeping on that bed.

Instead, she went to the foyer and grabbed her purse, pulling out her cell phone. She didn't consider, she just found the number and hit the call button, anxious for the sound of his voice.

TRACY SEEMED to have been waiting by her front door because she opened it as soon as he rang the buzzer. Brendan stepped into the foyer of the beautiful classic brownstone, the interior of which appeared to have been restored to the period in which it was built. But he didn't have time to take in the period details of his surroundings; he was too focused on Tracy and the look on her face.

He got the distinct impression that she wanted to hug him when he entered, but was barely managing to hold back. Instead she hugged herself, her arms tightly gripping her own shoulders. She had obviously been crying.

"What happened?" he asked, looking around.

Her voice on the phone had been so urgent, damn near incoherent, so he'd been expecting something dire, some imminent danger when he arrived. But she appeared to be alone.

"I ... I just needed someone here," she said.

Brendan narrowed his eyes in confusion. "Why? What happened, Tracy?"

She looked up at him and he saw a flash of something in her eyes. Shame. And loneliness. No, that wasn't right. Not loneliness, *alone-ness*. He advanced toward her, putting his hands on her shoulders, gently opening her arms and pulling her slowly into his chest. At that, Tracy seemed to collapse in on herself, loud sobs wracking her body as she cried. Stunned, Brendan held her tighter, not moving until she stopped.

When she calmed down a little and he tried to lead her upstairs, she pulled back, shaking her head.

"Is someone up there?" he asked, looking up the staircase.

"No, no," she shook her head. "He left. He's gone."

Brendan felt his entire body grow tense with anger. "Tracy, did he ..?"

"*Rape* me?" she said. She laughed harshly. "No, he didn't rape me."

The way she kept emphasizing the word puzzled him. She walked toward the back of the house and Brendan followed her into a kitchen with chrome and exposed red brick. It was neat, and impeccably designed, as well put-together as he would expect from Tracy who was herself usually well put-together. She grabbed a sheet of paper towel and noisily blew her nose.

"Then what ..?"

She looked at him, and there was the embarrassment again.

"He just scared me, that's all," she shrugged. "I was scared and I had no one else to call who would ..." she paused.

Brendan leaned in, waiting for her to finish.

"Who would make me feel safe," she said finally.

"Who is he?" Brendan asked, his voice flat.

He didn't even need to know the details. Anyone who made Tracy—tough as nails, Tracy—react like this had to have done *something* that merited a beat-down.

"Some guy," she said vaguely. "It doesn't matter."

"The guy you were sitting with?"

"Brendan," she said firmly, sounding a little more like her take-charge self. "It doesn't matter."

"Then why won't you tell me?"

"What would it matter? What would you do about it?" she asked, her voice tired.

"I would fuck him up," Brendan said, looking her in the eye.

Tracy looked at him for a moment and then the next thing he knew she was crying noisily again. Brendan stood there for a moment and shaking his head, pulled her into his arms.

"I'm sorry," he said, stroking her hair. "You don't need any more drama. I'm sor..."

"No, you idiot," Tracy pulled back a little and looked up at him. "I wish you would. If I knew how to find him, I'd *love* it if you'd fuck him up."

And then they were both laughing, Tracy through her tears, and Brendan with relief. He kissed her on the forehead and held her tight.

"You don't want to go upstairs and get some rest?" Brendan asked.

Tracy said nothing but shook her head.

"You do realize you're going to have to go up there sooner or later," he said.

"Yes. Later," she mumbled against his chest.

"You want to go someplace else?" he asked. "Or stay here?"

"Someplace else," she said, right away.

BRENDAN COULDN'T BELIEVE he was doing this. He was dog-tired, having been up for pretty close to twenty-four hours straight. But still he hadn't gotten a wink of sleep since he brought Tracy back to his place.

She was sleeping a peaceful sleep, her head on his chest, one arm wrapped about him while he tried not to think about how well she fit in that space, how good it felt having her there.

And then he tried not to think about the many nights that Meghan had tried to maneuver her way into sleeping at his place; nor about how readily he'd offered up that privilege up to Tracy.

But she was scared, he argued with himself. *What was the alternative? A hotel?*

Yes, as a matter of fact. What difference would it have made? She just wanted out of her townhouse. She would have settled for the Holiday Inn if it came to that.

But instead, he made the call to drive all the way back across the Brooklyn Bridge and bring her here. Because he wanted to. She had stepped across the threshold and looked around, her face devoid of make-up, dressed in sloppy sweats and a t-shirt, and scuffed Keds that looked like she used them as house slippers. She took in the décor and turned to smile at him; a little smile, a sweet, very un-Tracy-like smile.

This is nice, she said. *I like it.*

And for some reason that pleased him. It pleased him more than it should have.

But he could tell she was tired. Her eyelids were slower to reopen each time she blinked. She had been up most of the night too, and he didn't much want to think about some of what she had to have been doing and with whom.

I don't have a guest room, he told her apologetically. *But you can have my bed.*

He led her into his bedroom suite where once again she looked around, taking everything in. Without all her usual finery, she was prettier than he'd ever seen her before, and he wondered whether she knew that; that she didn't need all those extras.

If you need anything, he said, feeling inexplicably nervous. *I'll be just out ...*

But Tracy just shook her head, and saying nothing, led him

over to his bed as if it were her own. She sat on the edge and extended a hand, pulling him down toward her. When he lay back, she fit herself in the crook of his arm, rested her head just over his heart and within minutes was fast asleep. He toed his shoes off and when she was asleep, Brendan did to same to hers, and just watched her for awhile.

The key, he told himself now, was not to think. Just go with it. He closed his eyes and concentrated on the feeling of his chest rising and falling, with the weight of Tracy's head. Her hair was damp, and smelled like coconut. He exhaled and felt a few strands stir with his breath.

She sighed as though mirroring his actions back to him, and moved even closer. Before long, Brendan felt the beginnings of a dreamless sleep begin to tug at the corners of his mind.

He awoke what seemed much later to the smell of bacon and was momentarily confused about where he might be. He didn't have a single thing in his refrigerator except for Vitamin water, of that he was certain, and in his freezer, there was only vodka. And yet someone was cooking? Who the ..? And then it came back to him. The long evening at Lounge Two-Twelve. The panicked phone call. The trip to Park Slope and then back.

Brendan sat up and rubbed his eyes. He was wide awake now, well-rested and clear-headed. He brought Tracy here but it was a mistake, made in a moment of weakness. She was feeling unsafe and vulnerable and he felt protective, but it was time to erect those boundaries once again.

He washed his face, brushed his teeth and headed up to his kitchen, taking the stairs slowly, hoping she didn't get all emotional on him when he told her he was driving her home. But when he got to the top of the stairs the sight that greeted him stopped him dead in his tracks.

Tracy had changed while he was asleep and was now wearing one of his dress shirts, which looked immense on her small frame, and she had belted the waist with what looked like his one of his ties. Her feet were bare and she had let her hair out so that it was a semi-kinky, wavy mass about her face, not the severely straightened bob he was used to seeing.

She didn't even notice him at first because she was so busy moving about the kitchen, taking strips of bacon out of the oven on a cookie sheet he didn't even know he owned. She bit into one slice and licked her fingers, closing her eyes in pleasure at the taste. Brendan had never seen anything so sexy in his life.

Shit.

Then she turned and noticed him for the first time and smiled at him, the same sweet smile as earlier. The same un-Tracy-like smile. Except now he was beginning to believe that it was very much a Tracy-smile, just one that she reserved for very few occasions, or very few people. And he wondered whether he would be one of the lucky few who were privy to it from now on.

"Hey," she said. "I didn't want to wake you so I just borrowed a couple of your things and went to get us something to eat. You do know that sports drinks are not officially a food group, right?"

Then she was taking a baguette out of a Dean & DeLuca grocery bag, along with eggs, juice and a wedge of soft cheese. She moved around as though she had familiarized herself with where everything was, and Brendan swallowed, trying to remember why it had seemed so essential that she leave.

Tracy looked up at him again as he made his way closer, sitting at the breakfast bar, watching as she worked, beating eggs, slicing cheese and bread.

"I got some olive oil spatter on this shirt," she said apologetically. "And honestly, I don't think it's going to come out." She winced as though she expected him to be upset.

"That's okay," he said shaking his head.

"It's one of your Armani Collezioni shirts," she said. "Sorry. But I couldn't find anything in your stuff that wasn't a designer label. Don't you ever just go to Target like normal people?"

"When was the last time *you* went to Target, Tracy?" Brendan teased.

"I *beg* your pardon. Riley and I go to Target at least three times a month," she laughed.

"Sure you do."

"You should come with me sometime. Best. Date. Ever."

Brendan smiled.

She was so busy with the cooking she didn't seem to notice that she said the word 'date' in connection with something they might do together. It was almost impossible to connect this woman with the calm, cool and collected ice queen image she usually projected. For whatever reason, for the moment she seemed to have let her guard down around him. Maybe this was who she was all along. The person only Riley saw.

For years he'd wondered how two women, so different could be so close. Riley was the personification of warmth; one of those rare, open-hearted people who loved you right away and had to be given a damn good reason not to. Tracy had always seemed like the just the opposite.

She grabbed one of the barstools and placed it in front of the cabinets where he kept his dishes, visible through the glass doors. Brendan couldn't recall having ever taken a dish out of that cabinet so it took him a moment to realize that Tracy intended to use the stool as a ladder.

"I can get that for you," he said getting up quickly.

The last thing he needed was to have her fall and break her

neck on top of everything else that had happened to her in the last twenty-four hours. By the time he got to her, Tracy was already standing on the stool and Brendan found himself face to face with pelvis. He hated himself for the twitch he felt in his groin; after all the trauma she had been through the night before. But a hard dick had no conscience.

"I got it," she said opening the cabinet and grabbing two dishes. She handed them down to him and he tried not to look too hard at the apex of her thighs as he took them.

"Placemats?" she asked.

Brendan looked at her blankly.

"Placemats, Brendan? You know? The things that go under dishes when you're eating?"

"Oh." He shook his head, coming back down to earth. "I don't think I have those."

Tracy rolled her eyes. "We are *definitely* going to Target."

They ate sitting at the breakfast bar, talking about Shawn and Riley's soon-to-be-born baby and making bets on who would be the pushover parent and who would be the hard-ass. And as they laughed and talked, Tracy got up and poured his juice, made him more eggs and then cleared up when they were done. Then she hung out in the kitchen with him while he rinsed the dishes and put them in the dishwasher, her legs stretched out and resting on his stool.

He kept reminding himself that he needed to get her out of his apartment, and kept giving himself deadlines to mention taking her back to Brooklyn. First it was, *in a half an hour*; then when they returned to his bedroom and Tracy turned on the television, it was *after the stupid chick flick she seems to be so into*.

And then she drifted off to sleep, curled around one of his oversized pillows and he changed the channel to a baseball game. Brendan didn't know when he fell asleep himself, he only knew that when he woke up, it was dark and Tracy was still sleeping, but this time she was curled around him and he was too tired to get up, or to think of waking her, or to even consider driving her all the way back to Brooklyn. And by then, he finally admitted to himself that he didn't want to.

SIX

"I don't like those," Brendan said swatting away the red linen placemats Tracy held up for him.

"This is the fifth choice you've vetoed," she said. "I'm starting to think you don't want placemats."

Brendan laughed. "You think?"

Tracy sighed. "Okay. Fine. We don't have to stay. Let's go."

She had dragged him to the Target in Harlem as a joke, and for some reason Brendan didn't seem to be getting the punchline. But she had been so taken over by the domesticity of the place, and the odd comfort of shopping for household items with Brendan that for a moment, Tracy forgot that she should probably be going home, and that by now he probably wanted nothing more than to get her out of his hair.

But going back to her empty townhome seemed like such a bleak prospect compared to yesterday and today, just hanging out with Brendan in his apartment, watching movies, sleeping and walking to the gourmet market to grab food for each meal. For some reason, Brendan was averse to stocking his refrigerator, so they'd gone to the market a total of four times, each time buying only enough for the next meal.

They didn't talk about why she was there, or when she would go home, but now it was clear that her time was up. It was Sunday afternoon. The weekend was drawing to a close and real life would soon begin again.

"I appreciate the thought," Brendan said following her toward the exit. "But I don't cook, Tracy. And if I'm in that kitchen at all, it's not to sit and eat a meal using a place ..."

"Fine," she said, cutting him off. "You don't have to explain. You don't want placemats. I get it."

She walked briskly, now wanting more than anything to get out of the store herself, feeling silly all of a sudden for coercing him there, acting out some asinine domestic scene that he had no desire to participate in.

"Tracy," he said. "*Tracy ...*"

"What?" she stopped and turned to look at him. "We're leaving, just like you wanted. So what *is* it?"

Brendan looked at her for a moment. "Are you sure you're okay to go home?" he asked.

Tracy shrugged. "Doesn't matter. I have to."

"But if you're really not ready ..."

"If I'm really not ready, then what?" she asked softly.

Tracy saw that there was real concern in his eyes. He was such a good guy. A good guy who had a girlfriend he probably couldn't wait to get back to.

"I'm okay," she said, forcing herself to sound more confident than she felt. "And he didn't hurt me, Brendan. At least not physically. He didn't ..." She trailed off into silence.

He reached up and touched her hair briefly, surprising her.

"You ever going to tell me what happened?"

She shrugged again but said nothing. She couldn't imagine telling Brendan what Kelvin said. Because what Kelvin said was true. And she didn't want Brendan to know about that side of her. Right now, he was treating her like porcelain, like she was something precious that might break if anyone dared utter even a harsh word in her direction. She couldn't remember the last time a man had treated her that way, or if another man ever had.

He extended a hand which she took, without hesitation.

The brownstone was as she had left it. All was in order downstairs, but upstairs the bed still bore evidence of Friday night's little encounter. The sheets were in disarray, and as soon as Tracy entered the room with Brendan, she hurried to pull them from the mattress, balling them up and tossing them aside. Once stripped, she remade the bed with clean, fresh sheets and lit a scented candle. Brendan watched her from the doorway, stepping aside when she dashed downstairs, returning with a large dark trash bag into which she deposited the sheets she'd stripped from the bed.

"There," she said, her voice falsely bright. "Done."

She knotted the garbage bag and tossed it down the staircase.

"So," Brendan said. "You straight? How're you for dinner? You need to go out and grab something for later, or ..?"

"I'm fine," Tracy said shaking her head. "I'll walk you out. I need to drop this bag at the curb for trash pick-up tomorrow anyway."

"You have anything else that needs to go out?"

"Yeah. Kitchen trash," Tracy said. "Could you grab that for me?"

When Brendan turned to head downstairs, she kneeled by the bed and looked around until she found what she was looking for. Until Brendan mentioned other stuff that might need to go out, she'd forgotten the used condoms. She vaguely remembered Kelvin dropping them unceremoniously next to the bed when they were done. She stuffed them into her bathroom trash and grabbed that bag as well, knotting it tightly and then joining Brendan downstairs by the front door.

They walked together to the curb and dumped the trash bags near the growing pile of refuse that Tracy's neighbors had already put out for Monday morning. Then it was undeniably time for Brendan to go.

For a moment, they stood there awkwardly, neither of them knowing what to say or do. Tracy felt as though they'd turned a corner, crossed into new territory. However you wanted to say it, it was obvious that whatever they were now was something very different from what they had been just forty-eight hours earlier.

"You took really good care of me," she said. "Thank you."

"You know it's no problem, Tracy." He didn't look her in the eye, and seemed almost embarrassed to have her mention it.

"I want to thank you properly," she said. "Maybe we can have dinner or something this week? If you want. If you have time."

"Yeah." He nodded. "Sure. Call me. If this week isn't too slammed, let's do that."

Tracy watched as Brendan got in his car and started the engine, and was still standing there when he drove away. Then, remembering that she was once again all alone, she dashed up the steps and back into the townhouse, locking the door and setting the alarm.

TRACY SIGHED, glancing down at her cell phone, wondering why it hadn't rung. It was four hours since she'd called Brendan and left him the message inviting him to dinner. Four hours and he hadn't so much as texted his acknowledgment, let alone an acceptance. And here she was, sitting at lunch with a client, looking at her phone every five minutes instead of politely listening to how great the man's trip to the South of France had been.

The truth was Tracy didn't much like her clients. They were generally over-privileged people who had so much money that now their money made more money, eliminating the need for them to do any actual work. They were soft and indolent, and with a sense of entitlement that was often sickening to witness. They were rude and patronizing much of the time, even to her; because even though she helped them keep and grow their wealth that was all she was to them: help.

The current asshole she was lunching with was Jason Miller, a thirty-five year old dotcom millionaire who had sold his company and was now living on the interest of the proceeds. He occasionally played with chunks of his fortune, almost like a gambler, curious about whether he could double, triple or quadruple his money in ever shorter periods of time. Having only been wealthy for about eight years or so hadn't stopped him from behaving like he was one of the Rockefellers or Rothschilds. His net worth was rumored to be around $80 million, but his investment with Tracy's funds totaled only about five hundred grand.

Glancing at her phone, she wondered whether it was worth it to piss him off by ducking out for a moment so she could try Brendan again. Maybe he hadn't gotten her message. She had done herself that in the past, let a message linger without listening to it. Maybe he didn't even know she'd invited him to dinner. That seemed far more likely than the possibility that he was just failing to call her back, or ignoring her.

"Ms. Emerson," Jason Miller said with a smile. "I'm getting the impression I don't have your full attention."

And God forbid.

Tracy smiled back at him. "Of course you do," she said, sliding her phone into her purse and setting it aside.

Unlike most of her colleagues, she walked a very fine line with her clients. Not only were there very few Black hedge fund managers to begin with, there were very few women. And as someone who was both those things, she was constantly on guard, making sure she not only met but exceeded every expectation or goal set by her clients and employer. It was a tricky thing to accomplish with investing, because no one could predict the markets, so even her missteps had to be spun to look like something else entirely.

Jason Miller, she suspected, just liked to dabble. He liked feeling like he was a mover and shaker and had perhaps grown bored now that he wasn't actively managing or building a business. These lunches, where he could bring people like her to heel, and remind them that they worked for him, were probably just one way he maintained his sense of self-importance. Tracy was prepared to indulge him, however painful it might be, because behind his five hundred thousand dollar investment could be much, much more.

After lunch, there were two other meetings and then a conference call with a group of European investors, so it was well after eight that evening before Tracy was able to leave the office. She checked her phone and there were five missed calls. Three were from Riley and two from her mother. She called Riley back as she was riding in the car service's Lincoln, on her way home, hoping that she would be on the line long enough to make a call to her mother in Georgia impractical because of the lateness of the hour. Thankfully, her mother was still old-fashioned enough to believe that it was ill-mannered to call past nine p.m. unless it was an emergency.

"You're not in labor, are you?" she asked Riley when she picked up.

"No, unfortunately not," Riley said groaning. "And I'm losing my mind from boredom over here. I don't know what's going on at work, and Shawn watched me all weekend like a hawk. Come to think of it, where the hell have *you* been? You never called me back. I wanted to hear how the opening of the club was on Friday."

Oh. That's right. She hadn't told Riley about the weekend. But for some reason she didn't want to subject it to examination just yet.

"The opening was fine. They did a great job with the decorating of the space. And of course, your husband left as soon as he could."

"Yeah, he got back early. That's why I wanted to talk to you. I wondered how it was with Brendan. Was Meghan there?"

"She was. And I found other company."

"Oh."

Tracy let that hang there for a moment. Even if she didn't feel ready to share everything, she wasn't planning to lie to her best friend either. She just hoped like hell, Riley didn't ask any pointed questions.

"Well I'm still at the condo if you wanted to stop by this week," Riley said after a few more moments of silence. "Shawn is in Philly with Brendan for a couple of days, so we can have some girl time."

Brendan was in Philly? He hadn't mentioned that he was going away. But of course, why should he? If he did mention it to anyone, it would be to Meghan. Still, it felt unexpectedly hurtful that they spent all that time together and she'd mentioned dinner and he didn't think to tell her he would be out of town.

Tracy went through the rest of the conversation with Riley on auto-pilot and when they were done she called Brendan's number, opted to go directly to voicemail and left him a very nasty message about his failure to communicate. Doing that made her feel tons better and once home, she was able to eat her dinner with gusto and after a shower, fall directly into a deep and dreamless sleep.

The cacophony of a dog barking woke her up around two in the morning and Tracy sat upright in bed, wondering who was out in the street with their dog at this ungodly hour. It took her a moment to recall that the barking was the ringtone she'd set for Brendan's number. *Now* he wanted to call her back? *At two thirty-six a.m.?*

She grabbed the phone from the charger and hit the answer button.

"*What is it?*" she hissed.

"What *is* it?" he repeated, his voice calm. "You call and leave me that shitty message and then you want to know why I'm calling you back?"

"I don't think it was shitty," Tracy said, trying to clear her mind and bring it to full wakefulness. "It was direct. I was letting you know how I felt about ..."

"About what Tracy? The fact that I didn't share my travel itinerary with you?"

She said nothing. Well, if he wanted to look at it *that* way.

"You are so *spoiled*," he said. "I told you I had stuff this week and that I might be slammed, didn't I?"

Tracy said nothing. *Oh, yes.*

"Didn't I?" he insisted.

"Yes," she said meekly.

"Then *what* is your fucking problem?"

She normally might have objected to having him speak to her that way, but there was an undertone in his voice, an amused indulgence, like he was saying she was spoiled but didn't actually mind spoiling her. And besides he was calling now. He hadn't even wanted to wait until the morning, and that made her feel somewhat smug. She liked the idea that he may have struggled all evening with the urge to call her and not been able to sleep until he did.

"Tracy," he heaved a deep sigh and mumbled something to himself that she couldn't hear.

She waited.

"I'm back on Wednesday afternoon," he said finally. "I'll pick you up at your place for dinner at eight."

"Okay," she said quietly, stifling a smile.

"*Alright?*" he demanded.

"Yes," she said louder. "Okay."

"Good. And Tracy?"

"Yes?"

"Don't leave me any more shitty messages," Brendan said before he hung up on her.

Tracy put the phone back on the charger and turned to hug her pillow once again, smiling into it.

SHE DIDN'T NEED anything new and it wasn't as though tonight was a date or anything, but Tracy felt compelled to shop, and it was an urge she rarely resisted. She moved through the boutique, slowly, taking in the shape and cut of each dress, each pant, each blouse, pointing out to the sales consultant, which she wanted to try.

"This is a lot of effort to put into a 'quick bite to eat'," Russell said from behind her.

Tracy shot him a look. Russell was her and Riley's former housemate, from way back when they first moved to the city after college. For the past year he had been living in Atlanta where he thought—mistakenly it turned out—that he would meet what he called "an interesting new crop of men." But after several months of dating men he referred to as "flaming drama queens" he returned to New York where, after all, Tracy believed, he really belonged.

"I like having new things," Tracy said.

"Hmm," Russell said skeptically, looking at his nails. "Whatever you say. It's obvious you're into him."

"He's a good friend," Tracy said pulling out a short orange linen tunic. She remembered having the distinct impression that Brendan liked her in that orange maxi.

"No. *I'm* a good friend. *Riley* is a good friend. You would never go shopping just for a quick bite to eat with either of us," Russell pointed out.

He paused to regard himself in a nearby full-length mirror. Tracy couldn't blame him. He *was* pretty damn cute. The color of dark chocolate with eyes as black as coal, and the physique of someone who spent many vain hours in the gym.

Needless to say, Russell and Tracy had a lot more in common than Russell and Riley did. He was the one Tracy consulted about fashion, hair, make-up and all things trendy since Riley was hopeless in that arena.

"Why couldn't *you* be straight?" Tracy said glancing him over. "I think it's aggressive to be as fine as you are and not like women."

"You're trying to distract me with flattery," Russell accused. Then he paused. "But go on. How fine am I again?"

Tracy laughed and nodded to the sales consultant, letting her know that she was ready to try on her selections.

"No, but seriously," Russell said. "I'm still trying to wrap my mind around why you're not all over this dude."

"Because he's just not ... right for a long-term relationship. I could never see myself married to someone like him."

"Someone like who? A man who dropped everything and

drove like a bat out of hell to Brooklyn to rescue you from unspecified danger?"

Tracy had shared with Russell only some of the details of Friday night's misadventure; just enough so that she could tell him about Brendan's visit, but not sufficient information to make him alarmed and go blabbing to Riley. As far as he knew, it was just some guy who wouldn't leave; a predicament Russell himself had plenty of experience with.

"He's in the entertainment business," Tracy said. "He's a player. He travels to a million places, sits around in clubs sipping Dom Perignon and socializing with music video girls and models."

"And yet here you are, acting like you're going to prom when all you're doing with him is getting a so-called quick bite to eat," Russell pointed out.

Tracy looked at him but said nothing. It was true. There was no way to account for, or explain why she was feeling this giddy about seeing Brendan. All she knew was that she liked him more than she remembered ever liking any man, and more than that she liked the way he made her feel like a little girl who, when she was with him was totally safe; and like a sexy, desirable woman too because when he looked at her, he so obviously wanted her. It was an intoxicating combination and one that she was not accustomed to. Men who wanted her had never made her feel safe. In fact, often, it was strikingly the opposite.

Russell followed her unselfconsciously into the fitting room, ignoring the raised eyebrow of the sales consultant, and Tracy smirked. Russell had probably seen her undressed more times than all her ex-boyfriends combined.

It gave her a kick to sometimes be completely naked in her bedroom walking around getting ready for some event, curiously checking his package every now and again as he lay across her bed, waiting for her to get done. One time he'd caught her looking and rolled his eyes.

Nope, he quipped. *Still gay.*

"Did you ever tell Riley what happened that night?" Russell asked as he helped her with the zipper of her first selection, a cream Reem Acra pantsuit.

"No. I was planning to at first and now it seems like it might be too late. She'd be pissed if I told her now, several days after ..."

"Well *yeah,*" Russell said. "I don't understand why you didn't call her that day."

Tracy lifted her hair and turned in front of the mirror, checking out her derriere. She seemed to be losing it. Maybe a size two had been taking her diet and exercise routine too far.

"Riley's life is different now," Tracy explained. "And when the baby comes it'll be even more different. She's thinking about babies and nesting and here I come with some seedy story about my one-night stand."

Russell nodded. "I know what you mean. You see I didn't show up for that brunch baby shower thing she had. I mean, what the heck would I be doing out in Jersey *oohing* and *aahing* over silver rattles and shit?"

Tracy laughed. "It actually wasn't that kind of party. But I get your point. She hasn't turned into some kind of Stepford Wife or anything don't get me wrong. It's just that she's happy, y'know? And all my self-inflicted drama just doesn't seem to ... fit."

"Yeah but you were there for her drama. She at least deserves to have the chance to be there with you for yours."

"Oh shut up," Tracy said reaching back to unzip the pantsuit. "I hate it when you're all reasonable like that."

"She's still at the condo, right? We could stop by and bring her a cup of coffee or something. Last time I talked to her, she told me woke up to find her precious Lamborghini espresso machine missing."

"Ah, the joys of obsessive love," Tracy sighed. "I think her husband needs to be committed to a mental institution honestly." She would never admit it out loud but she was beyond pleased that Shawn was taking such good care of her friend. If anyone deserved it, it was Riley.

After settling on a Stella McCartney poplin dress with a very demure neckline and a very short skirt, she and Russell took a cab to Central Park West and Riley's place. These days, you had to punch an elevator code to get to their floor, a security feature for which Shawn and the only other tenant on their floor had agreed to split the cost.

Upstairs, Riley looked even bigger than she had been just the prior week and Tracy's eyes involuntarily widened upon seeing her. Russell, never one to mince words, clapped a hand over his mouth.

"Oh my god, girl, you are *huge*!"

Riley rolled her eyes. "Yes. Thank you. I am well aware."

She hugged them both and made her way over to the sofa where she had clearly been camped out, reading magazines. She eyed the Starbucks coffee cup Tracy was holding and her eyes lit up. Tracy held it out of reach as though Riley might pounce.

"Before I hand this over to you, I need to know two things. One; how's your blood pressure?"

"Slightly high within range of normal for pregnancy," Riley said promptly, moving toward her.

"You're not lying are you?"

"No Tracy, I'm not lying. What's your second question?"

"You aren't going to rat me out to Shawn? I need to know that if you feel the need to confess, that you won't bring me down with you."

"Done," Riley said.

Tracy handed her the cup and watched as she took a sip, eyes closed as though in bliss. Then she took a deep whiff of the aroma and handed Tracy the cup.

"That's all I needed," she explained. "And Shawn's right. I don't want to take any chances."

Russell and Tracy exchanged a look.

"What?" Riley laughed.

"We know you're going to tell him," Russell explained.

Riley shrugged. "Shawn and I don't keep secrets from each other."

At least not anymore, Tracy thought uncharitably.

"And besides, he's on his way home right now. He and Brendan should be here any moment, so it would put a real damper on our reunion if he walked in and I'm holding a venti americano."

Tracy's head whipped around to the front door.

"Brendan's on his way here now?"

"Yeah. He was with Shawn in Philly," Riley looked confused at her agitation. "They were checking out this guy they're thinking of signing."

"Well I knew they were there together. I just ... so *now*? He's on his way now?"

"Yes."

Tracy noted Russell's amused and smug look but didn't have time to get into it with him. She had to leave. She didn't want to run into Brendan before their da... before he stopped by that evening. It would be too weird.

"Okay, so I'm leaving," she said. She kissed Riley on the cheek. "Russell, you're hanging out for awhile, right?"

He nodded. "Sure. But what's the hurry, Tracy?" he challenged.

"I'll deal with you later," she said, heading for the door.

As she pushed through the front door, she heard her friends behind her.

Riley asked "Why do I feel like I'm out of the loop?"

And Russell's laugh. "Girl, you have no idea."

FADED JEANS, worn brown boots and a white t-shirt. He looked damned good in those jeans, but still. *Jeans*, while she was standing there, feeling stupid in her hot little Stella McCartney number. Tracy opened the door and stepped aside to let Brendan in, her face studiously neutral.

He laughed at her expression and held his hands up. "You never told me where you wanted to go."

"So you assumed what? A cookout?"

Brendan shook his head. "I can think of any number of really nice establishments that would be happy to have me, even dressed like this. In fact, I have one in mind, just across the bridge ..."

"Where?" Tracy demanded.

"You don't have to be in charge all the time, Tracy. C'mon, let's find you something else to wear."

And before she could stop him, he was taking the stairs two at a time and heading for her bedroom. She really had to start putting her foot down about these liberties he liked to take, she thought following him.

When she got there, he was in her closet. Tracy watched as he moved things around on the racks.

"You talk about me and designer stuff? Where your jeans at?"

Tracy breathed an impatient breath and shoved him aside, pulling out a tiered hanger. Brendan grabbed a random pair of jeans and started hunting for a top.

"I was supposed to be taking *you* out for dinner," she said. "So I should be able to ..."

"Yeah, I thought about that. And that didn't sit well with me."

Oh god, he was about to tell her about him and Meghan.

"I don't feel right about you thanking me for doing something that any decent man would do," he said, still looking through her tops. "So I'm taking *you* to dinner."

"A lot of men aren't decent, Brendan."

"Maybe you need to pick a different kind of man," he said pausing to look at her.

Finally, he pulled out a sleeveless orange blouse and she smiled. She knew he'd liked her in that orange maxi. She took the top and jeans into the bedroom to change.

"Where's your tennis shoes?" Brendan called after her.

"Downstairs in the mud room. But I'm not wearing them. Tennis shoes are for tennis courts, running or the gym," she called back.

"Okay, so these then," Brendan emerged with her pewter ballet flats in hand, just as she'd shed the Stella McCartney, so she was standing in front of him in just her bra and underwear, the dress pooled at her feet.

After a reflexive urge to cover herself, she decided not to bother. This was a man who had come face to face with the most private parts of her body, so what was the point?

Brendan seemed to sense that decision and a small smile crossed his lips. He placed the shoes at her feet just as she pulled on the jeans and shrugged the top over her head.

"I wanted to dress up tonight." She pouted one last time.

Brendan sat on the edge of the bed and looked at her.

"Tracy, you don't have to dress up," he said shaking his head. "You could wear a sack-cloth and blow every other woman out of the water."

She blushed, wondering why his compliments seemed to mean so much more than almost anyone else's. She went to her dresser and grabbed a ponytail holder, reaching back to scoop her hair up, and was surprised when Brendan appeared behind her in the mirror. He put his hands over hers and raked his long fingers through her hair, pulling it all back into a high swing ponytail and taking the elastic from between her fingers, expertly fastening it.

Tracy almost hadn't taken a breath while his hands were on her scalp. No matter where and how he touched her, it felt good. She turned to look at him but he was still standing so close that she had to look up to see his face.

"Am I ready?" she asked.

"Are you?" he asked.

Tracy's heart thundered in her chest and she waited for him to kiss her. He was definitely looking at her like he wanted to. But he didn't. Instead he put his hands on her shoulders and steered her out of the room, and toward the stairs. Tracy swallowed her disappointment.

At the curb he opened the door for her and let her into the car before getting in himself. As he walked around to the driver's side, Tracy recalled that Brendan had always done this for her: opened doors, took her hand when she was in heels going down steps, and walked with his hand resting on her back when they entered a room together.

Not too many other men she knew did that kind of thing. And many of them who did, seemed to be forcing it just to impress her. With Brendan, it was effortless, it was just who he was.

They drove for awhile in silence and Tracy watched as he reached out to get some music going. His hands were large, his fingers long. When he'd kissed her in L.A., he put a hand at the back of her head, palming it, cradling it so she felt enveloped by him.

The music that resounded throughout the car surprised her; it was restful, smooth jazz and was an artist she had on her playlist as well. Tracy wondered what else she had failed to notice about Brendan. This evening alone, she was racking up quite a list.

"It's not worth wasting the night driving around looking for a place to park so I'm going to park at my building and we'll take the train," Brendan said.

Tracy sat up. "What?"

"The train. You know. The subway?"

"I haven't taken the subway in ages," she said.

"Well good thing it's like riding a bicycle," Brendan said, unimpressed. "Once you get the hang of it you never forget how."

An hour later, Tracy was still somewhat irritated as Brendan held her hand and led her out of the foul depths of the 72nd Street station and toward Broadway. When she saw that he was headed directly toward the iconic neon sign she stopped and looked at him.

"Are you serious?"

"What? Who doesn't like hot dogs? And Gray's Papaya has some of the most famous hot dogs in the western hemisphere."

Tracy sighed. "This is so not what I had in mind for dinner tonight."

"Sometimes you have to let go of your preconceptions," Brendan said as he dragged her out into the street, dodging traffic so that Tracy was forced to stick close to his side or risk getting picked off by a yellow cab.

Brendan found an empty place at the counter and ordered two 'Recession Specials' which consisted of two dogs and a drink, giving Tracy the seat and standing just behind her so that she was shielded from the crush of native New Yorkers and tourists.

He ate standing up, leaning over her shoulder, and after a couple of exploratory sniffs, Tracy found her mouth watering. One bite of one of her dogs, smothered in sauerkraut and onions, and she was sold. Fine, she would eat the damn hot dogs. And anyway, they would help her get back to her preferred size four and restore her ass to its former glory.

"Good?" Brendan asked from behind her.

"Uh huh," she admitted, her mouth full.

"I knew you'd come around." He nudged her.

Tracy smiled in spite of herself and took a long swallow of the almost sickeningly sweet soda Brendan had ordered for her.

Afterwards, he put a hand on her shoulder, leading her back out to the street and they walked aimlessly for awhile, neither of them speaking, but Tracy was comfortably full and content. The evening was warm and the sidewalks crowded with people enjoying the summer evening. As they got closer to Central Park, the crowds grew thicker and Brendan took her hand, pulling her closer to him and out of the fray.

"So how're you liking being home a lot more?" she asked.

"I'm liking it more than I thought I would," Brendan admitted. "I was getting sick of running to catch flights, fighting Shawn into going to every single appointment. This is a lot less stressful for sure."

"But now you're one of the decision-makers about who gets record deals, so that's got to be exciting."

"Yeah, it is."

"Who was in Philly?"

Brendan looked at her and smiled. "All of a sudden you're interested in the music business?"

"I hope I was never that self-centered," Tracy said, stung.

Brendan said nothing.

"I mean, I was always interested in what's going on in your life, Brendan."

He said nothing, but with his fingers still laced through hers, the silence that fell between them was companionable. Even in the crowd and with the aroma of roasted peanuts and of street food permeating the sidewalks, Tracy believed she could detect a scent that was uniquely Brendan; woodsy and masculine. It made her want to take his shirt off and press her face against his chest. It was a scent she associated with safety, but also, paradoxically, with sex. Paradoxical because she had never considered sex to be 'safe.' And right now, she didn't even care where he was taking her as they walked because she trusted him implicitly.

"I want to go back with you to your place," she said.

Brendan stopped walking and for a moment she wondered whether she'd made a mistake. He was being nice to her and that was all. She had practically forced this little 'date' and he was being gracious about it, but maybe this last bit was assuming too much. And he was involved with Meghan for heaven's sake; a fact he had never tried to hide.

If she thought about it, he had never done anything with her that was inconsistent with him seeing someone else. So he let her stay at his place when she was scared to go home; so what? It wasn't as though he'd touched her in anything other than a brotherly way that whole time. And even now, he held her hand because he was gentlemanly, not because he was feeling anything approaching the feelings she had.

Maybe he didn't even want her? Maybe the vibes she thought she was picking up at her house were all wishful thinking.

Brendan turned her to face him, and letting go of her hand tipped her chin up so she was looking at him. His eyes were questioning, like he was trying to figure her out. Around them, pedestrians muttered impatiently as they blocked part of the sidewalk. Tracy's eyes met his and she took a deep breath.

"I just want to be with you," she said, before he could speak. "I don't want to examine it, or label it, or think about what happens later or tomorrow or next week. And I don't want to mess up anything else you might have going on with ... with anyone. All I know is, I like being with you."

Brendan's brow was furrowed and he pursed his lips as though concentrating very hard on something.

Tracy waited.

If he rejected her, she would be humiliated. What she'd just said was the most honest thing she had ever said to a man, the most naked and vulnerable she had ever allowed herself to be. But every word of it was true. Brendan might not be her future, but she didn't care. She had never known a man who was so completely himself, who made her feel like it might be possible for her to do the same. Everything he did, everything he said to her called out for her to open up and let him in, and she wanted to. Even if just for a little while.

THIS COULD ONLY END BADLY.

For the second time in less than a week, Tracy was sleeping in his bed, and he had shut off his phone to avoid interruptions, not wanting to wake her and—this part was much more difficult to admit—not wanting anyone to burst the little bubble they had formed around themselves. Like last time, there was no sex. Not that he didn't want it, but the memory of her last encounter was too fresh in his memory and probably in hers too. He couldn't imagine entering her body, knowing that not too long ago, some other guy had been there; someone who scared her enough to make her cry. If they had sex—and damn, he hoped they eventually would—she needed to make the first move.

Tonight, same as last weekend, they lay in bed together and watched television and Tracy moved over and pressed into him, wrapping her legs about his. And when Brendan turned to look at her, she kissed him, her lips exerting light pressure, the tip of her tongue tentatively pushing its way towards his.

He held back, taking it slowly, not wanting to alarm her, exploring her lips and mouth but being careful not to touch her too intimately otherwise. When the kiss deepened and became more urgent, it was because Tracy initiated it, opening further to him, capturing his tongue between her lips, gently sucking on it.

Then just as suddenly she seemed to decide to get a hold on herself and pulled back, sighing—he couldn't tell if it was in contentment or frustration—and rested her head once again on his chest. Brendan tried to ignore his almost painful erection and when that didn't work, thought about everything under the sun that could possibly derail sexual arousal, like the road-kill he and Shawn spotted on their drive back from Philly. That helped it go down for a minute but soon enough, she was kissing him again and he was a willing and enthusiastic participant.

He couldn't even remember what he and Tracy watched before she drifted off to sleep because every once in awhile she would turn and raise her chin once again, and they would share more slow, sweet kisses as he inhaled her coconut-scented hair. Sometime in the middle of all the kissing—he didn't even recall when—he reached up and pulled her hair free of the ponytail he'd fastened earlier, just so he could lace his fingers in it, his nails lightly raking her scalp. She moaned against his mouth that time and he was the one to pull back because that sound alone tested his resolve not to initiate anything until she let him know she wanted to.

So now she was asleep on his chest. It was past midnight on a weekday and if he wanted to get her home before morning he would have to wake her. But he didn't want to.

In Philly he spent a restless couple of nights remembering what it had been like sleeping with her in his bed. In sleep as when she was awake, Tracy was an enigma. She liked holding him, but she didn't want to be held. When he wrapped his arms around her, she murmured and swatted him away, but if he gave her too much space, she turned and draped a leg over his, an arm across his pecs, resting her head on his chest. He liked sleeping with her. Almost as much as he'd liked making lov ... fuck ... no, that didn't sound right either. That was the problem. He didn't know what to call what they did, didn't know what they were.

But one thing he did know was that it could only end badly.

Brendan took a deep breath and shook her gently, waiting until her eyes fluttered open. Apart from the beautiful eyes, he was greeted with a sweet-Tracy smile.

"Am I being evicted?" she asked, her voice soft.

"*No,*" he said quickly. "It's just that I figured you have work tomorrow, right? So I don't know if you need to get home, or ..."

"I'll go in the morning." She shut her eyes again, holding him tighter, and then after a moment they sprung open again. "Unless ... would you prefer that I go now?"

Yes! Now, man, Brendan told himself. *Do it now. Draw the line. It's one thing to spend time together but this is different. Tell her* right *now.*

"No," he said. "I would prefer it if you didn't."

Tracy said nothing but in response shut her eyes again and snuggled against him.

That was it. If there ever had been a line he'd long crossed it and it was so far behind him he didn't even know what it looked like anymore. But the truth was he was gone the minute she said what she said when they were walking in Midtown this evening.

It was like she climbed inside his head and read his fucking mind. He knew he wasn't what she was looking for, and if he was looking for anything serious, Tracy probably wouldn't be his choice either: she was high-maintenance, bratty, snobby and sometimes downright bitchy.

But there was something else, just beneath the surface that she gave him rare but tantalizing glimpses of; something that made him want to peel back all the layers of expensive clothes and make-up and private school manners. Something that made him want to strip her down to her rawest, truest self. What he might find there he had no idea, but the compulsion to find out was too strong to resist. For now, what he felt for her, he would label 'curiosity'.

HE WASN'T EVEN surprised when he woke up to the smell of cooking this time around. Except for the fact that it wasn't yet seven a.m., he almost expected it. Brendan stumbled out of bed and followed his nose, yawning hugely. Sometime during the night he removed his shirt and jeans, and slept in his briefs. Tracy, fast asleep next to him, had beaten him to it and already removed her jeans and was wearing one of his undershirts.

That was how he found her in the kitchen. She had a sandwich in her hand and looked bright-eyed and bushy-tailed, as though she had slept very well. Brendan was surprised to realize that he had too. Now that his eyes were open, he felt perfectly rested, something he didn't often feel.

"I grabbed you a regular coffee while I was out, and made

you a breakfast sandwich," Tracy said. "But I have to grab a car and head home to get ready for work."

"No, wait, I'll drive you," Brendan said turning to head back down to the bedroom.

"Don't," Tracy said smiling. "I have a car service from work coming to get me. They'll wait and bring me back. And it'd be hell for you trying to get back from Brooklyn afterwards."

She brushed by him and paused, coming back to get up on her toes and tilting her head backward so that Brendan realized that she wanted to kiss him and leaned in. She gave him a quick peck on the corner of his mouth.

"I'll let myself out. Call me later if you want to hang out."

Hang out? Brendan thought after she was gone.

Was that what they did? From where he sat, it felt like a lot more than that. But maybe she was right. No need to label it, examine it or question it. Just go with the flow. He grabbed the coffee Tracy had bought him and took a swallow, going back to the bedroom to turn on his cell phone.

As soon as he did, it started a series of chimes; there were plenty of missed calls and messages and only some of them were business-related. There was a message from Meghan asking how the Philly trip had gone and another from a woman he met at the opening of Lounge Two-Twelve. He remembered finding her attractive but not much else, so he deleted her message and returned Meghan's call, arranging to meet her for lunch at a pub they liked to go to.

As he was leaving the apartment for his morning meetings, he remembered the sandwich Tracy said she'd made him and ran up to the kitchen to grab it. It was egg, tomato and gruyere on sourdough and was the kind of thing he would do well not to get used to.

Meetings and a brief listening session with Shawn occupied his morning, and Brendan had very little time to think about anything but work.

Around noon, he drove Shawn to the condo for lunch with Riley. Brendan would have only twenty minutes to get back across town to meet Meghan and could have asked Shawn to cab it, but strangely, he liked listening to his friend talk about his marriage. Especially now that he and Riley were expecting the baby any day, Shawn was on constant alert, checking his phone every five minutes. Brendan tried to remember a time he had seen him so excited. Maybe the day he got married.

What he said to Tracy was true; he wasn't sure he wanted that kind of love. Shawn and Riley when they first got together were like a tornado. They either swept you into their vortex, or they wrecked all your shit. As tumultuous as it had been for Shawn in those days, it had been the same for Brendan because Shawn had been damn near impossible to manage. Every other week, he wanted to go off schedule to fly back to see Riley. Engagements had to be moved, people apologized to, contracts renegotiated. Brendan shook his head remembering it. At least now his boy was ensconced in a blissful domesticity, waiting for a baby.

"Most dudes want to run away from home when the wife is pregnant," Brendan observed. "You're the opposite."

"I know," Shawn said, grinning. "Picture that."

That was Shawn all over. Vague. If he wanted to know anything, Brendan would have to come out and ask it. So he did.

"It doesn't scare you ever?" he asked finally. "I mean, marriage is tough enough. But with the kid and everything, doesn't it feel kind of ... permanent?"

"Have you *met* my wife?" Shawn asked. "Why would permanent with her be scary?"

Brendan said nothing. Shawn still had The Fever, so he

should have known better than to expect a rational and objective response.

"But seriously though," Shawn said, sensing that his answer had not satisfied Brendan's curiosity. "I don't think about forever, B. All I know is that with her, at the end of every single day, I'm glad she's there and I don't know what I would do if she wasn't."

"Even when she's eight months pregnant and crazy as a loon?"

"She's not though," Shawn shrugged. "When she was working, maybe a little bit but now she's real chill, calm like she's preparing y'know? Getting her head into the game."

"The game being what exactly?" Brendan asked. "Parenthood?"

"Nah, man. Not just parenthood. *Life*. Real life."

Once he'd dropped Shawn off and was heading back, Brendan thought about that. The funny thing was he knew exactly what Shawn meant. For some dudes, the way Brendan lived now—the way Shawn used to live—was the ultimate. The luxury apartment, the traveling, the high-profile career and the women were what they aspired to.

Brendan had never been that guy though. A lot of how he lived felt like the wind up to the main event; to a time when he could slow down a little bit with someone who made slowing down worth it. The way Riley had done for Shawn. He just wasn't sure he wanted to walk through hell and back to get that though. Maybe it was better to embrace the calm and certain, like Meghan.

She was waiting for him in the booth they always sat in, and had already ordered the spinach and artichoke dip he always got. Wearing a brown suit and cream silk blouse, she waved when she saw him. Brendan kissed her quickly and slid into the seat opposite hers.

"So now that your Philly artist is out of the way, are we clear for planning Labor Day weekend?" she asked, smiling at him.

Brendan remembered now that they'd been talking about going out of town for Labor Day. Way out of town. To Puerto Rico to stay at the villa of a friend of his. Suddenly—and he didn't want to think about why—Brendan wasn't sure he wanted to go.

"We'll see," he mumbled, avoiding her eyes. "Something else might come up."

"Well, you were the one who said we'd want to get it locked in early," she pointed out.

There was a slight petulance in her tone, which Brendan couldn't recall her having had before. Women had great intuition about stuff like this. Could she sense something was different? But hell, he didn't even know if anything was different. He'd kissed Tracy, but nothing more. And Meghan was certainly free to see other people and kiss whomever she wanted, so ultimately, everything was just as it had been before. Or so he told himself.

SEVEN

TRACY CLIMBED OVER BRENDAN'S SLEEPING FORM AND headed for the shower. She could probably run out to Dean & DeLuca before taking one, but right after they ate, she was going to go to yoga, no matter what. Ever since she had fallen into the habit of hanging out with Brendan a couple nights a week and some weekends, she slacked off on Bikram. And especially with Riley her regular yoga buddy so long out of commission, it was easy to make excuses to skip. She had been trying to regain some weight but honestly, the snugness of her size four stuff was beginning to cause her some concern.

It was *his* fault, of course. Pushing big juicy steaks and assorted other crap onto her whenever they went out to eat. When she reminded him that he could afford to eat like a horse, given that he was six-five, he corrected her.

Six-three, he said.

What? Tracy asked. *Either way. You're tall.*

Yeah, but six-five would put me in the NBA, so ...

He was always like that. Going off topic, cracking jokes, making her forget whatever the hell it was that she'd been annoyed about in the first place. Which brought her to her other annoyance—Brendan's refusal to go actual grocery shopping so they didn't have to make multiple runs each weekend.

He explained it by claiming he had some bad experiences where he'd been traveling for weeks and come home to unidentifiable items covered in fungus. One time he told her, it was so disgusting that he replaced the refrigerator rather than face the task of cleaning it. So sad. And just crazy enough that it was precisely the kind of thing he would do.

She smiled.

"I'll come with you," a voice, still thick with sleep said from the bedroom, just as she was about to undress for the shower.

Tracy paused. *To shower, or to the store?*

"To the store," Brendan said, as though he read her mind. "But if you need some help in there, feel free to holla at me."

Tracy shed his shirt, pilfered from his dresser the evening before, and turned on the water, getting into the shower. She kept forgetting to bring a shower cap so invariably wound up with puffy or shaggy hair all weekend, which didn't bother her as much as she would have expected. And Brendan actually seemed to prefer it that way. Not that his preferences were a factor in how she wore her hair or anything.

His joke about coming to give her some help was, Tracy knew, probably just that. For some reason that she could not figure out, Brendan still had not made a move to try to get her to sleep with him. Well, they slept together all the time. That was the problem they *slept*. There hadn't even been heavy petting. It had been more than two weeks and all they'd done was make out like teenagers, carefully avoiding each other's genitals when they touched, as though uncertain of what went where. She wondered whether it was because of what happened after the Lounge Two-Twelve launch event. Or—and this was by far the more disturbing possibility—he was sexually monogamous with Meghan.

"You're going to be a prune in a minute. Hurry your ass up!"

Tracy started at the sound of Brendan's voice reaching her over the din of the water. It was only then that she realized she'd been in there for awhile, daydreaming. She shut the water off and grabbed one of his plush bath towels, going back out into the bedroom where he was fully dressed laying on the bed, with only his feet hanging over the edge to avoid soiling the sheets with his tennis shoes.

"I'm going to yoga today," she said firmly.

Brendan smirked. "Good luck with that."

"I am," she insisted.

"Good."

"I know you don't believe me," she said grabbing her gym bag. She held it up in triumph and pulled out her yoga pants and matching racer back top. "Hmm?"

"Putting on the clothes is one thing," Brendan said. "Walking out on a *Law & Order* marathon is another. And other things have a way of popping up. Or out."

"What are you talking about?" Tracy wrinkled her brow in confusion. "And there's a *Law & Order* marathon?" she asked, wincing.

"I texted you yesterday," Brendan yawned and sat up.

"Well you text about all manner of minutiae, Brendan, so honestly I've stopped reading them," she lied.

Actually, she loved it that he texted her about meaningless stuff. Loved that she might be in a client meeting and her phone would vibrate. She would apologize effusively and pretend it was something urgent and then have to stifle a smile when she read yet another absurd and irrelevant musing of Brendan's that she could scarcely believe he'd taken precious time out of his busy life to type.

Sometimes he was like a big kid; a big kid with Attention Deficit Hyperactivity Disorder maybe. Once, he actually texted to ask her why she thought the words "good" and "mood" were pronounced so differently despite having the identical letters "ood" at the end.

"Well it's your loss," he said, his breezy tone making it clear that he didn't for a minute buy her claim that she didn't read his text messages.

"If you actually texted me something that mattered, I would drop dead of shock," Tracy said. She pulled her underwear on without removing the towel and did the same with her yoga pants. For the top, she simply turned her back to Brendan and pulled it on quickly.

"Wait, I'm about to send you one right now," Brendan said, pulling out his cell phone. "And I promise you, it'll be something that matters."

"I'm sure it won't, but do feel free," Tracy smiled at him.

She went back to the bathroom to brush her teeth and when she returned, grabbed her cell. Brendan went into the bathroom himself and she heard running water as she looked down at her phone. Silly man. He really had sent her a message. Prepared for another joke, Tracy read the message: *Riley had the baby this morning 5:13 a.m. Boy 8 lbs. 3 oz.*

She shrieked and ran into the bathroom where Brendan was spitting toothpaste into the sink.

"Are you *serious*? When did you hear this? Who ..?"

"Shawn called while you were in the shower," he said, rinsing and spitting.

"How can you be so calm? Let's *go*! I want to see my godson!" Tracy jumped up and down beating a drumbeat onto Brendan's back while he finished up at the sink.

"Okay, okay," he turned finally. "Now I'm ready, so let's go."

All the way down in the elevator, Tracy was literally squealing her excitement. She wasn't sure she would be able to stand the ride to the hospital. She couldn't wait to see Riley and ask her what it the delivery had been like, and to kiss the baby and see which of his parents he looked like.

"We're *godparents*, Brendan!"

Riley was in a private room, and when they entered, Tracy was thrilled to see that the baby was there as well, in his own little bassinet. Riley's mom, Lorna, was sitting next to Riley's bed, watching her daughter sleep and Shawn was standing over the baby, looking down at him with something like awe. Putting aside their awkward history, Tracy went to him at once and hugged him close.

"Shawn, I'm so happy for you guys," she said, squeezing him tight.

She turned to look into the bassinet and saw that the baby, even though a newbie was already recognizably like his father, and already with a shock of dark, silky hair peeking out from beneath his nursery cap. His nose was definitely Riley's, but everything else, especially that pouty, full mouth was from his Dad. His Dad. Shawn was someone's *father*.

Tracy turned and smiled at him again, squeezing his arm.

"Brendan, come look," she said, "he's so beautiful."

Brendan had just gotten done greeting Lorna and came over to hug his best friend and peer into the bassinet.

"Looks just like you, man," he told Shawn.

Shawn grinned and nodded, looking like he was dead-tired but resisting sleep. Tracy went over to Riley's bed to allow Shawn and Brendan some space. Her friend was sleeping, her face peaceful. Someone had pulled her hair back and French-braided it. Not Riley herself, Tracy knew, because Riley was hopeless with hair, even her own.

"Hey," Tracy said to Riley's mom, her voice hushed. "How'd she do?"

"She was a warrior," Lorna said. "Refused the epidural."

Tracy rolled her eyes. "Why am I not surprised?"

Lorna laughed. "I thought Shawn was going to pass out when she started active labor with all the screaming and puffing."

Tracy glanced back at Shawn, feeling a rare surge of affection for him. No one had to tell her that he would have been beside himself to see Riley in actual physical pain.

"She looks so pretty," Tracy said, stroking Riley's hair. "For someone who voluntarily pushed out a nine pound child without the benefit of narcotics."

"Eight pounds three ounces," Riley croaked, opening her eyes. "And I barely had to do a thing. That kid was coming out, no matter what I did."

"Yeah, right," Tracy said, pulling up a chair to get closer to her. "How do you feel?"

"Like someone kicked me in the gut and then stomped on it with all their weight."

"Lovely. Well next time drugs, huh?"

"Next time? Oh *god*," Riley groaned.

Tracy laughed. "Oh, you have to make another one. This one is perfect, but I'd love a little goddaughter for a matched set."

"You sound like Shawn," Riley said, struggling to keep her eyes open. She held out a hand to Tracy and pulled her close, whispering in her ear. "Tracy. When he saw our son, he *cried*."

"So I guess you'd better give him as many as he wants," Tracy said.

"I guess I'd better," Riley said, and then she yawned loudly.

The sound of Riley's yawn called Shawn's attention back to

her and Tracy watched as he smiled. The love on his face was enough to make her heart quake.

Riley smiled sleepily, extending a hand to him.

"You've been up all night, baby," she said. "Come sleep with me."

That was everyone else's cue to make themselves scarce, so Tracy and Brendan said their goodbyes and Lorna went to sit next to the bassinet while Shawn shed his shoes and shirt and climbed into the hospital bed to sleep next to his wife. The sight of Riley's head on his shoulder, her arms about his waist, and Shawn's quiet contentment made Tracy's heart feel so full, she was grateful to leave before she burst into tears.

Yoga was out of the question after all that. And besides, Tracy was on too much of a high, so she and Brendan picked up take-out breakfast platters from a diner and headed back to his place. As they walked in, Tracy deposited her food on the table in the foyer and pulled out her cell phone.

"I'm sending messages to some of our friends," she explained.

Brendan grabbed her food and with his, walked it into the bedroom. Tracy followed and toed off her shoes as she typed out an email, sitting on the edge of the bed. Then she felt Brendan's hands under her arms, dragging her backwards to the top of the bed so she was bolstered by the headboard. She leaned against it still typing rapidly.

"Best yoga intentions shot to hell once again," she said. "I guess I should just give in to the fact that every weekend I spend with you, we'll be in bed eighty percent of the time." And then hearing how that sounded, she blushed and glanced at him. "You know what I mean."

"Well we do spend eighty percent of our time in this bed," Brendan said, his voice low. "Not that anything much ever happens here besides sleep, pillow fights and TV-watching."

Tracy paused her typing.

"Was that a complaint?" she asked carefully, not looking up.

"Just an observation."

"I wish I thought to take a picture of him," she said, focusing on the email again. "Wait a minute. Did they say what they planned to name him?"

"No. And the picture would've been on the internet within twenty minutes of your sending it out to your friends, so maybe it's better that you didn't take one."

"Oh crap, you're *right*. I keep forgetting they're famous." Tracy hit 'send' on her email and put the phone aside, turning to look at Brendan who was suddenly being uncharacteristically quiet.

"It's a whole new life for them now, isn't it?" she said. She couldn't seem to stop herself from smiling.

"Yup," he nodded slowly.

"And did you see Shawn? How happy he was? Riley said he cried when he saw the baby. I mean, doesn't it just make you love them both that much more when you see them together? I almost ..."

Before she could continue, Brendan's mouth was on hers, and by the nature of the kiss—as different as night and day from those sweet, almost chaste kisses they had been sharing these past weeks—Tracy knew that all talk of Shawn and Riley, or anything else for that matter was over with for the duration.

HE HELD out as long as he could. Brendan had been waiting for almost three weeks for her to give him a sign that she was ready for him and still wasn't sure whether he was reading her correctly. She undressed in front of him, but Brendan wondered and even worried that she thought of him as a brother more than anything else. If so, it was his own dumb-ass fault. You didn't let a woman, especially not a woman like Tracy, into your bed and give her the impression she could sleep in panties and a flimsy top with impunity.

But he had, and then once it had gone on for a time, it was tough to maneuver his way back to reminding her that he was one hundred percent a man, and could not have boobs pressed against him all night without wanting to slip her the high hard one. So he'd been strategizing, trying to think of a way to reintroduce sex into the equation with her.

In all fairness though, he hadn't been thinking about sex this whole time; he liked being with her, talking and laughing with her, watching television and making occasional grocery runs. It actually kind of scared him how much he'd liked doing all that stuff, none of which had anything to do with getting into her panties.

Still, he had already decided that today was going to be the day, and then Shawn called. Going to see a newborn when you weren't ready for kids of your own should have been a surefire way to shut down his libido, and at first it had been. But then he saw the way Tracy reacted, and something inside Brendan shifted.

Her joyfulness for Shawn and Riley had been completely selfless and the look of instant love for their new little person had been unmistakable. It was as though he witnessed her expand the reaches of her heart right there in front of him.

Looking at Shawn and Riley's little man, Tracy's face seemed to say, *You too. I welcome you into my heart, too.*

For the first time since he'd known her, she was consumed by something that had absolutely nothing to do with her. And yet she was happier and more excited than he had ever seen her before. Brendan watched her and he wondered whether she realized this about herself; that she had a hidden generosity of spirit. He wanted to tell her that he saw it, that he saw her. But she would probably have been embarrassed and may even have closed herself off again, and made one of her signature glib comments. And of course, there was also the possibility that she had been this generous and open and loving all along, but that he was the one who had misjudged her, believing her to be selfish and self-centered when she was anything but.

So he said nothing, and watched it unfold, and thought about how he had only begun to scratch the surface of the love she was capable of. He wanted to see more. And that was why he broke his promise to himself not to initiate. Because he couldn't help it. He wanted to see more of Tracy as she had been in that hospital room and since.

When he kissed her, she put her hands up right away, and he thought at first that she might try to push him back, but instead she gripped his shirt and held on for dear life as though she had been waiting for just *this* moment.

Brendan lowered himself over her and continued his slow, sensual exploration, moving from her lips to her neck, moving his hands over the smooth, snug fabric of her yoga top. He could feel her moan in the back of her throat as his fingers brushed her nipples and she pressed against his hand, encouraging him. Though he wanted nothing more than to have her naked, soon, he forced himself to go slow. There could be no ambiguity in their coming together. She knew he wanted her; she would have to show him unequivocally that she wanted him too.

Soon enough, she did. Tracy gripped the back of his shirt and pulled it up, tugging it impatiently over his head and then practically lurching for his chest. Brendan remembered this about her; she was demanding and assertive in bed, and would leave no room for error to get what she wanted. Now, she held on to his forearms and hoisted herself up to reach his nipples, tonguing and licking them, testing his resolve to take things slow. If he went purely on instinct right now, he would grab those goddamn yoga pants at the waist, rip them off and pile-drive the crap out of her.

Tracy raised her head even further and without warning bit him on the traps, just above his shoulder.

"What are you waiting for?" she breathed.

Brendan's eyes flew open at the combination of pain from the bite, and excitement at the urgency in her voice. He slid her yoga pants off with her underwear and reached down to touch her, to make sure she was ready. She was. So much so, he almost couldn't help but feel cocky. So to speak.

Her knees parted, almost as if in relief at his touch and he slid a finger inside her and then another, unable to stifle the sound from his throat when her inner muscles gripped them, almost pulling them in.

Tracy sighed and Brendan moved his mouth back to hers. She put one hand at the back of his neck, using her weight to pull him down to her, all while her hips undulated against his fingers. He added yet another and she moaned into his mouth, rolling her pelvis against his hand even faster. Just when he thought he would literally explode if he didn't get inside her Tracy pulled back and kissed him against the corner of his mouth.

"I hate it when you make me wait," she said, and her voice was low and husky and sexy as all get out.

She pushed against his chest until he realized what she wanted and lay on his back. Tracy straddled him, her thighs locked just above his pelvis, some of her weight on her knees. Brendan could feel her wetness against his stomach. Keeping her eyes fixed on his, Tracy reached behind her with both hands and slid his sweats down, just enough to free his erection.

With remarkable balance, she kept her position on his stomach but stroked him with both hands, running her hands up and down his length. The entire time she kept her eyes locked to his, and though he wanted to close his—because it felt *that damn good*—Brendan found that he couldn't.

The sight of Tracy sitting astride him, beautiful, magnificent, nipples erect, back arched and focused only on pleasuring him was a sight he would be a damn fool to pass up. It was so fucking erotic, he found it impossible to maintain a coherent thought except for one word: *more*.

Then Tracy was moving her hips back and forth, sliding herself against the line of soft and coarse hair on his stomach. Brendan could feel her heat and as her breath quickened so too did the motion of her hips and hands. Deciding that it was his turn to take charge once again, Brendan grabbed her by the hips and lifted her, rearing forward to impale her on him. But one word, breathed urgently stopped him.

"Condom," she said.

Brendan paused. *Shit.*

He had forgotten all about that. *Forgotten.* Something he never did. The last time he'd gone raw was with Tracy herself in L.A., what now seemed like dog-years ago.

"Oh my god," she groaned, misreading his face. "Don't tell me you don't have any."

Brendan laughed softly. "No, I do. Medicine cabinet."

Tracy moved so quickly, if he blinked he might have missed her. "Don't you *fucking* move," she said.

Brendan smiled. She only ever used that word when she was in the act, he now realized.

Momentarily she returned with a row of condoms. Six to be

exact. Brendan raised his eyebrows as she resumed her position astride his hips.

"Damn. You must think a lot of me if you believe I can live up to those expectations," he grinned.

"Brendan," she said leaning forward to slip her tongue in his mouth and then, smiling against his lips. "I think you just need to apply yourself."

Ah. *Humor*. The mainstay of his and Tracy's relationship, if that's what they had. Well, he was going to make sure she had nothing more to laugh about.

Brendan grabbed the condoms from her and ripped one open, sitting up while she wrapped her arms about him. He pulled it on and in one quick motion pulled her backward, burying himself inside her. Tracy's mouth fell open and her eyes shut. Brendan didn't move for a long while. Just watching the expressions that crossed her face and feeling himself inside her was enough.

Once again, he managed to wait her out. It was Tracy who took the initiative, placing her hands on his shoulders and pressing down on them, using them as leverage to raise and lower herself against him in a squatting motion. Brendan leaned back, propping himself up with his elbows, letting her take charge of her own pleasure, feeling himself enveloped by her.

"You're making me lazy," he said. Even getting the words out was hard, she felt so fucking good.

"You don't have to do anything," Tracy breathed. "Just ... stay just like that."

Something about that made him alert once again. Brendan fought his way back from the delicious distraction of being encompassed in Tracy's warmth and watched her for a moment more, her eyes closed, moving against him. She was *masturbating*. He was just the human dildo she was getting off on.

Was this what she was used to? Using men to get off, not seeing them, and not caring if they saw her?

The thought was depressing and he could feel himself getting marginally softer. It explained something. The night of the Two-Twelve launch, the guy who scared her. Suddenly Brendan understood.

Some men would not stand for being disappeared this way. Their egos, their very sense of their own manhood, could not stand for it and they would find another way to assert that manhood. Like maybe aggression.

"Tracy," he said, firmly. "*Stop.*"

"What?" she breathed, her voice impatient, still engrossed in her own pleasure. "*Why*?"

She moved faster, trying to reach completion. Brendan sat upright and held her by the hips, stilling her.

"Open your eyes," he said.

It made sense now that she only used the word 'fucking'. That's all this was to her. Maybe all it had ever been. He wondered whether—as beautiful as she was—Tracy had ever had a man make love to her. She opened her eyes, almost unwillingly and looked at him, confused.

Brendan's intention was to tell her his theory, to ask her what happened the night of the launch, just to confirm his suspicions. But when he looked into her eyes he was almost certain that she didn't know why whatever happened to her had happened. This kind of sex was probably all she had ever known.

A woman who looked the way she did, he could imagine got lots of offers; and most men who got her into bed were probably so damn happy to be there they used her to live out their porn movie fantasies. With sexual experiences like that, would it be any wonder that she would learn to take her own pleasure, just as they seized theirs?

So instead of talking about what she hadn't gotten from men before, Brendan decided he would be the one to give it to her. Make love to her the way she deserved to be loved.

"Brendan?" she said. Her voice sounded almost apprehensive, and she looked worried.

About what? Did she think he was upset with her? That she wasn't pleasing him? *What was going on inside that head of hers?*

"What's wrong?" she asked.

He tried to smile to reassure her, and gently raised her, pulling her off him. She looked alarmed, as though convinced now for certain that she had messed up somehow.

"Nothing's wrong, sweetheart," he said kissing her softly on the corner of her mouth. "I just want to go slow. Okay?"

She looked surprised at his use of the endearment. He said it because she *was* sweet, even if she didn't know it. Then her expression changed from surprised to puzzled for a moment, and then apprehensive once again. Almost like it was her first time. Brendan felt something inside his chest clench painfully.

"Let's just go slow," he said again.

"Okay," she said after a long while.

He stroked the side of her face and pulled her to him, holding her for a long time.

BRENDAN KNEW he was going to get in trouble with this woman and now he had. *Big* trouble. He could chalk it up to the emotional morning with Riley's baby being born and Tracy being so affected by it, but in his heart of hearts he knew that wasn't it. After his epiphany about her sex life, he just held her, nothing more, until he felt her stir against him, growing excited just from being held. He wanted her to know that it was possible, that there was arousal to be found in tenderness as well.

Then he kissed her, resisting when she immediately wanted to touch him, or have him touch her. Just kissing, with her nakedness against him, was difficult but he did it, for as long as it took for her to stop going for his package and just be in the moment.

When finally he touched her, he didn't let her reciprocate, not for awhile. He lay her on her back and ran the tips of his fingers over every part of her–face, shoulders, arms, breasts, hips, thighs–every part of her except the part that she tried desperately to get him to touch. The puzzlement never left her eyes and Brendan realized with wonder that she really hadn't had anyone do this for her before. It seemed inconceivable when he would have happily done only that for hours on end.

When she closed her eyes, he told her to open them again. He wanted her to see him, to see that he wanted her but could take pleasure in her pleasure; to see that he could wait until she had everything she needed; that she didn't need to rush frantically toward orgasm because he could be trusted to make sure she got there.

And he made sure she did. With his fingers, with his tongue; three times before he would allow her to touch him and even then, he would not let her use her mouth on him. That was too much for now, and ran the risk of making him forget who this was about, and what he was trying to do. When she did touch him, she was different. Slower, more patient, remembering the way he had been with her.

Brendan made sure he was on top, looking right into her eyes when he entered her, kissing the side of her face and her neck, telling her she was beautiful, reminding her to open her eyes again whenever she shut them.

Once inside her, he moved slowly, so, so slowly, and when

Tracy tried to increase the pace, wanting to slam her hips hard against his, he held her still. He moved inside her one slow inch forward, two back, making her focus on the finely-tuned and delicate sensation of welcoming him into her body. When he couldn't stand it himself, and was so hard he thought he might lose consciousness from the pressure, he moved a little faster, pushed a little deeper, but only marginally.

When he didn't hear her, Brendan pulled back a little, swallowing hard, still fighting to maintain his own control.

"Baby ..." he breathed. "You okay?"

Brendan was stunned when she reached up and pulled him down, both her hands on the sides of his face.

"Please," she said over and over again. "*Please.*"

At that, he finally gave in, thrusting hard and fast, and allowing her move at a pace of her choosing. It was only moments afterward that she exploded about him, calling his name, either as curse or endearment, he wasn't sure, and her arms wrapped tightly about his neck.

When the tremors inside her stopped, he moved slowly once again, finally feeling it was safe to reach his own satisfaction. But Tracy was quivering beneath him and for a moment, Brendan thought he'd misread the cues of her body and that she was still in the throes of orgasm, but when he looked down, he saw that she was crying, deep but quiet sobs wracking her body.

He tried to pull out of her but she wouldn't let him. She wrapped her arms even more tightly about his neck as though she never wanted to let go, pressing herself closer, pulling him even deeper inside her.

EIGHT

When your own home started feeling like a place where you didn't belong, you had to sit up and take note, Tracy thought as she opened the door. The air was a little stale and it took her a moment to remember that she'd turned off the air before she left for work on Thursday, and she had been gone three nights. She turned it back on and headed upstairs to look for something to wear. Though she got away with wearing her suit from work on Friday to the church for the baby's blessing, she needed something different for the party at Shawn and Riley's later this afternoon.

As much as she had wanted to go back to Brendan's with him after church and hang out till it was time to go to Jersey, it wasn't possible. She didn't keep clothes there, and had been careful to leave nothing behind, ever, not even a toothbrush. That was becoming a lot more challenging since over the past month she had gone from spending one or two nights over, to an average of three. Each time, it seemed spur-of-the-moment; she only planned to have dinner with him, having brought over something from Zabar's or his favorite restaurant and a bottle of wine.

They usually ate dinner in the kitchen and he talked to her about his work which she found surprisingly interesting. Then they'd go with the wine into his bedroom to watch some television and Tracy fell asleep with her head on his chest. Or, if they were feeling frisky (which was almost always) they fooled around until she was squirming and moaning and almost begging for it. Okay, not almost. She did beg for it.

No one had ever made her feel the way he did in bed. Like she was completely and utterly out of control. Somehow he knew how to touch her in a way that made pleasure radiate throughout her entire body, no matter where his hands actually were. His fingers brushing across her face were enough to make her push her hips toward him, anticipating where he would take her and how. *And the stuff he said!*

Despite her experience, Tracy had never been much into talking in bed, and if a man talked, she invariably wished he would shut the hell up and get on with it. But with Brendan it was different. She *liked* talking to him. And not only did he like talking, he was always saying the kind of shocking things that would have made her blush if she wasn't so damn turned on by it all. And despite that, nothing with him felt dirty or taboo, it just felt ... right.

Two weeks ago, while they were making love, she had been overcome with the desire to feel him, not a rubberized version of him, but *him*. And she told him so.

When she said the words, he hesitated, and for a moment she was sorry she'd brought it up, her face burning with shame.

Okay, he said finally. *So we'll go get tested.*

She nodded, relieved that he hadn't recoiled at the idea altogether.

And you're on the pill, right?

Of course, Tracy had laughed.

Well, you know I had to ask, Brendan said. *You look at Cullen and you get that hungry look those women who don't have babies sometimes get.*

Tracy had reared back and slugged him with a pillow. *Oh you should be so lucky as to have babies with me, Brendan Cole.*

Well they would be beautiful babies, he said seriously. And then after a pause. *But to be clear, you* are *on the pill, right?*

I am, she told him again, looking him in the eye. *But there's one other thing.*

Isn't there always? Brendan asked, lowering his head to take one of her nipples between his lips.

If we do this, you understand you still have to use condoms with any other partners you might have, right?

He froze for a moment and released her nipple looking at her for what seemed like a long while. She couldn't figure out what his expression meant. But finally he nodded and lowered his head to her breast once again.

Tracy swallowed her hurt.

Now she had all the confirmation she needed that he was still sleeping with Meghan. They had never discussed monogamy, or even what they were calling this thing they were doing. And it was fine, because she didn't know what she wanted the answer to be if they tried to define it. What she did know was that he was still the same man, and that he was not someone she could consider really being with. And it wasn't as though he said anything to indicate that he wanted to be with her in that way either. Which was totally fine.

She'd gotten what she asked for after all. They spent time together; lots of time. And he was still a really, really good friend. He never made her feel like he didn't want to be with her and if he had dates with Meghan, he was discreet enough that she never detected it. And she was mostly incurious about that. Mostly.

There had only been the one time when he was up in the kitchen and she spotted his phone sitting on the entryway table as she headed for the bedroom to change into one of his t-shirts. On the way back, she stopped and picked it up, not really forming any clear intention at all about whether to look at it. The face lit up and she was surprised that it didn't require a passcode to unlock it.

Tracy's finger slid, almost without her consent, down to the phone icon and before she thought about why, she tapped it once and began scrolling through the recent calls.

When you're done looking for whatever you're looking for in my phone, Brendan's voice called from above, *could you bring it to me? I need to return some email.*

Tracy had almost dropped the damn thing in fright, and her face became hot with embarrassment. She took a moment to regain her composure and go back up to the kitchen, handing him the phone and preparing for an angry—and completely justified—lecture about boundaries, trust and privacy. But all Brendan had done was take it from her with a mumbled, *thanks sweetheart*, followed by a playful grope of her butt. And when she sneaked a look at him out of the corner of her eyes, he indeed seemed to be returning email and by all appearances was not giving a second thought to her snooping.

She sighed now, fighting her frustration that she still hadn't figured him out. Normally, she would have had the benefit of Riley's thinking, but neither of them had told their friends what was going on. It hadn't started as a secret, but once Cullen was born the fact that they were sleeping together, it seemed so irrelevant to anything Shawn and Riley were going through that they just didn't mention it. And now that so much time had passed, it was going to be awkward to break the news.

Maybe at the house today, Tracy thought as she looked through her closet.

In that kind of setting, she seriously doubted Brendan was going to be able to keep himself from touching her in a way that made it apparent they were toge... well, not *together*, but whatever. Not that he was the jealous type at all. When he touched her, it wasn't about possession, but just about the fact that he didn't seem to be able to help himself.

Come to think of it, Brendan was disturbingly unaffected when other men looked at her. On one of their many trips to Dean & DeLuca last weekend some guy had been gawking directly and unashamedly at her ass, encased in tights, because she and Brendan had just come back from the gym. And instead of going ballistic, and becoming insanely possessive the way Shawn would have about Riley, Brendan only smirked.

On the walk back to the apartment, she had sulked until he finally asked her what was wrong, sounding more amused than concerned.

Why didn't you just give *me to him?* she demanded. *He clearly wanted me and you clearly didn't care.*

Why should *I care*? Brendan said.

Gee, thanks!

She stalked ahead of him, her eyes burning with unshed tears. Tears of anger, of course. Not of hurt, *anger*. Brendan hurried to catch her, which didn't take him too much effort, and put down the grocery bags, hugging her tight.

Why should I care if some dude wants to look at your ass for a couple seconds too long? he said, speaking into her hair. *All I know is two things: one, if he ever tried to touch it I'd fuck him up. And two, I'm the one who gets to take that fine ass home and put it on my chin.*

Tracy's eyes had opened wide at the lewd reference to what

he'd done to her just that very morning. But what he said did help her relax just a little. She relaxed even more when they got back to the apartment and after their shower, up against the bathroom wall, he showed her just how much he appreciated her "fine ass."

Shaking her head, she refocused on the matter at hand, finding something to wear for the party for Cullen's blessing. Brendan told her he secretly hated the name Shawn and Riley had chosen.

I love that name! Tracy protested.

White name, Brendan muttered.

Oh my god, Brendan, there is no such thing! Tracy had gasped, tossing a wad of unused toilet paper at him.

He had walked in on her as she was peeing and begun to shave; something he did so often now she didn't even notice or react to it anymore.

Okay, so what kind of name is Shanika? he challenged.

That's different, Tracy said wiping herself.

So there are Black names but no white names.

Well, the ... the ... Tracy stood at the sink next to him and rinsed her hands. *The difference is ...*

Thought so, Brendan said nodding. *Like I said. White name. At least his middle name is Brendan. A strong, masculine, race-neutral name that any kid could be proud of.*

Tracy had rolled her eyes and left him to finish shaving.

Okay, this was ridiculous. She needed to pick an outfit and stop thinking about Brendan. She'd only just left him about forty-five minutes ago for heaven's sake. Then her landline was ringing and she ran to grab it. He was probably checking to see she got home, okay. At least she wasn't the only one who was obsessing.

"Hello," she said, trying to sound bored.

"Tracy, I've been trying to reach you for several days now. I think it's rather inconsiderate of you not to call me back given all that's happening with you father."

Tracy closed her eyes and cursed herself for not checking the caller id before picking up.

"Sorry, Mom. It's been rather hectic at work."

"They have you working weekends now?" her mother demanded. "Seems rather unreasonable."

"How is Malcolm?" Tracy asked, sitting on the edge of her bed.

"Your father is fine," her mother responded, pointedly emphasizing the word 'father'. "Fine under the circumstances at least."

Three and a half months ago, her mother's husband had suffered a massive stroke, leaving one side of his body all but immobilized. Tracy had flown out briefly to provide her support, but managed to leave after only a few days when her aunts had shown up. She had pointed out to her mother that as a practical matter, they were better equipped to stick around and offer help because they were retired, and she on the other hand had to work. She promised upon leaving that she would fly home to Georgia at least every other weekend but had not been back since. Hence her avoidance of her mother's calls.

"And Riley had her baby last month," Tracy said, to further bolster her alibi. "Today was the blessing, and as the godmother, I had to, y'know, do ... stuff."

"Hmm." Her mother sounded unimpressed. "How she stayed married to that rap performer after everything, I'll never understand. And now to have a baby with him. I suppose she's made her bed."

Tracy swallowed hard. "Shawn is an amazing husband. And he's going to be an amazing father."

"Yes. Well. I'm more concerned about your father, Tracy. It

hasn't escaped his notice that you've not been here. Just because he can't speak doesn't mean he can't think. Or feel."

"I know. It's just been so crazy. I'll make plans to come soon."

"How soon, Tracy Ann?"

She hated when her mother used her first and middle names like that. Tracy could just see her face when she said them; her thin lips pinched, her powdered face drawn into a frown. Her mother frowned quite a bit, and whenever Tracy thought of her, it was with a look of disapproval, bordering on distaste marring her otherwise handsome and attractive features. Occasionally, to her horror, Tracy would walk past a mirror and see a trace of her mother's angry, disapproving face looking back at her.

"I'll find a date and make a reservation next week. I'll call you when I know what it is," Tracy said.

"Good. And please don't make me hunt for you again, Tracy. It worries me. And I have enough worries as it is."

"I'm sorry," she mumbled.

"Don't be sorry, Tracy Ann," her mother said, as she always did when Tracy apologized. "Just do better."

She hung up and Tracy felt the tension leave her shoulders. Talking to her mother always made her feel like she'd failed in some fundamental but unspecified manner. Today at least, her failure was clear: she was a bad daughter for having not come to see Malcolm, for not returning calls, for avoiding going back to Georgia to join the vigil at the bedside of a man who, however damaged, would probably outlive them all.

Tracy turned to more pleasant matters, finally choosing to wear her emerald green, stretched silk, sleeveless Akris dress with the jeweled neckline and ribbed pleated skirt that stopped just above her knees. With it she would wear her nude pumps, the ones that made her legs look incredible. Having settled on her outfit, she jumped in the shower. Her hair, which she had allowed to go practically wild lately, would take some work so she would need to start soon, before it was time to drive out to Jersey.

ACROSS THE ALREADY CROWDED ROOM, when Tracy walked in, she honed in on one person and one person only. Meghan. Holding a wineglass and wearing a pretty white blouson top and black pencil pant, she was talking and laughing with Robyn Crandall, one of Shawn's attorneys. Next to her, but engrossed in a separate conversation was Brendan. But he was *next to her*.

"You made it."

Tracy turned toward Riley's voice and hugged her friend. Riley looked amazing to have just given birth a month ago, but her boobs seemed to have gotten larger.

"Breastfeeding," Riley said following her eyes and shrugging. "You can't imagine how thrilled Shawn is."

"With the breastfeeding or the breasts."

Riley thought for a moment. "Both. Come see Cullen."

There was no way to graciously admit that at the moment she was more interested in staying downstairs and watching to see whether she could figure out whether Meghan came here with *her* man. Yes, yes, so he wasn't *officially* her man, and he'd never told her he wasn't seeing Meghan any longer, in fact she told herself that she accepted that he probably was. But even if that was the case, did he have to *rub her face in it?*

And after this morning, when they barely wanted to get out of bed long enough to go see their godson blessed ...

"So here's one for the books," Riley said as she and Tracy ascended the stairs to the nursery. "The man who's been badgering me to get someone to help around the house suddenly doesn't want anyone here at all. Claims we can do it all on our own."

"He's just being overprotective," Tracy said, her mind elsewhere.

"But what the hell? It's not like I'm superwoman, or anything. So we're actually fighting about this now. Except now I'm the one who wants to hire someone if you can believe that."

"You two *thrive* on fighting," Tracy said impatiently. "So please stop acting like you don't enjoy it."

Riley stopped and looked at her. "What the hell's gotten into *you*?"

Tracy looked at her and sighed. "I'm sorry. My mother called just before I got here. I don't know why I'm taking this out on other people ..."

"No, it's okay." Riley squeezed her shoulder. "I know I've become one of those women who only ever talk about their husband and their baby. And you've got a lot going on as well."

You have no idea.

"So tell me; how's Malcolm?"

"He's stable, I guess. My mother wants me to come home to visit though. Which you know I would rather stab myself in the eye with a pencil than do."

Riley laughed. "So you're all out of excuses not to, I'm guessing."

"I used you and the baby as my excuse this morning but she wasn't buying it."

"You can use me anytime," Riley joked.

When they got to the nursery, Cullen was fast asleep on his back, still wearing his charming little christening gown, breathing long, quiet breaths. Each day he was getting cuter and rounder with the face of a cherub and a beautiful honey-colored complexion; a real golden boy.

Tracy smiled in spite of her earlier annoyance. It was impossible not to smile when looking at her little guy.

"I just want to suck on those cheeks," she whispered.

"I can't stop kissing them," Riley admitted. "I look at him and feel like I invented this kind of love. Like no one has *ever* loved a kid in the history of motherhood as much as I love him. But every mother probably feels that way."

"Hah. I doubt *my* mother ever did," Tracy said dryly.

"Tracy," Riley turned away from the crib. "Your mother loves you. She's just hard on you because she wants you to be better than she thinks she was."

"That's not a very high standard. As much as she likes to pretend she's perfect."

Riley seemed not to know what to say to that. Tracy sympathized. Riley's own relationship with her mother could not be more different than Tracy's with her mother. How *could* she understand?

"Anyway," Tracy said, putting her out of her misery. "Let's go down and enjoy the party. When did Brendan and Meghan get here?" she added casually.

"Pretty early on. I came downstairs and they were already here," Riley shrugged.

That bastard, Tracy thought. Then she smiled at Riley and followed her out of the room and back down the stairs.

The house was becoming more crowded now, with about a hundred and fifty guests or so, and Tracy no longer saw Meghan or Brendan. Riley drifted off to greet her new guests while Tracy speculated that maybe they'd stolen off someplace for some alone time. The very idea of it made her chest constrict. Rather than examine why, or what that feeling meant, she wandered over to grab herself some finger food.

And that was another thing. She was easily a size six now. Not her fighting weight for going into the fall. Everyone knew you gained weight when the weather cooled down, and she did not want to gain weight.

"You look amazing in that dress."

His voice, right at the shell of her ear, caused her stomach to flutter. For a moment, Tracy forgot that she was angry and when she turned to look at him and it got far worse. Lately, every single time she looked at him, she noticed something else that made him damn near impossible to resist. Like the single dimple he had in his left cheek.

"I hope it comes off easily though," Brendan said against her neck, his fingers scanning the zipper at the back of her dress. "Because later, I'ma tear that ass u.."

"I haven't seen Shawn yet," she interrupted him, her face growing warm, not from embarrassment, but in spite of herself, from excitement. "Do you know where he is?"

"Someplace outside I think," Brendan said.

He was still looking at her with that appraising look, the one that told her he wanted to be doing very, very naughty things to her. Things she wanted him to do. But he was such a *fucking asshole.* To do what they'd done this morning and then bring Meghan here?

"I'm going to look for him," Tracy said. She rushed off before he could say anything else.

Funny that Brendan wasn't the rapper instead of Shawn. He was extraordinarily ... verbal. In bed and out, he liked to talk about what he was doing, what he wanted to do to her and what he wanted her to do to him; sometimes using language that was so frank and so *coarse* it made her blush and wonder if she should instead be offended.

Maybe she wasn't offended because his repertoire was so vast and his range so broad. One day they might have raw, crazy, Olympic sex, punctuated by dirty talk and the next he was so tender, and said such beautiful things, she cried as she climaxed. He had her head spinning like a top and she didn't know how to make it stop. She wasn't sure she wanted to.

But tonight? Tonight she was *livid.* Because he had come to the party with Meghan. The last thing she remembered was them planning to meet back at his place later tonight. So how, why would he bring Meghan? What was his plan, exactly? To take Meghan home and kiss her a sweet goodbye at the door, then come home and take *her* spread-eagled across his living room floor?

She found Shawn outside, talking to few of his business associates whose names she forgot as soon as she was introduced. Tracy hugged him, making nice for a few minutes as was her duty to do as his son's godmother. But that wasn't the only reason. The truth was, she'd warmed to Shawn considerably over the past month, and for his part, he seemed not to be simply tolerating her anymore. She dared say he was beginning to like her a little bit.

"So Riley told me you don't want to get someone to help out around the house," she said casually.

Shawn shook his head. "No, what I told her was we'll get someone to help out with the house, but I don't want anyone else looking after the baby. I don't think that's unreasonable."

There was a question in his tone, and Tracy tried not to smile. Unless she was mistaken, Shawn was *asking for her opinion. It was official, hell had frozen over.*

"Well, it depends. I mean, she wants to go back to work soon, right? So when she leaves, don't you think it'll be strange to just leave the baby with someone who you never got a chance to see in action, taking care of him while Riley was around to supervise?"

"I was thinking she'd take him to work with her," Shawn said.

Tracy couldn't help herself. She laughed out loud. But Shawn didn't look amused.

"She's the boss," he shrugged. "She can do whatever the hell she wants."

"Only if she's prepared for everyone who works for her to ask for the same privilege," Tracy pointed out.

Shawn rubbed his chin. "Or she could just work from home from now on."

"She would hate that and you know it," Tracy said quietly.

"Yeah, you're probably right."

Hell was getting colder by the second.

"So I guess you've got to give her this one," Tracy said wryly.

Shawn smiled and shook his head. "She gets 'em all, Tracy."

"Tracy?"

She turned to see who had spoken her name, and her smile faltered when Meghan approached.

"Meghan. Hello," she said.

Meghan leaned in to kiss her cheek and Shawn's. Funnily, it was her kissing Shawn that was more bothersome. These were *her* friends, and Brendan was her ... whatever he was. And where had this woman come from anyway? Meghan had only known Shawn and Riley for a hot minute and here she was acting like a long lost friend or something. And then, to make matters much, much worse, here came Brendan.

Tracy sighed. If she had to watch them together, she was going to lose her shit, right here in the middle of this high-profile party.

Luckily, Brendan seemed more interested in talking to the men Shawn had been conversing with but she sensed that he was hyper-aware, of her or of Meghan she wasn't sure. Probably of Meghan. The *real* girlfriend.

"So, I missed you at the church," Tracy said to Meghan, her voice sweet as pie.

She knew full well that Shawn and Riley had limited attendance at the church to very close friends and family. There had been only Lorna, Brendan, Tracy and two of Shawn's cousins from Baltimore in attendance. Only the smallest nucleus of their inner circle.

"Oh, no I wasn't at the church," she said, oblivious to Tracy's intent to embarrass her.

But Shawn had narrowed his eyes, sensing that something was afoot. He turned and exchanged a look with Brendan who in turn looked at her. Whatever. She didn't read faces, or minds for that matter.

"Hmm," Tracy said. "Now that I think about it, it was a small, intimate group."

Meghan smiled, but looked a little unsure of herself for a moment, as though she sensed a change in tone but had no idea what might have caused it.

"Shawn can tell you more than I what it's like," Tracy continued. "Having just random people at important life events like that, and the next thing you know, everything that was said winds up in a tabloid somewhere."

Meghan nodded and looked at Shawn. "I can imagine that must be difficult. Knowing who to trust."

"No, you can't imagine," Tracy said. "When Riley was three months along, someone in her doctor's office leaked it along with some made up story about her having a venereal disease. She cried for a week."

"Well, I'm sure Riley knows that I would never ..."

"Does she?" Tracy seized on the comment. "How does she know? She doesn't know you at *all*, Meghan. In fact, none of us do. Except for *maybe* Brendan."

"Tracy!"

The tone of Brendan's voice was one she had never heard him use before. Not with anyone. Apparently someone was a little peeved that she was going after his girlfriend.

"Well it's true," Tracy said, trying to sound unaffected. "There are all manner of opportunists around these days, so ..."

Meghan just stood there looking shell-shocked and confused. Brendan stood next to her, glaring down at Tracy like she was some kind of lab specimen. And Shawn just looked like he was enjoying the show.

"Tracy, shut the hell up," Brendan said. *"Stop it."*

She stared stubbornly at him for a moment, turned on her heel and walked away, shoving her way blindly through the crowd. Inside, she collided with Riley, on her way out to the backyard.

"Riley, I hope you don't mind if I ..." she began, but then she felt a hand on her arm and the next thing she knew, she was being pulled along like a recalcitrant child.

Brendan pushed open the door that led to Shawn's studio and kept walking until they were in the privacy of the live room.

"Why're you being such a bitch?"

"How am I being a bitch?" she asked. "By pointing out that this woman is a little late to the party, so to speak? That she's someone Riley and Shawn don't know at all? Someone who's insinuated herself into ..."

"She hasn't *insinuated* herself into anything, Tracy."

"No, that's right. She hasn't. Because *you* brought her in the front door."

"I don't even understand what we're talking about. What, you think Meghan's a spy for TMZ or some shit?"

Tracy rolled her eyes.

"Then what? Help me out with this Tracy. I'm trying to figure out what has you trippin' and I'm coming up blank!"

"Because you're an *idiot*," she said.

And then Brendan did something that further enraged her. He actually *smiled*. That thoroughly disarming smile that made her weak at the knees.

"I *am* an idiot," he said, still smiling. "Because I put up with tantrums like this from you at least weekly. And I keep coming back for more. So I guess you're right, I'm an idiot."

"Well you don't have to put up with them any longer, Brendan," she said, trying to get her voice to stop shaking. "We're done."

"*Done*?" he asked, his voice bored. "What are we done with? We were never anything anyway, right?"

Tracy swallowed the golf-ball sized lump in her throat. "I'm glad we're on the same page."

"We aren't even reading from the same book, sweetheart," Brendan said, his face impassive.

"Then there's nothing else to say," Tracy said, turning to leave. She only hoped she could get away before she did something stupid like start crying. But Brendan grabbed her arm again.

"You already embarrassed yourself tonight. Don't make it worse by embarrassing Riley too," he said. "They have speeches and a whole thing planned. As the godmother, you're going to have to find some touching shit to say.

"So what you're going to do now is, you're going to stay here for a minute, pull yourself together and then come outside and do something for someone else for a goddamned change."

And then he left her there.

TRACY WEARILY CLIMBED the stairs to her bedroom and kicked off her shoes. *Fine*. So she and Brendan were done. She couldn't complain about not having closure; there was that at least. And she was sure that strange void in her chest would dissipate soon.

After she left the sanctuary of Shawn's studio and returned to the party, Riley had quickly assembled the guests in the loggia—probably alerted by the scene with Brendan that she'd better do it quick because something was about to blow—and there were toasts and thanks and general good wishes.

Just as Brendan had warned her to do, she made a sweet speech about how much she loved her new godson, and how much she loved Riley and had come to love Shawn as well. Then Brendan took his turn as the godfather and didn't look at her the whole time. After the speeches were done, she made her excuses to leave, taking care to do so while Riley was occupied with other guests and couldn't take the time from them to interrogate her.

As she left, she saw Brendan talking to Meghan, his hand on her shoulder as though comforting her. Probably apologizing for the unprovoked attack she'd suffered at the hands of the crazy woman in a designer dress.

In her purse, her cell phone rang. She groaned.

No. Not now.

If Riley wanted her to explain, she just didn't feel like ... Then she realized it was Brendan's ringtone. She let it ring until it went to voicemail and ignored it when it rang again. The third time, she picked up, but said nothing, just listening.

"Open the fucking door, Tracy."

She hesitated. *Open the door?*

Still holding the phone to her ear, she went to the top of the stairs, looking down at the front door, but couldn't see anything but someone's legs from that vantage point.

"Open the door," he said again, his voice calmer this time.

The only thing that made her decide to do it was the realization that he had to have left almost immediately after she did, or driven very, very fast. That had to count for something, surely.

He crowded his way in as soon as the inner door was open a crack, and Tracy shut it behind him, leaning against it, afraid to look up at his face.

"You make me fucking crazy, you know that?" he demanded.

Tracy said nothing, focusing on his shoes. He had great taste in shoes, and they all looked very expensive. Shoes and shirts were his vices. And that ridiculously pricey car. As vices went, she supposed that wasn't so bad. She had definitely known worse.

"Meghan didn't come to the party with me. She came because Riley invited her. She came on her own."

Slowly, she raised her chin and looked at him.

He looked no less angry than he sounded. So he'd finally figured out what made her mad, huh? Or, more likely, Riley told him she was fishing around for information about when he had arrived with Meghan.

"You didn't have to go off on her like that. If you were pissed at me, come at me. Why be a bitch to someone who's never even done anything to you?"

She has done something to me, Tracy thought. *The fact of her existence does something to me.*

"You need to handle your shit, Tracy. Because tonight? That mess was just ... sloppy."

"I'm sorry," she said finally.

"Why are you even here?" he continued, his voice softer. "We were supposed to meet back at my place."

"Because we ended it." she said quietly.

"Oh you meant that?" he said, his voice impassive and sounding unconvinced.

Tracy said nothing. No, she didn't mean it. She didn't mean a word of it but had been worried that he believed she did, and that her foolish pride would prevent her from taking it back.

She shook her head.

"I didn't think you did. So I expected you to go to my place," Brendan said.

"If you thought that," she said, hesitant to challenge him in his current mood, "why did you come here?"

"Because Tracy, whenever I think of the rational thing a person would do, you generally do the opposite."

She couldn't help it. That made her smile.

"It's not funny," Brendan said. He ran a hand over his face and sighed. "Anyway, I'm drained from all this shit. I'm going home and going to bed."

He came toward her and moved her gently out of the way, opening the door. Then he paused and placed something on the entryway table.

Tracy looked at it and almost couldn't believe her eyes.

"Brendan," she said.

"That's a key to the apartment." He explained what needed no explanation. He didn't turn to look at her as he spoke. "Your key."

"I didn't come to the apartment," she admitted, "because I thought maybe you'd have Meghan there. Especially after what I said about us being done."

"Meghan doesn't come to my apartment, Tracy," he said, his voice tired. "Not for a long time. And no one sleeps there. No one ever has. No one but you."

She was glad his back was still turned, because she couldn't contain how overjoyed that news made her, even as she wondered why it should matter so much.

"Brendan ..."

"Goodnight," he said, cutting off whatever she'd been about

to say. "And don't use the key to try to come over tonight, either. I think you've shown me enough of your ass for one day."

He shut the door quietly on his way out, which was almost more condemnatory than if he had slammed it.

Still, once he was gone, Tracy permitted herself the pleasure of a wide, self-satisfied grin.

NINE

Five days. It had only been five days. And why was he even counting?

Not too long ago, he had slept every single night in this very bed, alone. And preferred it that way. Now Brendan found himself delaying the part of his day that involved going home to his empty apartment even though it meant he could watch basketball uninterrupted instead of flipping back and forth between NBA TV and the Home Design Channel to satisfy Tracy's insatiable and inexplicable appetite for information about how other people decorated their houses.

Late last week when they were eating out for dinner for a change she mentioned casually that she had to go home to Atlanta "for a couple of days" and Brendan told himself that he was a little relieved; that it would be good to get a break and be alone for a little bit once again. Tracy was beginning to get a little too comfortable at his place, he thought, and he was getting way too comfortable having her there.

Most nights now it was assumed—though never declared—that she would sleep over. It seemed natural now that she sometimes showed up around midnight after a work event or a dinner with clients, just because she didn't feel like going all the way to Brooklyn.

And neither did she comment on those nights when he checked on Lounge Two-Twelve and came in just before dawn, crawling into bed next to her still reeking of alcohol but too exhausted to shower first. All she ever did was roll over and sometimes murmured something along the lines of, "*you stink,*" before wrapping her arms tightly about him.

So it's good, he told himself, *that she's going away.*

He could reset a little bit, get his head screwed back on, because as things stood, he was beginning and ending almost every day with her, and that could only end badly in the long run. But for now, he was alone in bed and "the long run" seemed like a long way off.

That afternoon, he had run into Meghan, or to be more accurate, she stopped by his office. Although she didn't say it—because Meghan wasn't one to push—Brendan knew she was wondering why he'd been so scarce lately. Instead she sat across from his desk and made small talk with him, her voice light but her eyes hopeful.

He felt like he owed her something, an explanation for his abrupt change of course where she was concerned, but he couldn't think of what to say. So he let the conversation go on until she had to leave, and even told her he would call her, though he knew it was lie.

It was only nine-thirty and he was home, with what suddenly felt like an abundance of free time. He tried to remember what he used to do before he had a woman to come home to. The clubs and parties were still an option—there was always someplace to go, events where he could find pretty women who were willing and excited and almost didn't expect to be taken seriously. A woman like that would take the edge off a little bit; the edge being his increasing discomfort with Tracy—who didn't even live there—being away.

Brendan slung his legs over the edge of his bed and resolved to find one of those events, and maybe even one of those willing women, when his phone rang. He reached for it and wasn't at all surprised to see Tracy's name on the console.

Smiling, he shook his head. Maybe she had some kind of radar or something. All he had to do was *think* about being with someone else and she materialized.

"I want you to come to Atlanta," she said as soon as he answered.

"Excuse me?" Brendan said. "Who *is* this?"

On the other end of the line, Tracy gave an exasperated sigh. "Brendan, I'm serious. Could you?"

"What's going on?" he asked, sobering up. "Are you okay?"

"No. I want you to come."

"What's the matter?"

"I just want you to come," she said again, as though that should have been explanation enough.

Brendan closed his eyes and shook his head.

All it took was for Tracy to want something, and like a sucker he wanted to give it to her. No matter the inconvenience or cost to his own priorities. If she was spoiled—and she was—he sure wasn't improving matters much.

"You're going to have to tell me more than that, sweetheart."

"Okay, never mind," she said, her voice listless. "You don't have to."

Fuck. Now he was going to have to figure out whether there was anything work-related he could accomplish while in Atlanta.

"When were you planning to come ho... back to New

York?" he asked, hoping there was a way to stave off a trip that already felt inevitable.

On the other hand, if she was going to be back in a couple nights, he could manage that. Piece of cake.

"Now it looks like the weekend or sometime around there," Tracy said.

Another *five* days?!

Brendan considered for a moment. Nothing to get all bent out of shape about though, right? He wasn't some lovesick *teenager*. He could go ten days without seeing his girlfr... without seeing Tracy. In fact, wasn't he just thinking that the break was what he needed? And he damn sure didn't have to fly all the way to Atlanta just because she called him pouting about something she didn't even want to tell him about.

He sighed. "What time was that shuttle you took out there?"

"Seven-thirty a.m.," Tracy said, her voice animated once again.

"I'm not taking a seven-thirty shuttle," Brendan said. *As if that was taking some kind of stand*, he thought bitterly.

"There's a nine as well, I think. They leave every couple of hours," Tracy said. "I'll book you one. How's sometime around noon sound?"

"Fine," Brendan said.

"Tomorrow?"

"No, not tomorrow. I need more time than that. Time to set up some meetings or something."

"Okay, so I'll go online and find you something as soon as we hang up and email it to you," Tracy said. "For Wednesday then?"

All of a sudden she'd turned into a travel agent when it came to getting something she wanted. But how could he get mad when what she wanted was him?

FIRST NIGHT IN ATLANTA, and Brendan was looking forward to getting the best sleep he'd had in almost a week with Tracy's butt pressed into his groin right where he liked it. In fact, he was almost asleep, and about to pull her into their usual spooning position when she raised her head from where she had been resting it on his abdomen and got up, heading for the bathroom, grabbing her dress as she went.

Through half-shut eyes, he watched as she smoothed her hair, taking extraordinary care with it—considering it was already past ten p.m.—before pulling her dress over her head.

"What're you doing?" he asked sleepily.

"I have to go home," she said.

"Curfew, huh?"

"Brendan ..." She sounded exasperated, and let her voice trail off into silence.

"So what time do you want me tomorrow?"

"Seven. We always have dinner at seven."

"So what's the set up going to be? Why am I there?"

She turned away from the mirror to look at him. "What do you mean?"

"What am I? You invite some guy over to your mother's house, there's bound to be questions, right?"

"You're a friend from New York who's in town for business," she said, as though it was obvious.

Brendan sighed.

He didn't do families and parents. Never had. Particularly not under these ambiguous circumstances. But if he was being the "friend from New York" he wouldn't be subjected to the same scrutiny as a "boyfriend from New York" so he felt pretty confident he could handle it, as much as he didn't want to.

"But why am I going, Tracy? I could meet you afterwa..."

"*No,*" she said quickly, coming to sit next to him on the bed. "I need you there."

Need. She said she needed him there. If she said 'want' he might have tried to wriggle his way out of this ill-conceived plan of him having dinner with her family. He might have been able to conjure up some other obligation, like getting together with some local producers or something. But to have her say she needed him; that was difficult to ignore.

"Okay," he said finally. "I'll be there."

"Thank you," she heaved a sigh, and leaned in to kiss him quickly on the lips before sliding her feet back into her shoes.

Her voice still held an edge that had been there from the moment she met him at the airport. She was different here; more like the Tracy he used to think she was at her very core—pulled together in a way that was almost severe—contained, and tightly-wound.

When they got to his hotel room she didn't spare a moment before undressing. On her face had been a look of almost solemn determination as she strained against him, relentless in the pursuit of release. Brendan knew she was working something out in their sex, like it brought her comfort somehow.

When she reached her goal of sexual exhaustion, he put a hand under her chin, turning her head so she would look at him.

"I'm right here," he said.

And her face had softened a little bit, and he kissed her, because there was still something in her eyes he couldn't read. Brendan didn't know why he needed to provide it, just that she craved reassurance.

After his kiss, as she looked at him, he felt her relief. A part of him was dancing just on the edge of panic, wondering why he had come all the way to Atlanta where he had little or no business, to be with this complicated and difficult woman who was very quickly—and scarily so—becoming an important part of his world.

Afterward, Brendan was looking forward to sleeping with her next to him again but that wasn't in the cards. It worried him that he cared so much, and that it wasn't just about the sleep but about the fact that he liked having her there, in the crook of his arm, her head on his chest.

Now fully dressed, Tracy leaned over the bed once again.

"I love that you came," she said. "Thank you."

"If I'm not mistaken, you came too. A couple times," he said, taking refuge in humor as always.

Tracy rolled her eyes. "So I'll see you tomorrow evening?"

"Yup," he made a popping noise with his lips as he said the word.

"Wear something nice," Tracy said as she shut the door. "Not a tie or anything, but nice."

As soon as she was gone, sleep seemed out of the question, so Brendan swung his legs over the edge of the bed and reached for his phone. There had to be some trouble he could get into in Atlanta.

TRACY NEEDN'T HAVE BEEN SO worried about Brendan coming over. He couldn't have been more perfect had she given him a script. He arrived at her mother's house ten minutes early, bearing gifts, no less; a bouquet of flowers for her mother and a bottle of wine for dinner.

The sweater over his shirt was overdoing the choirboy act a little for her taste, but when he winked at her as she greeted him at the door she knew he was hamming it up a little, making fun of her request that he "wear something nice." He was always dressed well, he seemed to be saying, but if she needed him to take it up a notch, he could do that too.

"Mrs. Emerson, you have a lovely home," he said, as her mother led him into the living room.

Tracy watched as her aunts and cousin took him in. He was arresting to the eye at first because he was tall, but when you looked closer, you saw the chiseled good looks framed by expertly shaped facial hair lining his jaw and ending at a neatly sculpted goatee.

Tracy had watched him from bed on many New York mornings maintaining it with the precision of a surgeon, running his small, electric razor about the perimeter and then down under his chin and over his Adam's apple. She liked kissing him there, right on that interesting and uniquely masculine bulge at his throat which seemed to be a particularly erogenous zone for him.

Tracy shook her head, wondering why she was even thinking about that while standing in her mother's showpiece living room, about to have what was sure to be an uncomfortable meal.

Looking up, she saw as her cousin, Jocelyn's eyes lit up at the sight of Brendan and for a moment regretted telling everyone that he was "just a friend from back in New York who's in town for a little bit." She even thought she saw Jocelyn stick out her chest a fraction of an inch further as they were introduced. Although she was just behind them, Tracy could tell from her aunts' and cousin's reactions that Brendan was turning on his patented panty-dropping smile. Internally, she rolled her eyes.

Her mother, she noticed, seemed to be somewhat affronted by Brendan's charm. She called men like him "showy", considering their good looks and easy manner with people to be vulgar in some unspecified way. But Brendan was not that kind of man, Tracy thought, offended by her mother's unspoken judgment. He was one of the most genuine people she knew, one of the kindest ...

"Is Mr. Emerson here?" Brendan asked. "I would love to meet him if ..."

"My husband is very ill, I'm sure Tracy may have told you," her mother broke in. "He's upstairs and has his meals in his room now. I'm afraid the only visitors he has now are close family and a physical therapist."

Tracy tensed, thinking about the uncomfortable fact of Malcolm in his bed upstairs, propped up by pillows, the left side of his face drooping grotesquely, his hand limp on a pillow at his side. She had followed her mother's directive to spend at least a half hour with him each day since she'd been home, and that time seemed to drag out for an eternity.

He could not speak, and only seemed to be vaguely aware that she was there at all. But still her mother insisted, and as always, despite being a thirty-year-old woman, independent and assertive in her own life, she felt helpless to refuse anything her mother told her to do. Particularly when in her physical presence. But having Brendan there relaxed her somehow, and she didn't quite understand why.

"I did hear he was ill," Brendan confirmed. "I was sorry to hear that."

But it was a lie. Tracy had only told him that she had to go home, and had carefully omitted why. She hardly talked about Malcolm with anyone, and certainly hadn't gotten into it with Brendan.

"Well thank you," her mother responded. "We're taking good care of him. Now everyone, if we could ..." She gestured in the direction of the dining room.

Tracy's mother led the way, followed by her Aunts Rose and Kay. When Brendan hung back to let them go first, Jocelyn fell into step next to him. Tracy tried not to eavesdrop, but heard as Jocelyn asked him if he had a chance to see any of the city, and Brendan replying that he'd been out with friends the previous evening.

What the hell? *Out with friends?*

Tracy recalled only that she had left him in the hotel looking like he was moments away from slumber. And then she caught herself. Why shouldn't he go out? He was in "Hotlanta" and it hadn't even been midnight when she left, prime-time for a young, single man of means.

"I could show you a little more of the city if you're interested," Jocelyn said. "Maybe later this evening?"

"Brendan has business in town, Jocelyn," Tracy said, her voice snippier than she intended. "He's not here to hang out with you and your girlfriends."

"Oh there'd be no girlfriends," Jocelyn said without missing a beat. "Just me."

Tracy glared at her. Jocelyn had been a thorn in her side since they were thirteen, and the sharp elbows that typified their relationship had not dulled with the passing of the years. While Tracy was the cool, aloof beauty, Jocelyn had more obvious, openly sexual good looks, all hips and boobs and big, Southern hair. She wore—for Tracy's taste—colors that were way too loud, and bright lipstick shades that only called attention to what was a full-lipped, almost lascivious mouth. But men seemed to like that, and Jocelyn had never lacked admirers, even when in Tracy's company. Because of it, they had grown up in a constant state of competition and one-upmanship.

Now, Jocelyn almost aggressively claimed the seat beside Brendan's at the table and Tracy sat near the end, next to her mother. At the other end, Aunt Rose had taken a seat as the eldest of the three sisters. She tended to want her recognition for that, much as her daughter Jocelyn seemed to crave attention for just about everything *she* did.

The meal began with a prayer, offered solemnly, as only Southern Baptists can. Tracy kept her eyes open, wondering at her mother's insistence on long prayers when she never set foot in a church unless someone had died or was getting married. Across the table, Jocelyn had a small smile on her face and Tracy wondered what she was up to other than plotting to get her claws into Brendan.

"So Brendan, what's your line of work?" Aunt Kay asked, as the food was passed around.

Aunt Kay was the sweetest of the sisters and was probably just making conversation, but Tracy cursed her for bringing up Brendan's profession. Her mother was sure to have a raised eyebrow at his answer.

"I'm a music executive," he responded.

Tracy did not look up, but out of the corner of her eye saw that her mother did.

"That must be very interesting work," Jocelyn said. "So I assume you know Tracy's best friend's husband, K Smooth."

"Yes. Very well," Brendan said. "Used to be his manager, in fact."

Next to her, Tracy could feel her mother visibly tense.

"Really? Oh, so that's how you and Tracy ..."

"Jocelyn, could we not interrogate him about his work and the music business?" Tracy interrupted. "Let's talk about something where everyone can participate."

"And heaven knows, I have nothing to contribute in a conversation about the music young people are listening to these days," her mother said, her voice dry.

"I don't know," Brendan said amiably. "It's not all club music and hip hop anymore, Mrs. Emerson. We're seeing a lot of new artists who have interesting similarities to a lot of names you'd recognize. Just last month, I signed a young man who, if your eyes were closed, you'd think was Otis Redding. Young kid out of Philadelphia. Big talent."

"Oh is that right?" Aunt Rose asked. "I always loved Otis Redding. What's this new artist's name? I may have to look for him."

"When we release his CD, I'd be happy to send you one," Brendan offered. "His name is Sam Gaston. I guarantee you're going to be hearing about him."

"Well I suppose even I know something about Otis Redding," Tracy's mother acknowledged, somewhat reluctantly.

Tracy smothered a smile and resolved to let Brendan look out for himself since clearly he was more than capable of doing so. Even with her mother sniffing for blood.

After dinner, she played the role of the dutiful daughter, helping to clear the table and putting away leftovers while her aunts and Jocelyn entertained Brendan and stuffed him with Aunt Rose's rum Bundt cake. From the kitchen, as she and her mother worked, Tracy could hear his voice and Jocelyn laughing a little too enthusiastically at something he said. She hurried with her task, going out to join them before her mother could ask her to do anything else.

When she entered the living room, Jocelyn was sitting next to Brendan on the sofa—a little too close—and listening to something on his phone.

Brendan looked up and smiled at her.

"Could I have a minute?" she asked him, her voice perfectly even.

"Sure."

Brendan stood and she walked him out to the foyer, turning to look up at him, arms crossed. They looked at each other for a moment until he shrugged, waiting for her to speak.

"Don't flirt with her," she said. "I swear she has a personality disorder or something. If anything with a penis is within ten feet she turns into the Black Marilyn Monroe. Don't encourage it."

Brendan looked amused. "Was that what I was doing?" he asked.

"Were you?"

He shrugged again. "I don't think so."

"Well, are you going out with her tonight?" Tracy challenged.

Brendan closed his eyes and slowly shook his head.

"Tracy ..."

"It would be well within your rights to go out with her if you find her attractive," she babbled on. "And for some reason, which escapes me, lots of men seem to."

Brendan waited for her to finish then sighed. "You're doing it again," he said.

"Doing what?" Tracy snapped. She could feel her nerves beginning to fray.

"Trippin'," Brendan responded matter-of-factly.

"*Am* I?" she asked. "You went out last night after I left, with Lord knows who, so maybe you want to hang out tonight too. And if Jocelyn, Ms. Thirty-eight double Ds in there is offering to ..."

Brendan looked over his shoulder to make sure no one was within sight and wrenched open the front door, pulling her outside with him by her forearm. Once he shut the door again he pushed her back against it and caged her in with his arms.

"God*damn* it, Tracy!" he said, losing his patience for the first time. "I'm not interested in your fucking cousin. While I'm in Atlanta, I'm not interested in anyone. Anyone but you. Is *that* what you want to hear?"

Tracy looked up at him, strangely aroused by his anger,

and perversely pleased that she was the only person she knew of who could—without fail—make Brendan lose his cool.

Then she realized what he said.

"Only while you're in Atlanta?"

"What?"

"You said you were only interested in me. While you're in Atlanta."

Brendan leaned in closer. His face was almost touching hers.

"We're going by your playbook, sweetheart. Are you telling me you want to change the rules? Because if you do, we can have that conversation."

His voice held the hint of a challenge. Tracy swallowed hard. Was he telling her that he was open to a conversation about being exclusive? And what if he was? Her heartbeat suddenly accelerated. She didn't even know if that was what *she* wanted, did she? All she knew was that when she thought about him touching someone else, it made her want to throw a screaming shit-fit.

"Thought so," Brendan said, quietly, nodding. "So let's just go back inside and finish the evening with a minimum of bullshit."

She pulled in her lower lip and her shoulders sagged, all of the fight gone out of her.

"You're something else, y'know that?" he said shaking his head, smiling.

And then before she could respond he was kissing her, an open-mouthed, full-on, usually reserved-for-love-making type of kiss, his hand spanning her neck, making her feel tiny. Then he replaced his hand with his lips and pressed himself against her. She could feel the beginnings of his arousal against her stomach.

"Does that feel like I want your cousin?" he breathed against her neck.

"No," Tracy admitted.

"So stop trippin'," he said, nuzzling her.

Then he opened the door and pulled her back in. Just inside the foyer, heading toward the front door, probably coming to find them was her mother. Tracy smiled guiltily and noted a flicker in her mother's eyes that quickly disappeared.

"Coffee for you, Brendan?" she asked, once again the unfailingly polite hostess.

"Would love some," Brendan said as he released Tracy's hand and followed her mother back into the living room.

When she walked him out to his rental car later, they didn't kiss goodbye, mindful that someone might be watching them from the house. Brendan leaned in and whispered in her ear, joking that Tracy should leave a ladder outside her bedroom window so he could climb in when her mother was asleep.

She blushed and shoved him away from her. Every time he looked at her, it was as though he was about to pounce, and what was scarier, she wanted him to. Thinking about the fact that he was flying back to New York without her in the morning made her feel a little uncomfortable.

I'm not interested in anyone else while I'm in Atlanta, he said. And tomorrow he would no longer be in Atlanta.

Back in the house, Jocelyn was waiting for her by the front door. She arched an eyebrow, and smiled at Tracy, shaking her head.

"So, nice cock-blocking," she said.

Tracy smirked at her. "Hard as it is to believe, Joss, he was not interested in you."

"And why would you care?" Jocelyn pressed. "I mean, since he's just a *friend* and all."

"He is," Tracy said trying to walk past her.

"So you won't have a problem giving me his number," Jocelyn said.

Tracy hesitated. "I told you, he's not interested."

"Men are notorious for changing their minds," Jocelyn said. "Especially if skillfully persuaded."

"He wouldn't be ..."

"Girl," Jocelyn said, turning to walk away. "You ain't foolin' nobody ..." she paused and looked back. "Except maybe yourself."

Tracy resisted the urge to smack her.

"And by the way," Jocelyn said as her parting shot. "Does he know about your ... issues?"

Tracy's face colored.

That Jocelyn knew anything about that was the result of an unfortunate lapse in judgment one Christmas break during college when Tracy had found herself stranded and with no one else to call after a spending the night with a guy she barely knew. Jocelyn had gotten up even though it was well past two a.m. and had driven twenty-five miles to fetch her after sneaking her mother's car out without permission. In a rare moment of candor, and largely out of gratitude, Tracy had told her cousin considerably more than she should have.

And Jocelyn had never forgotten it. She only rarely alluded to what she knew, but when she did, it was always intended to embarrass or take Tracy down a notch or two.

"I'm guessing he doesn't know, huh?" Jocelyn said with mock sympathy. "The way he was looking at you, he probably thinks you're exactly what you pretend to be—better than every-damn-body."

GETTING relaxed enough to sleep in her high school bedroom was difficult. Tracy was surrounded by pink, lace and posters that reflected the naïve dreams of her fourteen-year old self. The following year, the year she turned fifteen was the last year she could recall having had anything resembling a girlhood fantasy about the male of the species.

That was the year she lost her innocence in more ways than one, and she hadn't been the same since. But now, and much to her surprise, some of what she used to believe—that one day someone would love and want to take care of her—was slowly being revived. And there was no escaping the fact that it was all because of Brendan.

For a while Tracy entertained the idea of slipping out to go spend his last night in Atlanta with him. She didn't expect to miss him as much as she did when she left New York. And for sure, she didn't anticipate that just seeing him walk across the Hartsfield terminal toward her would lessen the awful weight on her heart that she didn't even realize was there.

He was one of the last passengers to disembark and was carrying a large brown leather duffel, wearing a white button-down open at the neck with a t-shirt underneath, and khakis. Upon seeing her, he smiled and it had taken every ounce of her self-control not to run to him. When she hugged him, it was hard to let go. He kissed her on the top of her head and they walked out of the terminal together with his arm about her shoulders.

At the hotel, she'd scarcely been able to wait to get close to him. Feeling his weight on her was like being enveloped by a security blanket. And what was most stunning was that it wasn't even about the sex, it was about the sense of connection, of seeing him and being seen by him as she truly was.

But Jocelyn's words reminded her that Brendan didn't know who she truly was. He didn't know anything of her long and sordid history of men with blurred faces, and even blurrier names, dates and circumstances. Could he look at her the way he now did, if he knew any of that? Would he still spoil her and tease her and indulge her as he now did, if he knew that she was precisely what Kelvin had called her that night? Funny how she remembered his name now—Kelvin. It would have disappeared from memory like all the others had he not said about her what she always said about herself: *she was a fucking whore.*

Unable to sleep even after lying in the dark for over an hour, Tracy crept out of bed and headed downstairs. The house was quiet and the only light that remained was the dull glow, escaping from under the door, of the lamp in Malcolm's room that stayed on all night so her mother could slip in and check on him.

Sleeping with the light on didn't seem to disturb him. His days and nights all seemed to blend seamlessly one into the other now. On the odd occasion over the last week that Tracy had stopped in to visit with him, he barely acknowledged her presence. She tried to talk to him, but only about the most superficial things, like the temperature in the room and whether or not he wanted her to turn on the radio or television.

He responded when she asked direct questions but the most effective were those that permitted him to respond with a 'yes' or 'no'. Beyond that, and he would seem befuddled, or force out an answer that was as likely as not to be nonsensical. What was most striking was the utter absence of emotion on his mangled face. He seemed neither happy nor sad. He was just there. His lack of emotion seemed a mirror image of Tracy's. She neither loved nor hated this man, and could not even muster sufficient feeling to produce sympathy for his plight. There was just ... nothing.

In the kitchen where Tracy had gone to cut herself one

more slice of Bundt cake and make a cup of tea, her mother was waiting. Wearing a powder blue housedress, she looked as well composed as she had at dinner, not a hair out of place. On the table in front of her was a cup of coffee and the remnants of her own late night snack on a saucer. She looked up as Tracy entered.

"Who is he to you, really?" she asked without preamble.

Tracy had not expected this conversation tonight, but was unsurprised that they were having it.

"I told you," Tracy said, opening the refrigerator. "A friend."

"What kind of friend, Tracy Ann?"

"Why does it matter? I'm not *sixteen*. I can date whomever I want."

"So you are dating him."

"He means something to me," Tracy confirmed. "And honestly, Mom, what do you care?" she demanded, going to grab a knife for the cake.

"I suppose I shouldn't care," her mother acknowledged. "After all, he's gainfully employed. Very gainfully, I would guess. He's good-looking, articulate."

"And yet you still disapprove," Tracy couldn't help adding.

She hated that it still mattered what her mother thought, even when she had more than enough evidence that it shouldn't.

"Good-looking, oozing charm, talks a wonderful game. Works in a glamorous, high-profile field. *Loves* the ladies. Never an objectionable word to say about them, and promises you the world. I wonder why I would disapprove," her mother said, her voice bitter.

"Are you sure we're talking about Brendan?" Tracy said. "Sounds like someone else we both know."

Her mother's face darkened. "Tracy, you think you have it

all figured out. You always have. But I have the benefit of many more years experience than you. And as soon as I saw that man walk through the door, I knew his type."

Tracy's breath was coming in short bursts, she was so angry. This was one of the reasons she didn't want to come home ever —the criticism disguised as concern, the prophesies of doom and gloom.

"I bet he treats you like no one else in the world is as important," her mother continued. "Like he doesn't see another woman, can't see another woman, because you're *just* that special."

"Or maybe I am that special to him."

"You want to believe you are. Choosing a mate is an art, Tracy. And the fact that he sets your stomach aflutter shouldn't even enter into the equation. Take it from one who knows."

"Who said anything about choosing a mate? He's my ..."

"Oh for heaven's sake, Tracy Ann. I'm your mother. I saw what it was like between you two. Don't tell me again that he's just your friend. It insults me, and diminishes my view of you as an honest young woman."

"I'm not honest at all," Tracy said. "You have no *idea*."

Her mother looked puzzled for a moment and for what was not the first time, Tracy was tempted to let it all come pouring out, telling her mother that all work and lectures and platitudes had been for naught.

Everything you told me fell on deaf ears, she imagined telling her. *Because despite your best efforts, I still turned into a slut.*

But even she was not that cruel.

It had always been easier just to stay away. But Malcolm and his damned illness had made that impossible. All the wounds, carefully covered up all these years would begin to bleed again if she stayed too much longer. She could feel the urge to confess building up in her with each day she spent in the same house as her mother.

"I know it probably feels possible, doesn't it?" he mother said, almost sympathetically now. "Especially with your friend, Riley and her husband. You're thinking that you may be able to make it work, and oh, what a cozy little foursome you all would make. As soon as he told me he worked with Riley's husband, I knew that's what you were thinking. As soon as I saw what it's like between you, I knew."

Tracy's face flushed. She desperately wanted to ask her mother what she saw, because she thought that with the exception of her little outburst (which had been done in private after all) she did a great job keeping her distance from Brendan at dinner, as had he. But she could not bring herself to give her the satisfaction by asking.

And truth be told, she was pretty sure she knew. If she and Brendan were within reach, there was a charge between them, not always a constructive, positive or even sexual charge, but a latent energy that, to Tracy at least, was so thick, it sometimes felt like she could barely draw a breath.

"If you pursue things with this man, you would be making a very grave mistake, Tracy Ann. A very grave mistake."

"And what makes you so sure of that?" she asked, her voice shaking.

"Because I was you once. And boy did I ever pay for being the kind of fool you're being right now."

Tracy felt her heart ache. "You wound up with precisely what you wanted in the end," she said, her voice cold.

"But at what cost?" her mother said. She turned to leave the room. "So perhaps you ought to consider the cost to you, Tracy Ann."

TEN

Tracy never understood why Jason Miller insisted on personal service for the somewhat small—by his measure anyway—investment he'd made with her. He almost never wanted to talk about it on the phone and had on countless occasions insisted that she schlep all the way over to his office, or out for lunch.

Today he'd invited her to yet another lunch, which was fine since a girl did have to eat sometime. But looking over his file earlier, Tracy saw that his investment was performing about as well as expected and so she couldn't figure out what the purpose of the meeting might be. Unless he was about to fire at her. And that was always a possibility. Some new hotshot might have accosted him at a party and gotten in his ear, or a friend on the golf course gave him a tip, and rather than risk new money, he may have decided to move his modest stake with her someplace else. In her business it happened all the time.

Tracy walked into Dorcas, at precisely the appointed time, smoothing her skirt several times as she waited for Jason Miller in the entryway of the exclusive restaurant. She had refused the hostess' offer to wait at the table because she preferred to greet her clients while standing, from a position of power. In Jason Miller's case, though, it was probably a fantasy that she could ever be in anything resembling a position of power. His wealth made it more than clear who held all the cards. So perhaps a position of equals was more achievable, though even that was a stretch.

When finally he walked in, only five minutes behind, Jason Miller was smiling apologetically. He ran a hand over his head as though harried and busy and then placed it at the small of her back.

"I hope I didn't keep you waiting long," he said.

"No, not at all." Tracy smiled back at him.

The hostess hurried to seat them before he even said a word. Clearly he was a recognized and valued patron here. The restaurant was one of those highly exclusive places where the reservation wait-list was rumored to be months long. Tracy had never been, and would have been somewhat excited at the prospect of the meal if she wasn't so apprehensive about the cause of his summons.

As soon as they were seated, Jason Miller ordered for them, not even requesting a menu. She tried not to take offense, and instead smiled and nodded when the waiter glanced in her direction. When they were alone once again, Jason Miller turned all his attention to her and formed a steeple with his hands, resting his chin on them.

"So," he said. "This is very difficult."

Yup. She was about to be fired.

"I've decided to move my investment with you."

"I was afraid of that," Tracy admitted. She took a sip of her water. "May I ask why?"

"This is the difficult part," he said.

"So it wasn't difficult to fire me?" she asked, managing to smile winningly at him.

"No, it's more difficult to work with you," he said flatly.

Tracy's face fell and she put her glass back on the table. "Mr. Miller ..."

"Jason."

"Jason. I have no idea why you feel that way, but I assure you, if there's anything I've done, and anything I can do to ..."

"I can tell you've already misunderstood me," he said waving a hand to silence her. "You've serviced my account impeccably. And so far the investment has performed well beyond what I expected. And if your boss were to ask me, I would say that you're one of his best assets in the firm."

Tracy wrinkled her brow. "So I don't understand."

"I've been trying now for six months to ask you out," he said baldly.

Tracy leaned back in her chair.

Wait, what?

She hadn't picked up on that. At all. Now granted, over the last four months she had been otherwise occupied, but this was still a surprise. Not to mention that Jason Miller called her 'Ms. Emerson' in that awful, condescending voice that only her most difficult and high-maintenance clients used. Usually, she had great radar for when men were attracted to her, and Jason Miller had never treated her any differently from her average rich jerk client.

"I've surprised you," he said sounding surprised himself.

"Yes."

"This can't have been the first time a client asked you out," he said.

"As a matter of fact it is," she said truthfully.

"And?"

"I can't pretend to be happy about it if it's the reason I'm going to lose your business," she said.

"You could lose the investment and gain a boyfriend," he suggested.

Tracy couldn't help it. She laughed. "Are you saying you want to be my boyfriend?"

"Of course not. We barely know each other," Jason Miller said. "I'm saying I'd like to take you out and see how it goes. But I'm hoping it goes well. I'm betting that it does."

He was okay looking, she supposed. Like a young college professor, complete with the black-framed glasses and perpetual pensive look, as though he was always thinking deep thoughts. But his clothes were considerably better tailored than a college professor could afford.

If she could get past the supercilious mannerisms, she might be able to find him attractive, she supposed. But *why*? After all, she was very happy with ... She stopped herself from completing the thought and turned her attention to Jason Miller once again.

"I *might* gain a boyfriend and would *certainly* lose your business would be more accurate," Tracy countered.

"Well, I can't promise you we'll be dating a year from now or anything ..."

"Obviously."

"... but I couldn't promise you my investment would still be here a year from now either," he pointed out.

"You don't waste time getting down to it, do you?" Tracy asked coyly. "I mean, we've only been sitting here for ten minutes."

"I had to work up the courage to do this," he said. "I've been working it out in my head for ages. And I'm sure you know that you're a little intimidating."

"I am?"

Jason Miller smiled. "Very beautiful, but you never smile. Men are suckers for that. We like the challenge."

"I do smile. In fact, I think I've probably smiled at you a dozen times since we sat down," she countered.

Jason Miller shook his head. "I'd like to keep my money invested with you, Tracy. But I'd much rather take you out to dinner."

It was the first time he ever used her first name. And it made all the difference in the world. Suddenly he seemed like a genuine ... possibility. She rewarded him with one more smile.

BRENDAN WAS upstairs in the kitchen when she let herself in, and looked over the railing down at her as she entered.

"Hey!"

Tracy waved up at him,

"Happy Friday," she said.

"Friday is when the work begins at Lounge Two-Twelve though," he called back. "You want to come with me tonight?"

"Maybe. I'd need to go back to Brooklyn to get something nice to wear though."

"What?" he called down as though he hadn't heard her.

"I'm coming up." Tracy went to join him in the kitchen.

He was standing by the refrigerator, wearing sweats and a t-shirt, drinking Vitamin water. He'd finally given up on the argument against her stocking it up, so inside there was fruit, veggies, meat for the breakfast sandwiches she made him almost every morning, juice, eggs and cheeses.

"I said I would have to go back to Brooklyn to get something to wear if I'm coming to the Lounge with you."

"Not worth it," Brendan said. "Go buy something new.

And the next time you go to Brooklyn bring back some stuff to leave here."

He said it so casually, like it was just a common-sense solution, that she almost missed its significance. Brendan was inviting her to leave clothes at his apartment. The key was one thing, this was one step even further. This was the step just before moving in.

"You have no room for me," she said quietly, sitting on one of the breakfast bar stools.

Brendan came over and grabbed her about the waist, planting a kiss on her forehead. "I'll make room."

Tracy's heart thundered in her chest.

Oh God, why did she want this?

She couldn't stop to dissect it right now, but she really, really wanted this. And what was worse, she couldn't remember ever having been with a man who she wanted to spend as much time with as she did with Brendan. For most of her adult life, she'd been convinced she wasn't the relationship type, because she was always eager to be rid of the men she was sleeping with after the sex was done.

And once she realized that she did want a relationship, she was frustrated that no one came along who measured up, who made her crave him. A couple of men lasted a month or two but when they were gone, their absence barely registered. In one case, she recalled feeling nothing but relief at the affair's end. Just her luck that she would find someone she did crave, but who might not even be real relationship material. Although lately, her reasons for thinking that in the first place were beginning to seem so obscure she could hardly recall what they had been.

"If I go shopping for something for tonight, will you come with me?" Tracy asked.

Brendan looked at her. "Ahm, no. I'm about to pick up a basketball game downtown."

Well, thank God. Because at least now she knew he wasn't *perfect* or anything.

BRENDAN WAS BACK from his basketball game by eight and they lazed around on his bed channel-surfing and eating a light supper Tracy picked up from Zabar's, of seafood salad and basil bruschetta. Even as she enjoyed it, she felt almost outside of herself, watching the comfortable domestic scene of a couple in bed, and scarcely believing that the calm and content woman who was one half of that couple was she. Even the crumbs that Brendan managed to scatter all over the Egyptian cotton sheets did nothing to dampen her mood. The few quiet hours they spent together until it was time to leave for the club were enough to make her night, no matter what happened once they got there.

Tracy's quick shopping trip had yielded an inexpensive but chic Michael Kors Ikat-print mini dress with a cowl neck and cut-out sleeves, and a pair of black heels while Brendan wore navy pants and black dress shirt. He was handsome in dark colors, Tracy noted; and she shocked herself when it sprang to mind that next time she went shopping, she might pick him up the shirt she had admired in a store window earlier that evening.

Just as they were about to walk out the door, Tracy remembered she left her phone in the kitchen and ran upstairs to grab it. On her way back down, Brendan, waiting at the foot of the circular staircase, watched her descent.

"You're looking up my dress," she sang, enjoying the clear appreciation on his face.

"Except I can't tell if you're wearing underwear," he said wrinkling his brow.

"I don't always." She shrugged.

She was almost at the bottom when he stopped her with a hand on her thigh. Just one step shy of having her pelvis directly in line with his face, Tracy could feel the pace of her breathing increase almost immediately. His touch did it, every single time, so much so that she was sure if someone hooked her up to an EKG machine, the damn thing would go crazy.

Brendan slid his hand slowly northward, his fingers lightly caressing the smooth skin of her inner thighs. His eyes never left hers as he hooked a finger at the crotch of her thongs, briefly and just barely brushing her clitoris as he did.

"This doesn't qualify as underwear," he said. "This is just a torture device."

"It's not torture at all," Tracy said, struggling to keep her voice even. "It's actually surprisingly comfortable."

"I meant that it tortures *me*," he said and in one quick motion he yanked it sharply down and away with a flourish, like a magician performing a disappearing trick. His movement was so sharp, the strings on the side simply snapped, but not before chafing her hip.

"Ouch, *Brendan!*" she said.

He held up her now-shredded panties.

"Useless," he said, letting them drop from his fingers and onto the step closest to the bottom. Then he ran his open palm across her lower abdomen.

"Where does it hurt?" he said. "Show me."

Tracy thought she would pass out just from how freakin' hot his voice made her. She put a hand down to her hip and over the fabric of her dress rubbing the sore spot.

"No," Brendan said, a smile playing about his lips. "Touch it. Show me."

Her breaths were short and shallow now, like she was having trouble getting air to her lungs, and when she looked at him, it got even worse. Brendan took her hand and put it under her dress so she was touching her skin directly.

"Right here?" He used her hand to rub a spot near her hipbone.

Tracy shook her head.

"Here?" He moved her hand lower.

Tracy shook her head again and he smiled a slow, sexy smile.

"So ..." he said, "where exactly does it hurt?"

Tracy moved her hand, still under his, so that it was directly over her *mons*.

"Maybe I should kiss it and make it better," he said.

And before she knew what was happening he had grabbed her by the waist and lifted her up one step higher and raised the skirt of her dress, putting his head under it.

Brendan was shrouded by her skirt so that when she looked down, all Tracy saw was the mound that was his head, moving back and forth. But she felt him. *God did she ever.* He had captured her clitoris between his lips and was gently working it with just the tip of his tongue, making her feel as though she would dissolve into a pool of warm liquid at his feet.

With each licking and suckling motion he made, his head bobbed and her knees threatened to buckle under her, so she gripped the stair railings, hanging on for dear life, which was just as well since Brendan had put his hands on her inner thighs and was spreading her, burrowing closer as he took more and more of her into his mouth.

Tracy felt her hips beginning to buck uncontrollably against him, and he moved his hands, palming her buttocks and holding her so she couldn't escape if she wanted to. He held her there, his tongue lashing against her, his lips simultaneously sucking, and just when she thought her heart might literally stop from the intensity of it, Tracy cried out his name. Still, he didn't stop, though he slowed a little, lessening the pressure, the strokes more delicate until she came down from the crest of her climax and could feel sensation in her legs once again.

After a moment, he lifted her skirt and using the hem, dabbed his mouth like someone in a fine dining establishment and licked his lips.

"Wow," he said, his voice surprisingly steady. "It was hot under there."

Tracy looked at him, and using the hem of her dress as he had, dabbed away a few tiny beads of perspiration that had formed on his forehead.

Holding her by the waist once again, he lifted her off the staircase and deposited her on the floor next to him, but not before pausing to kiss her briefly on the lips. She looked up at him and something deep in her chest literally ached. Breaking eye contact because it was just too intense, she noticed for the first time the protrusion in Brendan's slacks and looked back up at him.

"*Oh* no," he laughed pulling away as she reached for him. "If we go there, we won't ever get out of here tonight and as much I'd rather stay here, I need to go. Our PR people invited a bunch of bloggers to come check the Lounge out."

"Well, you can't very well walk out of the building like that." Tracy said smiling.

"I'll concentrate," Brendan said. "It'll go down by the time the elevator hits the ground floor. 'Cause I'ma Jedi mind-trick it."

Tracy rolled her eyes. "Okay, why don't you start on that while I go put on some underwear?" she said.

"No. No underwear. I want you just like you are. Raw, and wet."

Tracy's eyes opened wide for an instant, wondering whether she would ever get used to him saying things like that.

THE RATIONAL PART of her knew that Brendan was just that kind of guy who people were drawn to. Men wanted to hang out with him and be his friend, and women wanted to be much more than that. It was obvious from the way they exploited his basic touchy-feely nature. He was the kind of guy who hugged you when he greeted you, who touched you, or nudged you, or took the fabric of your blouse between his fingers and tested the texture when he talked to you. Some women misinterpreted that. They got a bright, glittery look in their eyes and played with their hair, lengthened their neck, straightened their backs to showcase their chest, and worst of all, they *touched him back*.

After what happened on the staircase at the apartment, Tracy should have been mellower and more tolerant but far from it, she was tense, overexcited, and felt incomplete. She still needed to feel Brendan inside her. But she was stuck here, wanting him still, and having to watch these bitches crawl all over her man. Okay, so he wasn't *technically* her man, but dammit, he was *her* man.

Coming to the Lounge had been a blunder. It only made sense if the goal was to drive herself crazy with jealousy. She had never come with him before when he was working and as long as he came home afterwards, hadn't spared a thought about what it was like for him in the club, surrounded by scantily-clad women who mistook his natural friendliness for interest in their skanky asses. Now she would never be able to let him go alone again. If she did, her imagination would run wild, so she may as well be there to see with her own eyes what she was imagining anyway.

And to make matters worse, she was going to be forced to pretend it all didn't bother her because if she breathed a word of complaint, Brendan would tell her she was "trippin' again." But who *wouldn't* trip? She made a mental note to ask Riley to send Shawn to the club more often. It wasn't fair that Brendan was carrying more of the burden for managing what was supposed to be a joint venture.

Tracy leaned forward a little from her vantage point in one of the semi-private VIP areas and watched as Brendan grinned one of his signature grins at some woman in a white bodysuit. Anyone who wore a white bodysuit in a club that had black lighting was just an exhibitionist plain and simple, because everyone knew that the black lights made lighter colors glow. She sighed and leaned back in her seat so Brendan and the tramp in white were out of view once again.

What seemed like a long while later he came back to her, and Tracy smiled blandly at him. After pulling the gauze curtain to close off their sitting area, he collapsed next to her on the sofa. After a moment he slid his hand along her leg and Tracy clamped her thighs shut.

"Uh oh," Brendan said, leaning back. "What did I do now?"

"Nothing," Tracy said. She reached for her glass of champagne.

"You sure?" Brendan asked, leaning into her line of sight.

"Positive," she said, taking a sip and avoiding looking him in the eye.

"Okay, nothing's wrong," Brendan said, nodding his head thoughtfully. "So if I wanted to do something to fix the 'nothing' that's wrong—hypothetically speaking of course—what would I have to do?"

Tracy tried, but couldn't prevent herself from smiling. No

one made her smile this much, or laugh as hard. No one made her feel as good as he did, or as bad as he could, or as beautiful, or as sexy, or as angry, or as jealous, or as alive. Or as completely herself. Ah, to be *herself* with a man—what a revolutionary notion.

Sensing that she was somewhere else, Brendan leaned closer.

"Huh? What can I do to fix it? Hypothetically."

"If something *were* wrong," Tracy said, playing along, "you could, *hypothetically*, kiss me. Maybe that would make me feel better. If something were wrong, that is."

Brendan smiled and leaned in, brushing his lips lightly against hers and nuzzling her nose with his. When Tracy leaned forward to make contact with his lips again, he leaned just out of her reach.

"It's a good thing then," he said, "that nothing's wrong."

Tracy reached for him, putting a hand at the back of his neck and pulled him toward her. His lips opened for her and she slipped her tongue into his mouth, kissing him almost desperately. As he always did when she got this way, and maybe because he knew it would drive her crazy and make her want him even more, Brendan pulled back and slowed things down, taking his own sweet time exploring her, his hand lightly caressing her hip. When he moved his hand around, and down between her legs, this time she opened up for him without hesitation.

"*Whoa*. Better stop," he said against her lips. "In a few minutes I might not be able to. And I still have some celebrity website bloggers to entertain."

He stood and pulled her up, leading her out of the VIP area.

"C'mon, I want to show you off," he said against her ear.

"You're the most beautiful woman in here, Tracy. I want everyone to know you're with me."

Somehow, he managed to pretend her neurotic insecurities were neither neurotic nor insecure. He never tired of it, and she wondered sadly how long that would last. A thought flitted through her mind and was gone in an instant, that maybe it wasn't Brendan who was not good enough for her; it was she who was not good enough for him.

The Lounge had filled up nicely in the time since they got there, and Brendan continued to play the perfect host, but this time kept a firm grip on Tracy's hand as he made his rounds. When he introduced her, he only told people her name, and didn't clarify the nature of their relationship in any way which made Tracy strangely disappointed, even though she wasn't sure what she would have had him say. Still, to even the casual observer, it would be obvious that they were together and that was good enough for now.

When one of his conversations, with the blogger from CelebHotSpot.com began to exceed her attention-span, Tracy pulled her hand out of his to head for the bar. To her surprise, Brendan excused himself and turned to her.

"You okay? Where you going?"

"To get a drink. You stay here," she said. "I'll be fine. I'll come find you in a few."

He nodded and turned back to his conversation and Tracy smiled as she walked away.

See? Women are easy, really, she thought. *All we need is a little acknowledgment sometimes.*

She was fairly certain that she would be able to make it through the rest of the evening without getting irritated when women got pushy with Brendan again. Because now, one would have to be an idiot not to have seen that Brendan was most decidedly taken.

The bar was crowded, but one of the bartenders who Tracy thought might even be the young woman who had served her and Brendan on the launch night, approached her right away and took her order for a Two-Twelve martini, which had a fruity taste that Tracy was still trying to identify. When she tried to pay for her drink, the young woman smiled.

"No charge," she said. "Earlier this evening Mr. Cole told me to make sure I take care of whatever you might need."

"Thank you." Tracy smiled.

She stood by the bar sipping her drink, taking everything in, including more than a few celebrities and a couple of radio deejays she recognized from posters around the city. There were even a few professional athletes among the crowd. If this was representative of the average Friday night, Tracy had no doubt the club was going to be a huge success, something that was no longer a foregone conclusion just because the owner was a celebrity like Shawn.

And Brendan was of course a natural at making people feel welcome. Watching him greet someone else who had joined his conversation with the blogger, she felt something suspiciously like pride. Tracy never thought much about how good he might or might not have been at his job, but seeing him in action now, she could only imagine how essential he had been to smooth over the rough patches and run interference when managing someone as moody as Shawn. She made a mental note to begin telling her clients about the Lounge; something she often did with restaurants and nightspots around town that she liked and could vouch for.

"I don't recall putting that sweet of a smile on your face," someone said close to her ear.

Before she even turned around, Tracy knew it was him. Her body reacted before her mind did, maybe because of that scent he was wearing. She hadn't been able to get it out of her nostrils for days afterward. It was a scent she now associated with shame.

Swallowing hard, Tracy turned to face him.

"You remember me, don't you baby?" he said, his face closer to hers than she expected. "KEL-vin. Not Kevin, but KEL-vin."

Tracy said nothing but shot a desperate look in Brendan's direction.

She didn't know why, because the last thing in the world she wanted was to have Brendan know who Kelvin was. Not just because she was ashamed—though she was—but because she knew how important tonight was to the Lounge, and felt certain that Brendan would still do something stupid like haul off and hit the guy.

Kelvin followed her quick glance and nodded. "Yeah, I saw him," he said. "That your man?"

His breath smelled strong, like cognac, and his eyes were bleary. Tracy tried to recall what he told her he did for a living, and wondered why he would be a regular at the Lounge. God forbid he should be in the same business as Brendan, know people in the same circles.

"Your man know you can suck the skin off a dick?" Kelvin asked matter-of-factly.

Tracy felt her palm itching with the desire to slap him, but she didn't want to make a scene. Not here. Not tonight when Brendan had been so perfect.

"Kelvin ..." she began.

"Ah, this time she *remembers*!" he said, with mock-applause.

"... I know our night didn't exactly go well, but ..."

"Oh no, baby," Kelvin said leaning even closer, pressing his wet lips against her ear. "It went *real* well. I remember you riding me hard, like you was in the damn rodeo. I remember you deep-throatin' the shit outta me. So our night was pretty damn good if you ask me. The part that fucked me up was in the morning, when you tried to put a nigga out like he was last night's *trash*."

Tracy felt her entire body grow cold with humiliation as she recalled the things she had done with and to this repulsive man. Just having him as close as he now was made her want to recoil in disgust. The woman who had picked him up and taken him home seemed like a complete and utter stranger to her now.

"Sweetheart, you want to introduce me to your friend?"

BRENDAN FELT an immediate recognition when he saw the man leaning in way too close to Tracy, but he didn't know why. He definitely didn't like any other man getting that close to her and he damn sure wasn't crazy about the fact that dude's mouth looked like it was actually touching the side of her face. Still, he might have let it go but for the tension about Tracy's shoulders and the stiffness of her posture that made it clear she was more than a little uncomfortable.

It was only when he approached them, and Tracy turned at the sound of his voice and Brendan saw the look on her face that he realized who the man was likely to be. The immediacy of his anger startled him. He couldn't remember ever getting that enraged that quickly before and suddenly had a newfound understanding of Shawn's volatility. His friend had been known to go from zero to one hundred in less than thirty seconds, something Brendan had never experienced himself and so did not understand. But he understood it now.

Tracy's face was a combination of ten emotions at once, the predominant ones being fear and shame. Not embarrassment, but *shame*. And that was how Brendan knew in his gut that this was the man who had broken her down that night so much that Brendan scarcely recognized her as the woman he knew. But still, he needed confirmation from her before he commenced tearing shit up in this motherfucker.

"Introduce me," he said again, his voice sounding remarkably calm, even to his own ears.

"She don't never remember my name," dude said, smirking at Brendan. "But I'm Kelvin. And you are?" He extended a hand.

Brendan ignored it, keeping his eyes fixed on Tracy whose gaze was fixed downward at the floor. "I'm the owner of the club."

"Oh damn! The owner?"

"Tracy," Brendan said. "Is this ..?"

"Brendan, don't," she said, her voice almost inaudible.

"Don't *what*?" he asked, raising his voice. "I'm asking you who this is."

"He's nobody," she said.

"*Nobody*?" Kelvin pulled back as though shocked, but it was clear he was beginning to enjoy himself. "I wouldn't say all that, *Tracy*. See I always remembered your name. Woulda remembered it even if your man here hadn't said it."

Next to him, Brendan could almost feel Tracy shrinking into him, as though if she could, she would crawl under the crook of his arm and hide. And normally, he would pull her closer to him just because she wanted him to, but he was angry and didn't understand why she didn't just tell him that this was the guy so he could commence with the ass-whupping.

Brendan looked at Kelvin now, taking him in, studying his face. Maybe another day. If this was the dude, there would be other days.

"Kelvin, I'm going to have to ask you to leave."

"Oh yeah?" Kelvin said. Suddenly he was calm. Deathly calm. "Why's that, Mr. Owner?"

"Because you're making my lady uncomfortable," Brendan said.

And with a raised hand, he called over two of the club's security team, men in suits who looked deceptively dapper, but were well-trained to take out dudes twice their size and weight. Kelvin assessed them as they approached.

"Man," he said to Brendan. "If you think this here's a lady, you need to take a closer look. A *much* closer look." And then he was laughing and heading for the exit, flanked by the security team.

Brendan looked down at Tracy but she still wouldn't make eye contact.

"Was that him?" he asked, his voice tight with anger.

"Brendan ..."

"That's a yes or no question, Tracy."

"I don't want to talk about it right now," she said, heaving a deep sigh.

"Excuse me, *what*?" Brendan leaned in closer. "You don't want to talk about it?"

"Lower your voice!" Tracy hissed at him.

She was looking around like she was afraid to make a scene and Brendan couldn't for the life of him figure out why that would matter at a time like this. Hell, that was the *last* thing on his mind right now.

"Why wouldn't you say it in front of him?" Brendan demanded. "If that's him, why wouldn't you say it?"

"Because I knew you would react exactly the way you're reacting right now," she said. "Except much, much worse."

"So that's it then. It *was* him. I could go find that motherfucker right now ..." Brendan looked toward the exit and Tracy grabbed his arm, her fingers grasping at the sleeve of his shirt.

"No!" she said, her voice frantic. "Don't. *Please.*"

And he almost ignored her. Kelvin couldn't have gotten very far. Was probably less than a block away or waiting for the valet service to bring around a car.

But Tracy's face, her expression stopped him. She was an inch away from tears, and the last thing he wanted was to make her cry.

"Sweetheart ..." He touched the side of her face.

Tracy shook his hand away. "I don't want you talking to him," she said. "Just ... *don't*. Okay?"

"Let's go," Brendan said, taking her arm.

"Where?" She looked up at him.

"Home." And when she looked even more frantic. "My place."

"But what about ..?" She looked around.

"The bloggers?" Brendan shook his head. "I already hooked them up with bottle service and all that. We can leave. It's okay, I promise."

In the car, she leaned far away from him against the door, her face turned toward the passenger-side window. When Brendan glanced over at her, there were tears rolling down her cheeks, but by the time he pulled into his building's underground garage, the tears were no longer in evidence and she was instead stony-faced, almost emotionless.

Upstairs, they undressed in silence and when Brendan was stripped down to his boxer briefs, he got in bed and waited for her to join him. In the dark, when they were lying next to each other, he would hold her. He hoped that might help her open up to him.

Before, whatever had transpired the night of the launch party had been almost academic, abstract. Now it was real. That slimy little motherfucker had touched her, had fucked her

… and had in some way scared and humiliated her. Just the thought of it …

Brendan was distracted from his thoughts by the sight of Tracy nude and heading for the bathroom. He watched her walk away, taking in the utter perfection of her body, the smoothness of her skin. Thinking of someone else touching her, let alone someone as undeserving as that worm, made him want to start breaking shit.

"What're you doing?" he called after her.

"Taking a shower," she said, her voice dull.

She was in there for more than half an hour, until Brendan was sure she would have surely exhausted all of the hot water. He turned off the lights while he waited, so that the only illumination came from the bathroom itself.

When he heard the water shut off, Brendan sat up and leaned back against the headboard waiting for her to emerge. He didn't have a speech prepared or anything, but he knew they had to talk about it. If they didn't, he was going to lose his fucking mind. He had to know precisely what this dude had done to her, and in painstaking detail.

He had no doubt at all that he wouldn't be able to stand knowing, but not knowing wasn't feeling much better than that anyway. And at least when he knew, he would feel good about fucking Kelvin up the next time he ran across him. Next time, he wouldn't examine or hesitate.

But before he could even begin to formulate what he might ask her, Tracy had come out of the bathroom and pulled back the sheets. On her hands and knees, she dragged his briefs partway down his hips.

"Whoa, Tracy …"

Then her mouth was on him and she was pulling him in, sucking hard, making his eyes cross, it felt so good. She used one hand to grasp him, moving it up and down, Brendan could feel his climax approaching, mind-blowingly fast and pulled back. She was trying to distract him. The conversation she knew he needed, she did not want to have.

As he was about to say just that, Tracy pulled up, and grabbing his shoulders lowered herself onto him. Brendan exhaled sharply, instinctively holding her by the hips, fighting the impulse to thrust even deeper into her.

"Tracy," he said again, her name sounding like a gasp. "What's ..?"

"You still want me?" she asked.

The catch in her voice gave him pause and Brendan put his hands on either side of her face and found it wet.

Fuck, she was crying.

She wrenched from his grasp.

"Brendan?" she said. "Do you?"

Her hips were moving back and forth, almost of their own volition, desperately, and Brendan's mind spun in circles, lurching back and forth between pleasure and confusion, the desire to comfort her and to the urge to flip her over and finish what she'd started. But she was crying, so he held her still, then sat completely upright and with her still astride him, closed his arms around her.

Tracy struggled for a moment but soon went limp, and then the crying began in earnest, her chest heaving as she fought to catch her breath, her face buried in his neck.

Holy shit.

Brendan wasn't even sure what the fuck was going on anymore but he knew for sure something way deeper than Kelvin was operating here. Whatever the hell it was, it was way too deep to talk about, especially with her in this overwrought and emotional state.

He tried to pull out of her but she wouldn't let him; always, always she tried to work things out with sex. Or maybe she wasn't working anything out. Maybe she was telling him with her body what she couldn't always find words to say.

Then Brendan realized that she *had* said it. She wanted to know that he still wanted her, and he did, so all there was left to do was show her. And it was only then, when he gently lowered her onto her back, kissing her face and moving against her, that Tracy finally stopped crying.

ELEVEN

THE PEAL OF LAUGHTER FROM ACROSS THE POOL CAUGHT his attention and Brendan looked up to see Tracy holding Cullen, her face close to his, nuzzling his nose. Next to her, Riley reclined on one of the loungers, wearing sunglasses and a black tankini with boy-shorts. There was nothing boyish about the swimsuit Tracy had on, however. It was a little white thing that looked like Brendan could pop that sucker apart with very little effort. Maybe he would, later.

This was the first time they had come over to Shawn and Riley's place in Jersey together even though their friends were now well aware that they were ... involved. Brendan didn't even know what to call it still. All he knew was that he had finally given up on pretending that he didn't want to sleep with her every single night. And on those odd nights when she stayed in Brooklyn, it was an actual struggle not to call her, or just head on over there and drag her back to his bed like a caveman claiming his woman.

She *acted* like she was his woman that was for damn sure, the claws coming out if she so much as sensed that any other female had more than a passing interest in him. Brendan knew there were many things about herself that Tracy held back, but her possessiveness was definitely not one of them. What he always thought would have been a turn-off for him was a big turn-*on*.

Just that morning in the gym, some woman in pink shorts and a white sport bra had wandered over while he was doing bench presses and asked whether he needed her to spot for him. Truth was, he was definitely feeling himself on that bench press and would have readily agreed, had it not been for the sight of Tracy, across the room, working up a sweat on the elliptical machine, watching them both. Her eyes met Brendan's and she tilted her head to one side, looking at him like, *go ahead playa, let her touch you and see what happens*.

Brendan smiled thinking about it now.

"What the hell are you smiling about?"

Brendan looked up at Shawn. For a moment he forgot he was even there.

"Damn, she's got you, hasn't she?" Shawn laughed.

"I don't know what you talkin' 'bout," Brendan said, raising his Corona to his lips.

"Riley told me you gave her a key."

"I can neither confirm nor deny that," Brendan said.

Shawn laughed and shook his head. "Hey, who am I to talk? It's Labor Day weekend and I'm sitting here barbecuing in my backyard in the suburbs. Who the hell would've thought that would be in my future five years ago?"

"True story," Brendan said, distracted by the sight of Tracy standing and stretching her arms above her head before diving cleanly into the pool.

"Shawn, can you take him for a minute?"

Brendan watched as his friend went to join his wife and infant son. Before taking Cullen from Riley, Shawn leaned in and pressed his forehead against hers in a gesture Brendan had seen many times before. It was almost more intimate than a kiss. For one moment, they focused solely on each other to the exclusion of all others, even the baby they had made together.

As if in protest, Cullen wailed and Shawn pulled back abruptly, probably thinking he'd hurt him in some way. Riley handed him off and Shawn took over parenting duty while she joined Tracy in the pool.

"Brendan, come in with us," Tracy called.

Her hair was soaked through from her dive. He smiled remembering how one of the first times they showered together she screamed at him like a banshee because he pulled her in before she had time to put on a shower cap. She never used a shower cap now.

"Later," he said holding up his beer.

"Be a shame to let all those bench presses go to waste," she said with raised eyebrows, before she did a backstroke across the pool.

Brendan smiled and shook his head.

Right after the holiday he was taking Sam Gaston out to the West Coast to meet some folks. He would be gone for a month and while he was there, working long hours. With the time difference, there was no telling how often and when he and Tracy would get a chance to talk. Brendan was dreading and looking forward to it at the same time.

When he told her about the trip, she had changed the subject. The only other time it came up was when she asked him if Shawn was going as well. He was not. Shawn was probably her hope for a chaperone. Brendan was amused thinking about how their roles had switched. At one time, *he* was perceived as the level-headed one who was essential to keep Shawn in check.

When the steaks on the grill were done, he and Shawn ate

together under the loggia while Riley and Tracy sat with their legs in the water, Riley balancing her plate on one knee and breastfeeding Cullen while holding him like a football, tucked in the crook of her arm.

"You'd better not drop my son in the pool!" Shawn called out to her.

"I like the way you call him 'my son,'" Brendan said so only Shawn could hear. "Like Riley had nothing to do with it."

"I'm beginning to think she didn't," Shawn joked. "Have you seen how much he looks like me? Like I cloned myself."

"He does look like you," Brendan nodded. "Her nose though."

"Nah." Shawn shook his head. "All me."

"You're going to need to come take him in a minute," Riley said in a stage-whisper. "He's falling asleep. D'you mind putting him down?"

"*Damn*, baby, I did it last time," Shawn said. And then lowering his voice. "Best part of my day."

Shawn and Riley both wound up going to put Cullen down, so Brendan and Tracy were left alone. He joined her by the pool and kicked off his tennis shoes, sitting next to her and dipping his feet into the cool water. She was different lately; quieter and more subdued. Often when they were alone together, she seemed to be far away and Brendan didn't press, thinking it likely that she was still recovering from that crazy night, now a couple weeks back, that they still hadn't really talked about. But while it made Brendan want to hold her closer to him, it seemed to have caused Tracy to pull farther and farther away.

"So when you're in California," she said suddenly. "What ... what are we going to do?"

"As far as what?"

"A month is a long time," Tracy said. "I just wondered whether you would be ..."

"Socializing?" Brendan asked, preparing himself to talk her down from the ledge of jealousy once again.

"Yes."

"I'll be there to work. I don't think I'll have much time for that."

She was making little waves in the pool, lifting and lowering her feet in the water.

"And what about me?" she asked, casually. A little too casually, Brendan thought.

"What *about* you?" he asked, alert now.

"If I wanted to ... would you have a problem with that?"

No, he wouldn't "have a problem with that" but he would want to find the dude and bury a fucking meat cleaver in his head. Their little close encounter with Kelvin had helped him make a new and intimate connection to an emotion he had rarely if ever experienced before: jealousy.

"Somebody in particular you want to 'socialize' with, Tracy?" he asked, his voice tight.

She didn't say anything for a long time.

"Someone asked me out."

Brendan nodded. "Figured as much."

She said nothing in response so he looked at her.

"What?" Brendan asked. "You need my permission? Or are you telling me you're about to say yes?"

So all *her* possessiveness, jealousy and drama, what the hell had *that* been about? But then again, Tracy was never one to care about things like fairness and reciprocity. It was all well and good to keep him under lock, but made perfect sense for the rules to be different for her.

Forget the meat cleaver to this guy's head. He felt as though someone had already buried the damn thing right in the center of his chest. But what could he say? They had never labeled this bullshit quasi-relationship thing that they'd been doing the last few months. And while it was implied, she never voiced the expectation that he would be monogamous. In fact, jealous tantrums notwithstanding, she seemed to expect that he wouldn't.

Hell, when she wanted them to stop using condoms, she asked that he continue using them with "other partners." And he'd taken the bait and said he would when he knew good and well that even then he had already stopped being interested in sleeping with anyone else.

When Shawn and Riley returned, he went to sit with them and even managed to laugh and carry on a conversation as though nothing was wrong, as though his world didn't feel like it was about to come crashing down around him. Much later when he and Tracy finally set out for their drive back to the city, neither of them had much of anything to say to the other during the ride.

"You want me to drop you off in Brooklyn?" he asked.

Next to him Tracy's head whipped around. "No," she said right away. "You're leaving the day after tomorrow."

Either she was the best actress in the world, or she was genuinely confused by his suggestion that she go home. So she really believed in this arrangement they had going here; that it was possible to keep going like this, the two of them inseparable until and unless she decided it was time to do some dabbling in the dating world, just in case there was something better out there.

Back at the apartment he headed straight for the shower and stayed in there for a long time. She didn't join him and when he got out was already in bed. Without a word, Brendan covered her body with his, kissing the side of her neck and pulling the shirt she was wearing over her head.

She wasn't the only one who could fuck their problems away. His hands moved to her breasts and he kneaded them, his touch was more aggressive and caused her to wince, but he didn't care. When he put a hand between her legs, he was frustrated to find that she was still wearing underwear.

"Take it off," he ordered.

Her eyes were fixed on his as she complied. She looked a little uncertain, like she didn't recognize him, but he didn't care about that either.

"Brendan ..?"

She was forming a question in her mind, but he didn't allow her to complete it and pushed himself into her, keeping up a punishing pace, holding her by the calves and slinging her legs over his shoulders. When she began to meet his rhythm, he stopped and pulling a pillow from above her head, flipped her over onto her stomach and shoving it under her, entered her from behind.

Damn, she felt good, so fucking good.

Brendan tried to put out of his mind that she might be dating while he was gone; no doubt some dude whose goal would be to do to her precisely what he was doing now.

"*Brendan,*" she breathed. "Oh god, *Brendan.*"

Why the hell did she keep saying his name like that? It made it hard for him to concentrate on his anger. And it was essential that he concentrate on his anger because if he didn't, all that would be left was the hurt.

He wrapped both arms about her waist and reared back, pulling her with him so she was sitting on his lap with him still buried deep inside her. He could tell by the frantic clenching and unclenching of her muscles that she was nearing her orgasm so he grabbed her by the hips, his fingers digging into her, and hoisting her off him and back again, controlling the pace so that when he felt her about to come, he could stop it, keeping her close but making sure she never quite got there. Not until *he* was good and goddamned ready for her to get there.

She wasn't saying so much as panting his name now, and he knew he was about to explode himself, so he pulled out of her and let it rip, all over her back. His heart was pounding and he could scarcely catch his breath so he was only vaguely aware of her moving, away from him and curling onto her side in a semi-fetal position.

He fell onto his back, waiting for his breathing to subside, waiting for the ache in his chest to subside, a part of him marveling at how swift, certain and complete his new realization was that he was in love with this woman.

Not that it made a damn bit of difference now.

For the first time in a very long time, she didn't try to hold him, or get him to hold her, and instead grabbed one of his body pillows and coiled around it, her back to him. Brendan did the same, drifting off into a deep, but strangely restless post-coital slumber.

NO WAY WAS this going to work. It was a conviction that had come to him in his sleep; this just wasn't going to work for him. Something told him Tracy on the other hand could keep this going indefinitely; telling herself that it was casual, but slowly but surely changing everything about his life.

Just about every day, one more thing was different, like stocking up his fridge with groceries, even though he asked her expressly and repeatedly not to. The first time, she did it on the sly. It was actually kind of cute, the way she kept running ahead of him up the stairs to the kitchen whenever he headed in that general direction. It had taken Brendan a little while to figure out that something was afoot because she had always brought him food, and cooked for him, from the very first night she ever spent there.

If he had to guess, he would never have pegged Tracy as the kind of woman who liked to take care of her man domestically. But she did. Not only the cooking, but she dropped off his dry cleaning and picked it up without him asking, and he once overheard her chiding the lady from the cleaning service for doing what she called a "superficial job" on the stove, and the woman replying that she wasn't accustomed to seeing the stove in this unit used, so had mistakenly overlooked it.

The evening he figured out what was going on with the groceries, Tracy had made her third run up to the kitchen in a half hour to fetch him something, when Brendan finally followed her, ignoring her protests that she didn't "mind at all" getting him whatever he needed. When he opened the refrigerator and saw that it was stuffed to the gills with food, he looked at her. She grinned back at him with her shoulders hunched and then gave the cutest little grimace, as though she expected him to yell at her.

Brendan, she said. *We can't go to the store every single day. And if I'm not here one morning, I just know you're going to buy something junky from the deli near your office.*

He was touched that she cared whether he ate junk or not, but was more focused on another part of what she said.

Why wouldn't you be here one morning? he asked, eyes narrowed.

Well, she responded, looking almost shy. *I can't be here* every *night, Brendan.*

He just barely stopped himself from asking her why not. But it had to have been written all across his face because she'd gotten on her toes and looked up at him, and he leaned in to kiss her, right there in front of the open—and thanks to her—overstocked fridge.

But that kind of shit couldn't keep going on. Nope. Didn't work for him. Especially not when she was dropping little bombs on him like the news that "someone" had asked her out. What the hell did that mean anyway? Who was this "someone"?

They were together damn near every minute unless they were working. So that had to be it—someone at her job had asked her out. Working in the testosterone-driven environment that was Wall Street, he would be shocked if it didn't happen all the time. But she mentioned this someone because maybe she wanted to say 'yes.'

Before she could wake up, Brendan dressed for a pick-up basketball game and stayed out as long as he could. It was past noon when he turned, and by then he had been gone for a good number of hours, an uncharacteristically long period of time, knowing full well that she would be waiting for him—anxiously, he hoped—to return.

And she was. As he entered the bedroom, Tracy sat up, cross-legged in the middle of his bed, looking at him as though she'd spent the entire morning waiting to confront him, but had suddenly forgotten what she planned to say.

"Hey," he said; his voice was emotionless.

"You want to talk about last night?" she asked finally.

Brendan shed his perspiration-soaked shirt and looked at her.

"What part of last night? The part where you told me you're about to start dating?"

"Everything."

But she seemed not to have thought of anything to say. Good. That was good. He had her off balance, like he'd been knocked off balance by the realization that Tracy wasn't the woman he thought she was.

Tracy wasn't the one you got your fill of and let go; no, she was the one you *couldn't* get your fill of. She was the one you keep. And that last part was what killed him because he didn't know what that looked like quite yet. The epiphany was way too new. So thank God for Sam Gaston and this trip he was about to take.

"Look," he said wearily. "No heart-to-hearts necessary. You're off the hook. We made no promises, no commitments, and as far as I know, we told each other no lies. So let's just have breakfast and enjoy the rest of the day."

Tracy blinked a few times and Brendan turned away from her.

"I'm about to take a shower," he said. "You want to come with me?"

"No," she said, shaking her head. "I'll wait till you're done."

DID *he really not care if she went out with someone else?*

Last night, he'd been angry; very angry, she was certain of that. He didn't kiss her on the mouth when they were having sex, didn't wait for her to finish, didn't even seem to want her to, which was not just unlike him, it was downright cruel.

She wasn't even sure what had gotten into her bringing up Jason's dinner invitation. Maybe a perverse need to cut through the thickness of her growing feelings for him, to dilute it a little bit, maybe even to self-sabotage. A part of her wondered when she brought it up if he would dump her. If he did, it would be easier, because she wasn't sure anymore whether she would be able to walk away from him when the time came. And the time was coming, she was sure of it.

But this morning when she woke up and he was gone, without a word, or an attempt to wake her first, she felt a stab of hurt. That was not the kind of thing Brendan did, ever. He was almost scarily attuned to her moods, and could predict her reactions with such precision, she almost resented it.

Tracy recalled a Thursday evening a month earlier when she'd come in from work stressed and bitchy, and Brendan told her to get dressed so they could go out. As usual, he told her nothing about where they were going.

She had come out wearing three-hundred dollar Chloe jeans and some similarly pricey top with wedge heels and he'd gotten a dubious look on his face. Tracy remembered her exasperation.

It's all I've got, she snapped at him. *So we either go with me wearing this, or we stay in.*

No, Brendan said after a moment's consideration. *I think we definitely need to go.*

And then he'd taken her to Queens to an enormous warehouse. For paintballing. She'd been livid enough to refuse to get out of the car for twenty minutes while he cajoled, teased and finally coaxed her into it. There were goggles and smocks to wear over your street clothes but by the time they were done, her jeans were still ruined, as was her pedicure because she'd had to remove her wedges and play barefoot, which was against the regulations, but Brendan made her do it anyway so she wouldn't twist her ankle running in heels.

Tracy had laughed and squealed and ran like a kid, and Brendan had been merciless about hunting her down. They had hooked up with another group that was already there, and he joined the guys and she the women. When he ambushed her, just as she expected him to blast her with a pellet, he'd instead pulled her against him and kissed the living daylights out of her.

Traitor, she murmured against his lips.

Best date ever. It was precisely the kind of thing she needed, without even knowing it. The wild and reckless energy she'd expended paintballing had snapped her completely out of her funk. Back at the apartment, Brendan had washed paint out of her hair in the shower and even humored her when she asked him to help her blow dry it so that it was perfectly pin-straight afterwards; she always had trouble with the back near her nape.

The next day at work, when the receptionist told her she had a delivery, she expected flowers, but Brendan was never that obvious. He had sent over a gift-wrapped pair of brand new Chloe jeans, identical to the ones she'd ruined the evening before. That he had looked at her jeans and taken note of both the size and style had her staggered. But who cared about getting new jeans when the stained ones would always remind her of that night and of his kiss, behind the bales of hay, that took her breath away.

"What d'you feel like eating?" Brendan asked.

He walked out of the bathroom completely nude, and Tracy's mind went completely blank as she took the sight of him in. Long and lean, with that tapered waist and his ...

Brendan snapped his fingers in front of her face. "Chicken and waffles?"

That revived her. "Brendan, you know I hate that kind of heavy food."

"Just checking for signs of life," he said.

He seemed to be back to his old playful self she noticed; which would have been great but for the fact that now she was the one feeling unsettled. After his initial reaction to her dating, he'd let it go, like water gliding off a duck's back.

Was he really willing to leave for a month and let her date someone else while he was away?

Tracy brooded on that question the entire time she was in the shower and still hadn't made her peace with it by the time they got to the diner around the corner for brunch.

The waitress who served them was named Pam, and had served them many, many times before. She had the rolling hips of a woman who was slightly larger than the fashion magazine ideal but so completely comfortable with her body that Tracy almost envied her. When she walked away to put in their order, it was almost impossible not to watch the rhythmic sway of her gait. But this time, it annoyed Tracy to no end that Pam seemed to be flirting and that Brendan was having fun with it.

No surprise there. He was the kind of man women flirted with because his appreciation of their gender was so genuine, frank and non-threatening. While most men wanted to sleep with any woman they found attractive, not all of them *liked* women at their core. Brendan did, and somehow they knew it, and appreciated him back because of it. Some of that mutual appreciation was a little too apparent for Tracy's taste.

But she was hardly in a position to complain. She was the one who had announced that she was about to date.

The entire meal was nothing short of painful; not because it was awkward and filled with silences but because it was not. Brendan was himself again, as though liberated by some new realization. Or maybe just liberated.

With the last of her coffee, Tracy swallowed the fear that in telling Brendan she might go out with someone else, maybe she'd made the hugest mistake of her life.

AS SOON AS Tracy got to the door of the condo, she could hear Cullen's cries from inside, advancing closer as someone—obviously carrying him—came to let her in. Shawn was holding the baby with one arm against his bare chest and grimacing against the noise of his son's squalling.

Tracy instinctively reached out to take him but Shawn shifted so that Cullen was out of her reach.

"Nah, that's okay. I got him," he said.

"Oh. Okay," Tracy said, hurt.

Wow. He was really pissed at her.

"He just needs to be fed," Shawn explained. "I was about to get him something."

Tracy followed him to the kitchen and sat well out of his way. Shawn moved around in a practiced routine, sterilizing a bottle, warming what looked like breast-milk in a plastic pouch and finally transferring it to the bottle, all while holding a crying Cullen with one hand. He even tested the temperature of the milk on the back of his hand like a mom would before putting the nipple into his son's mouth.

"You're a natural," Tracy commented.

And it didn't escape her notice that even though Cullen had been crying for at least ten minutes, Riley hadn't once come out of the bedroom to check up on Shawn. They had become a team; so much so that Riley trusted that even if Cullen was crying, Shawn was handling it, whatever the problem might be.

It was a lesson she might do well to learn. If Brendan fumbled around with the coffeemaker for more than fifteen seconds, she always stepped in and took over, nudging him out of the way, never patient enough to let him do it on his own if she believed she might do it better.

And then she caught herself. She and Brendan—to the extent that there even was a 'she and Brendan' anymore—were a long sight away from being anything like the now well-oiled machine that was Shawn and Riley.

"Ready to go?"

Riley emerged from the bedroom dressed in a tan shirt and jeans with sandals and a beautiful soft brown leather bag that Tracy knew right away Shawn had probably bought her. It looked too plush, too luxurious to be anything her friend would purchase on her own. Riley paused to kiss the top of Cullen's head and the bicep of the arm Shawn was using to hold him.

In the elevator, she let out a deep, heartfelt sigh.

"Sometimes I just cannot wait to get away from them." And then she laughed at the look on Tracy's face. "What? You think it's sunshine and blue skies all the time? Oh girl, just you wait."

"I've been waiting a long time," Tracy said wryly.

"Don't get me started," Riley said. "I'm beginning to doubt that you want what you say you want."

"What does *that* mean?" Tracy looked at her.

"It means you screwed up. You leave the best thing you've had going for years to date some dotcom millionaire who probably thinks of you as just another pretty little toy he can buy?"

Tracy said nothing. It was true. She knew it was true. But she hadn't really left Brendan, he'd let her go.

"Riley, he wasn't exactly blockading the door to stop me, either."

"Why should he, Tracy? You told him you planned to date someone else!"

"We weren't exclusive."

"Oh my *god*! Not with that old line again. What are you? In high school? You need him to give you a promise ring? According to you, you slept at his place practically every night and you saw him just about every day? What more did you need?" Riley demanded.

Whoa. So clearly Shawn was not the only one who was more than a little pissed with her.

"Well, he'll be back in New York next week, and I still have a key, so ..."

Riley stepped off the elevator and Tracy followed.

"Walking or driving?" Riley asked.

"Walking."

They stepped out into the street and headed south.

"It's too late," Riley said.

"What's too late?" Tracy asked.

"With Brendan. It's too late," Riley said. "I overheard Shawn on the phone. I'm not certain but I think Meghan went out there."

Tracy stopped walking and turned to face Riley, her heart in her mouth. "No. I don't believe that. He's not interested in her anymore."

Riley shrugged and touched Tracy's arm.

"Well maybe I heard wrong." But it was obvious from her face that she didn't think so and was only trying to make Tracy feel better.

"Tell me *exactly* what you think you heard," Tracy demanded.

"Sure. But could we do that while walking? Because I'm starving."

Tracy could barely contain herself until they were in the Tea and Crumpets Café and Riley had ordered her breakfast. The idea of Brendan with Meghan had her stomach in a painful, tight knot.

"So what did you hear?" she asked again as soon as the waiter left.

"Not much, honestly. I heard Shawn say her name and then it was a couple moments later, I heard him ask something like, 'when did she get there?' or something along those lines. That was all."

"But it was enough to make you think she was there with him in California."

"Yes."

The waiter returned with water. Tracy took a sip of hers right away.

"I'll just call him when he's back in town. He'll ..."

"Why?" Riley asked baldly.

"What?" Tracy looked at her.

"Why're you calling him?" Riley asked, looking at her. There was a tightness about her mouth, more than a hint of disapproval, Tracy thought.

"I want to see him, Riley!"

"Yes, I get that. But where are you going with that, is what I mean. You want to see him, but do you want to be with him? Or do you want to be with Dotcom Man?"

"You know I don't want to be with Jason Miller," Tracy said.

"And yet you're dating him. So I guess I don't get it," Riley said, barely keeping the irritation out of her voice.

"I'm not sure where things can go with someone like Brendan, that's all. His lifestyle ..."

"What lifestyle? You mean the lifestyle where he comes home to you every night, treats you like a queen and indulges all your crazy behavior as though it's cute. *That* lifestyle?"

Tracy swallowed. Nothing about what Riley said was untrue.

"Tracy, you know I love you, but maybe you should just leave him be. If you're so concerned about this lifestyle thing, whatever the hell that means, and Meghan really cares about him. I mean, she told me ..."

"Wait. You've been talking to *her* about Brendan?" Tracy demanded.

"No," Riley said slowly. "A while back, *she* called *me* about Brendan. Seems he pretty much cooled things off for no reason and she was confused."

"And you didn't tell me?"

"As far as I knew, it had nothing to *do* with you. I didn't even know then that you and Brendan were involved."

"But you knew I ..."

"Knew you *what* Tracy? Liked to have him on a string in case one day you decided to give him a shot? Yes, you're right. That I did know. I guess I just didn't think it was relevant to him having an actual relationship with a really nice woman who genuinely cares about him."

Tracy felt as though she'd been slapped. She leaned back in her seat and opened her mouth to respond when the waiter returned, this time with their coffees. She watched as Riley prepared her espresso, adding milk and sweetener.

"*I* genuinely care about him," Tracy finally said, her voice quiet. And when Riley said nothing she shook her head. "You don't think I'm good enough for him."

"No," Riley said looking up right away. "I don't think that Tracy."

"I can hear a 'but' in there."

"It's just that, on the one hand you're spouting off all this nonsense about which men are and aren't suitable partners, and then on the other, you let yourself get used by a parade of men who think of you as ... less than nothing."

Tracy looked away.

She had never gotten around to telling Riley about the night of the Lounge Two-Twelve opening, but knew that her friend was speaking more generally, more historically. She *had* let herself get used by men who made her feel like nothing. And the one man who didn't make her feel that way was the one she pushed away.

"You know I don't know how to do this," Tracy said. "I'm just trying to figure it out, Riley. Same as everyone else."

"Brendan's not the guy you use to figure your shit out.

Brendan's the guy you hope you get once you *have* figured your shit out."

"IT DIDN'T TAKE *you very long, did it?"*

Brendan had rolled over and flipped on the lamp next to his bed, fumbling in the dark for a moment because of the unfamiliarity of his surroundings. He hated hotels, particularly hotels that he checked into late at night while exhausted. He always woke up sometime around three a.m. looking to use the bathroom and stubbed his toe on something.

This time, it was his phone that had awoken him, and he grabbed it more to stop the annoying ringtone than because he was interested in speaking to anyone at—he checked the clock—four-ten in the morning.

"Hello?" he croaked.

"You've been gone three weeks. *Three* weeks. And already Meghan's back on the scene. But of course, you never did say she was *off* the scene, so I guess ..."

"Tracy?"

"Yes!" she hissed at him.

"What time is it there, Tracy?"

"It's a little past seven, why?"

"So what time does that make it here in California?" Brendan asked.

There was a moment's pause while she absorbed what he was saying.

"Oh."

"Yeah, 'oh'."

"I'm sorry."

Brendan settled back against the pillow, rubbing his eyes

and yawning. Anyone else and he would have hung up on them already.

"Now what was it you wanted to say?" he asked after a moment.

"Riley told me that Meghan was out there with you."

"Riley's mistaken."

"So she isn't there?"

"No."

"*Was* she there?"

"Hold up. I'm still stuck on trying to figure out why you think I should have to answer any of these questions at all, let alone answer them before dawn."

"You're right," she said after a moment. "But you were the one who got angry with me, remember? Just because I was honest about being asked out by someone ..."

"No. Not about you being asked out," Brendan corrected her. "About you wanting to say 'yes'. That's the goddamned difference."

"You never said you didn't want me to go out with other men."

Brendan looked at the phone incredulously. "Oh, that's something I have to *say*?"

"I'd like it if you did," Tracy said, her voice barely audible.

"And if I did, you wouldn't go out on the date?"

"I don't know," she admitted.

"Tracy," Brendan sighed. "I'm exhausted ..."

"You didn't answer me. Was Meghan there?"

"Yes."

Brendan listened to the silence for a while. He didn't need to see her face or even hear her voice to know she was pissed. It made him feel good to know she was angry and jealous about Meghan. In fact, it just might make his whole fucking day.

"How about you?" he asked. "You go on your date with ol' boy?"

"Yes."

"Well then I guess I'm even more confused about why you're making this crazy phone call," Brendan said.

"Because it was very hurtful to hear that you saw Meghan, that's why. And for the record, it was also hurtful the way you treated me that night when I told you about being asked out."

Hurtful. For Tracy to admit that something had *hurt* her was nothing less than a breakthrough. Sure, she was jealous and irrational, but "hurt" was a new introduction to their relationship lexicon. It gave him hope in a strange way.

"I was hurt too," he said. "So I'm sorry. I shouldn't have ..." The image of himself wrenching out of her, denying her pleasure because he was in pain, flashed across his mind, and not for the first time he felt a stab of remorse. "I shouldn't have treated you that way."

"*Are* you back together with Meghan?" Tracy asked, ignoring his apology.

"No. And I was never with Meghan. Not in the way you mean it."

"I need ..." She stopped abruptly.

"What do you need?"

She said nothing for a long time. Brendan had no doubt that the answer to that question eluded her. Tracy didn't know what she needed. She *thought* she knew that he was bad for her, that much he was aware of. And he was also aware that she couldn't be persuaded otherwise. Tracy was the kind of woman who had to come to her own realizations, no matter how long and arduous a process that might be. The question was how long he was willing to hang in there and wait for her to do that.

One thing he did know was that it had been a shitty three weeks. Being away from her was one thing. Being away from her and having to entertain the likelihood that she was with someone else was a whole new level of discomfort altogether, and one that he would be more than happy to put an end to right now. But this was not his move to make, it would have to be all hers.

"Tracy, what do you need?" he asked again. "I'm about to go back to sleep."

"I need for you to not to see her anymore," she said finally.

Brendan couldn't help himself. He smiled.

"While you get to run around town with anybody the hell you want? Not a chance, Tracy."

"Okay then, 'bye."

And that quickly, she hung up.

The entire conversation had taken less than fifteen minutes but Brendan marveled at how much if changed the texture of his upcoming day, hell, his upcoming *week*. The ups and downs of being with Tracy were a little tough to get accustomed to and sometimes it seemed nothing short of insane, but there was no denying that for whatever reason, he wasn't exactly clamoring to get off the ride.

TWELVE

"IF YOU GO, I'M NOT SURE THERE'S ANY WAY FOR US TO move forward."

If he lived to be a hundred, Brendan would never understand women who issued ultimatums. There was no surer way to get a man looking at the front door than to give him a false choice, meant to blackmail him into choosing you. Had that strategy ever worked for anyone? He seriously doubted it.

"It's a funeral, Meghan."

"For a man who you just admitted you'd never met."

"For the father of a very good friend."

"Is that what she is now? A very good friend?"

Brendan tried to contain his impatience, wondering why he was even entertaining her questions. It wasn't like him to go back to a relationship that had played out already. And he hadn't. Not really.

When he was in California, Meghan had called him because she was doing an audit near L.A. and wanted to know whether he was interested in getting together for dinner. And he agreed because he couldn't think of a good reason not to. But he'd been puzzled, wondering how she even knew he was on the West Coast. Turned out she'd gotten Shawn at the club and he told her.

His first mistake was accepting the invitation to drinks, but the bigger mistake was accepting an invitation to go back to her room with her. Maybe he was thinking that it would be a definite step in getting Tracy out of his system, or maybe he was just horny. He couldn't even remember now what dumb rationale he'd come up with. But he'd gone back to the room with her, and from there, things had progressed: more dinners and drinks when he came back to New York, a couple nights at her place.

And now she thought she owned him. Where before she had been relaxed and permissive, Meghan had become suspicious and clingy, even though the only understanding they had at this point was a series of dates that—at least as far as Brendan was concerned—amounted to no more than that.

"Maybe it's time we talked about this 'moving forward' stuff, Meghan," Brendan said, massaging his temple while holding the phone in the crook of his neck.

"Yes?"

"I'm not sure I can give you what you seem to need," he said.

"Which would be what, in your estimation?"

That was another thing. She had turned sarcastic on him as well.

At first, all these changes seemed like what he deserved under the circumstances. From her perspective, one minute they were going hot and heavy and the next he had fallen off the face of the earth and was seeing someone else. Someone who once tried to humiliate her at a party, no less. So Brendan felt like he owed her something for that, and patiently absorbed her obvious frustration with him for the past month.

But now this was going too far. When Riley told him Tracy's father had died, there was no question that he had to go to the funeral. He had been in her family's home, sat down to dinner with her mother. He could send a wreath, sure, but it didn't seem like enough, not after what he and Tracy had been to each other, however ill-defined.

And it didn't hurt that he would get to see her either, he admitted to himself.

When he got back from the West Coast a part of him had fantasized that he would open the door to his apartment and she would be there. Like some kind of stupid-ass romantic comedy like the ones she used to force him to watch with her on Sunday mornings. But she wasn't there, and what's more, there was food in his refrigerator going bad that he had to toss out, which only reminded him of her more.

Turning his thoughts back to the conversation at hand, he took a deep breath.

"Meghan," he said now. "I'm pretty sure you know what's going on."

"But maybe I need the benefit of hearing you say it," she told him, her voice bitter. "Unlike last time, I want things to be crystal clear."

He had never said it. Not to anyone.

"I love Tracy," Brendan told her matter-of-factly.

The words, said aloud, felt like a weight off his shoulders. The only thing that could possibly feel better right now would be saying the words to her. But regardless of whether or not he went to her father's funeral, Brendan knew Tracy wasn't ready to hear them. So for now, they would have to be his burden alone.

Still, he would find a flight and go to Atlanta this weekend for her father's funeral. Just because they hadn't been in contact in six weeks didn't mean he wasn't concerned about her. And though she hadn't come out and told him as much, he sensed that Tracy's relationship with her mother was strained, so as many friendly faces as possible couldn't hurt. Riley was flying down and leaving Cullen with Shawn so there would be someone to act as a buffer if it came to that.

"Well, there's no arguing with love, is there?" Meghan said on the other end of the line.

Brendan gave a short laugh. Who was *she* telling? No matter how you looked at it, Tracy didn't make sense for him. But that didn't matter: the heart wanted what the heart wanted.

"Meghan, I'm sorry I couldn't ..."

"You were always a gentleman, Brendan," she said sounding weary all of a sudden. "You have nothing to be sorry for."

And just when he was starting to think how cool she was being about this, she had to go and add something more.

"But I can guarantee you, if you get together with that woman, she'll give you *plenty* to be sorry for."

And then she hung up.

In a way, that last comment was a gift, because it gave him license to stop feeling guilty. He had been a little less than a gentleman in the way he treated her before, but the piece of mean-spirited advice there at the end had pretty much evened out the scorecard as far as he was concerned.

"GOOD TO SEE YOU AGAIN, JOCELYN."

Brendan leaned in to kiss Tracy's cousin briefly on the cheek.

"Nice of you to come," Jocelyn said.

She was wearing a black dress that was marginally too close-fitting to be appropriate. Brendan remembered what

Tracy told him about her acting like "the Black Marilyn Monroe" and tried not to smile.

"Does Tracy know you're here?" she asked.

He nodded slowly. She had spotted him at the graveside standing next to Riley and her eyebrows had shot up for a split second before she resumed her somber expression.

As Brendan scanned the mourners, he noted that besides Tracy, her mother and her mother's sisters, nearby, and on the other side of the casket were two young women who bore passing resemblances to Tracy. But while they clung to each other as they cried, they didn't look at or speak to Tracy or her mother.

Curious, Brendan leaned in and whispered in Riley's ear, asking who they were.

"Tracy's sisters," she responded.

Sisters? Tracy never mentioned siblings. In fact, he was pretty sure that when he was talking about being an only child, she had commiserated as though her experience had been precisely the same.

"Will we see you back at the house?" Jocelyn asked, her expression calculating.

"I'll be there." Brendan nodded.

He looked around for Riley who was chatting with a group of women, wishing she would come rescue him.

"I have to admit, I didn't believe Tracy the last time you were here and she told me you two weren't involved," Jocelyn said taking a step closer to him. "But this time since she brought along her boyfriend, I guess I have to ..."

"Excuse me, what?" Brendan gave Jocelyn his full attention for the first time.

"Jason," Jocelyn said. "You know him, I assume. He's from New York as well."

"No," Brendan said, his voice wooden. "I don't know Jason."

"Flew in at the last minute is my understanding," Jocelyn said. "Anyway, I'm riding with the family, so I'll see you over there?"

"Sure." Brendan nodded once again.

So Tracy had a boyfriend. Well, he shouldn't be surprised. Once you cracked the surface, there was a lot to Tracy that would make a man want to lay his claim to her. Except now he was preoccupied with just how much cracking dude had managed in the last six weeks.

Was she sleeping with him?

"Brendan. You ready to head over?"

Riley's hand was on his arm and he turned to look at her.

"Why didn't you tell me Tracy had a boyfriend?" he said.

Riley looked confused for a moment. "She doesn't."

"Her cousin Jocelyn seems to think she does. Some guy named Jason?"

Recognition entered Riley's eyes but it took a moment for her to shake her head. "He's not her boyfriend, Brendan."

"But she's with him."

Riley sighed and looked exhausted. "I don't know what to call it. I'm not sure she does either."

"Yeah, I'm familiar with that set-up," Brendan said nodding.

"It's not ... it's ..."

"None of my business," he said, holding up a hand. "Let's just go to the house and pay our respects. I might be able to get back home on the red-eye and get some work done tomorrow."

No point pretending he wasn't pissed. But mostly, he was pissed at himself. He had been hoping for more than a chance to say he was sorry about her father's death, and that was the truth. So he played himself. Wouldn't be the first time.

All along both sides of the street outside Tracy's mother's home, cars were lined up, and it took Brendan and Riley some time to find a place to park, which wound up being three blocks over. As they walked back to the house, they joined dozens of other mourners making their way toward the classic colonial.

Mrs. Emerson, Tracy's mother, was greeting them at the front door. As he and Riley drew closer, Brendan saw that Tracy was standing next to her, and behind Tracy, a man he didn't know.

Beside him, Brendan could feel Riley's apprehension but she had no cause for it. It wasn't as though he was Shawn after all. In his day, Shawn would have had no compunction about starting an out and out brawl if he felt someone was moving in on Riley, but that had never been his style. As shitty as this might feel, he could only assume that at least for this moment in time, Tracy was precisely where she wanted to be, and with the man she had chosen to be with.

"Mrs. Emerson." Brendan took her hand as he entered the house. "I'm sorry for your loss."

"Thank you." She blinked, looking surprised to see him, and then—Brendan was sure he hadn't imagined it—she cast a worried look behind her in the direction of Tracy's companion.

He was wearing a dark grey suit, which Brendan recognized as expensively tailored, and his shoes were a pair Brendan himself had. Also very pricey. He had a serious, almost stern face, clean-shaven and was a little on the thin side. It was hard not to try to get the measure of this man, his competition. He would have spent more time sizing dude up if he didn't have to keep the line moving.

Then he was standing in front of Tracy and if he didn't know better he would say she looked relieved, and maybe even a little elated to see him. When he held out a hand, she hugged him instead. He wanted to hug her back. But now that they were standing face to face, he was too angry and felt a revival of the same hurt as the night she told him about this guy in the first place.

So instead, he awkwardly patted her back, mumbling something about condolences and moving on. Briefly, in the back of his mind he wondered where her sisters were, but foremost was how quickly he could get the hell out of there.

Three hours it turned out.

Although he was pretty much ready to go the minute after he made himself known to the family, Riley was not. She had known many of Tracy's family members for years, and hadn't seen them in a while, so she spent long minutes talking with each one, catching them up on her life, getting them caught up on hers, and showing off pictures of Cullen. Brendan hung on the outskirts of these conversations, gauging from each one just how much longer she was likely to be.

Once or twice, he considered leaving her, but knew he wouldn't. Even though she was among people she knew well, Shawn would not take kindly to his wife being left behind anywhere. The entire afternoon, apart from following Riley around, his remaining focus was directed at avoiding Tracy.

She had a shadow of her own. Wherever she was, Jason was there as well, a supportive hand on her back. Rather than break the hand off, Brendan decided it might be better to just not look at them.

Finally, at dusk, Riley was ready to go, and only because she needed to get back to the hotel and relieve herself with her breast pump. Just when he thought they were home-free, she turned in the foyer remembering "just one more person" she needed to speak to. Brendan stood waiting, juggling the keys to the rental car, looking eagerly out at the street.

"We never got a chance to talk," a voice behind him said.

He turned and looked at Tracy, taking her in fully for the

first time. She was wearing a conservative black suit and low-heeled black pumps with dark pantyhose. In her ears were simple pearl earrings and around her neck the matching necklace. She had pulled her hair back into a bun and wore only minimal make-up. It was hard to look her in the eye.

Brendan could feel her wanting something from him, a response that he was obviously failing to produce. She kept trying to hold his gaze even as he looked over her head, searching for Riley, wishing she would hurry the hell up.

"You're still angry with me," she said.

He looked at her. "I was never angry with you."

"Really?" she asked, skeptical. "So that last night we were together? What was that about?"

"I *was* angry," he admitted. "But more at myself than at you."

"What for?" she asked, her voice barely audible.

"For lying to myself about what you and me were."

"What did you think we were?" she asked.

Brendan looked over her head again. "Tracy, this isn't the time or the place. You just lost your dad ..."

"He wasn't my 'dad'," she said, her voice hard. "Not by a long shot. And I want to know." She held his arm. "Tell me what you thought ..."

"It doesn't matter anymore, does it?" Brendan said. "You've got somebody and he looks ... he looks like a good guy."

"I don't have somebody, as you put it. And Jason is a good guy. I guess. Just not ..."

"Okay, so are we ready?" Riley was back. She looked from Tracy to Brendan and then apologized. "I can come ba ..."

"No," Brendan said quickly. "I'm ready.

And he was. It was already too much—all the back and forth of emotion; it was exactly what he didn't want. What with the dead father, the new boyfriend and her interminable ambivalence about him, he was fucking exhausted. His life never used to be like this, marked by sharp lurches of feeling, up and down, forwards and backwards.

It used to be that he was the happy-go-lucky guy, who nothing got to. Well, she'd fucked *that* all up. Or he had. But either way, it was time to get his shit straight again.

Brendan decided right then that when he got back to New York he would have left all this behind him. And the next time he showed up at Shawn and Riley's, and Tracy was there, looking the way she did, he would absorb the emotional blow that seeing her would undoubtedly produce, and then he'd just keep on stepping.

"Brendan ..."

"It's okay, Tracy." He touched the side of her face, and attempted a smile. "It's all good."

During the car ride back to the hotel, Brendan could feel Riley wanting to say something. He stayed silent, hoping she wouldn't, but at the same time wishing she would. His hold on this new resolution to stay away from Tracy was tenuous at best, and all it would take was one encouraging word from the person who knew her best before that resolve would crumble and disintegrate entirely. He waited, but she said nothing.

At the hotel, they paused in the lobby.

"You okay for dinner?" Brendan asked her.

Riley nodded. "I'm a little tired so I'll probably do room service. You?"

"Same," Brendan nodded.

"You'll call me before you decide about leaving early?" Riley asked.

"Already decided, Riley. You want to get on the same flight?"

"No, I'll stick with the one in the morning."

Brendan hesitated.

Shawn would not appreciate him running away from Atlanta to avoid Tracy, and leaving Riley alone to take an airport taxi at seven a.m.

"Y'know what, I could use some sleep too," Brendan said. "I'll meet you down here in the a.m. like we planned."

"Okay." Riley smiled at him and squeezed his arm before heading for the elevators.

He wasn't sure how he felt about all the sympathy being lobbed his way. He would drink himself silly tonight and tomorrow would be a new day.

"ARE *you going to open the door?"*

Brendan sat up in bed and listened for a moment as it began to dawn on him that Tracy's voice wasn't in his head, but in the real world where things were considerably fuzzier since he polished off almost all the little bottles in the mini-refrigerator.

At the peak of his drunkenness he had laughed aloud at himself, remembering how he watched Shawn go through this same mad dance, and felt sorry for the dude. This was his punishment.

"Brendan? You're making me worried now. If you don't open up, I might have to call hotel security."

That spurred him to move a little more quickly and he swung his long legs over the edge of the bed and went to open the door. Tracy was standing there in jeans and a t-shirt, her face clean of make-up.

"You're flattering yourself," he said as he walked back into the room.

"I wasn't implying you would hurt yourself ... because of me," she said.

"Not for *any* reason," Brendan said. "I happen to be one of my favorite people." And with that last sentence he knew that he was still pretty fucking drunk.

By the tiny smile on her face she was trying to hide, Tracy knew it too.

"You're one of my favorite people too." She shut the door behind her and sat on the edge of the bed next to him. "I didn't like how we left things."

"Which time?" he asked.

"None of them," Tracy said after a moment.

"So you need *closure*?" Brendan asked. The word didn't roll off his tongue as easily as he hoped it would. "Whatever the fuck that is."

"I'm not trying to close anything," Tracy said.

The stubbornness in her voice made him look at her, and she looked right back at him her chin tilted slightly upward, the way it did when they argued and she was refusing to back down.

"Y'know Tracy, to be the prettiest woman I ever knew, you sure have a lot of ugly inside you," he said.

The effect of his words was immediate. She blinked as though he had punched her in the gut and tears sprang to her eyes. And then he felt like a shit for making her cry.

Brendan sighed and reached out, pulling her against him, burying his face in her hair.

"I'm sorry," he said. And because he was too drunk to censor himself he went on. "I'm hurt so I'm hurting you, and I'm sorry."

Her head snapped back and she looked at him, her eyes strangely hopeful.

"You're hurt?" she asked.

"Fucking crushed," Brendan admitted. He used his nose to nuzzle hers. "Wasn't it obvious?"

"I knew you were angry."

"But only because I was hurt. I thought we were okay. I thought we were ... starting to get each other. And then out of left field, you tell me *that* shit? That you want to date?"

"I didn't know what to do."

"About *what*?"

"About you. About everything. I didn't know what to do. It was just too much. It wasn't what I expected."

"What did you expect?"

"Not to feel anything."

That knocked him back a little.

"What does *that* mean?"

"It means," Tracy said slowly. "That I'm used to not feeling anything. With men. That's what I'm used to."

Brendan struggled to wrap his alcohol-addled mind around that, not sure he understood what the heck she was talking about. Tracy, probably seeing his confusion, stood and went to sit instead on one of the armchairs a few feet away, so that they were opposite each other and could look each other more easily in the eyes.

"I want to tell you some things about me," she said. "Things that only Riley knows. And when I'm done, you have to promise me that you won't try to respond. At least not now."

Brendan was even more confused, and Tracy seemed to read that on his face too.

"I know it doesn't make sense yet. But when I'm done, maybe you won't want to see me again. Or you will. But I want you to promise not to try to give me an answer tonight."

She looked terrified. Even in his inebriated state, he could read that expression.

Whatever it was she wanted to tell him, it was clearly not something she shared lightly. Brendan could feel sobriety battling for supremacy in his brain because he wanted to hear and understand what Tracy said, even though another part of him dreaded it.

"I promise," he said.

Tracy's chest heaved as she took a deep breath and began speaking.

THIRTEEN

Tracy would never have thought in a million years that Brendan would fly all the way to Atlanta for Malcolm's funeral. After all, he had never met him, and even if he had, things hadn't exactly been left on a high note between them.

And Riley, in true form, hadn't breathed a word. But seeing him there at the graveside, in his black suit, wearing a tie—Brendan in a tie—had been the sweetest thing. And as she stood there, listening to the preacher intone, she realized that all the "sweetest things" anyone had ever done for her, *he* had done. In the few months they had been together, the list seemed endless.

What she had known for at least a month came crashing down on her again in that instant. *She loved this man.* She loved him and she didn't care one whit about what her mother or anyone else might think. She loved him, and she was pretty sure he might love her too. But there was the reality of Meghan who he had begun dating again, and Jason who had breezed into town, looking like he expected a medal for showing up.

Over the last few weeks of dating Jason Miller, half-heartedly and more out of inertia than anything else, she figured him out. He was the Prince of the Grand Gesture. He wanted to take her to the best, most expensive restaurants, in the newest luxury car, and to the exclusive-run ballet where tickets were *impossible* to get for mere mortals. It all felt a little too contrived, as though he didn't enjoy doing these things for her so much as he enjoyed how doing these things for her made *him* look.

Even coming to Malcolm's funeral had been a big showy thing. He had gone to great pains when he was in New York to apologize with flowers that he couldn't be there, and then at the last minute chartered a jet to fly him in, because he just "needed to be there" for her, "no matter the inconvenience." She almost rolled her eyes when he said it. For heaven's sake, they'd only been on about five or six dates. A nice card and a wreath would have sufficed.

But her mother of course had loved the whole bit, and looked approvingly at him when he explained his ordeal getting there. *My god,* Tracy thought, *can she not see through this guy? He's everything she thought Brendan was!* And the way he stuck to her throughout the reception was nauseating, acting the part of the solicitous boyfriend, basking in everyone's approval.

Watching him reminded Tracy of the way he asked her out in the first place. That was a Grand Gesture too. *It's worth half a million dollars just to have you go out with me.* What a crock of shit. And she'd fallen for it, because she was just that stupid and thought it must mean he believed she was worth something.

And the person who *really* thought she was worth something, and who had shown her that every day, was across the room, avoiding her and obviously itching to leave. Every time she looked up at him, Brendan was gazing longingly toward the front door, or impatiently at Riley; and her heart ached because all she could think about was having him hold her, and how much she missed that.

He made her feel so small, but so safe when he held her. If she moved across the bed in the middle of the night, he would drag her back toward him, sometimes even grumbling at her, though half-asleep.

Where you goin'? he might say, sounding annoyed.

And she would smile and push back against him, wedging her butt into his groin.

Letting Brendan leave and fly back to New York where they would both once again be pulled away from focusing on each other was out of the question. But when she tried to talk to him at the door, he was back to being the Brendan she ran into at Shawn and Riley's baby shower brunch months ago—nice, cordial, friendly, but closed off to her in some fundamental way. That was not going to happen. She would not let him send her back there, into emotional exile.

When she called Riley later, she was scarcely sympathetic. She, also, had been thrown by Jason's presence.

"What should I say to him?" Tracy asked her, feeling desperate. Riley was always her life preserver, and she was refusing to play that role this time."He won't *talk* to me."

"Tracy, I'm tired, and I miss my husband and kid. I don't know what you should say. Try the truth."

"I tried to tell him before ..."

"Oh, you mean the night you told him you were going back into the dating pool to find better fish? That time?"

Tracy said nothing.

"Goodnight Tracy," Riley said, her voice bearing a note of finality. But then before she hung up, because Riley could never truly *not* be her life preserver, she said, "he's in room 2018."

As soon as she could, when various and sundry family members were occupied with tending to her mother's needs, Tracy changed and slipped out of the house. Finding Brendan drunk had been a blessing, really, because part of her hoped that when she was done talking, he would remember only the spirit of what she said, the generalities rather than the awful, sordid details.

And he was—as she should have known he would be—an adorable drunk, an emotional one, not a mean one, despite that one comment about the "ugly inside" her. God, she only got all teary-eyed because it was true. And now she would have to tell him just how true.

TRACY TOOK a deep breath and looked at Brendan sitting across from her, his elbows on his knees, hands clasped between them, waiting.

"Y'know the old joke about the man who has a perfect family in the suburbs? And across on the other side of town a whole other perfect family?" Tracy said.

She could see Brendan's eyes already narrowing in confusion.

"Well, I'm the punch line to that joke. My mother and I. For twenty years, my mother was the mistress. She had been for three years before I was even born. And then for seventeen years after that.

"The thing of it was, we didn't live clear across town from my father's family. We lived fifteen minutes away. I had a single mother. So what? Lots of my friends did. So I never noticed anything until I was about twelve and I started to make the connection between those nights my mother would get dressed up and prepared for company, and I would be sent to my Aunt Rose's house."

Tracy paused and took another breath. Brendan said nothing, still listening.

"I figured she had a boyfriend, and I didn't care. I was glad she did, because she was happier on those nights and even if the day after, she seemed a little moody, I assumed it was just because she missed him.

"When I was fifteen, I was in the same grade as a girl who everyone said looked like me. We thought it was funny, she and I. We weren't close friends, but we joked about it sometimes, saying we were cousins or whatever.

"And then one day, her mother came to the school and there was a big scene in the administrative offices and this girl who looked like me was pulled out of my homeroom. And by the end of the semester, she was pulled out of the school altogether. I think I knew, vaguely, that she had a sister and that her sister was a senior who'd graduated that year."

Tracy saw something pass fleetingly in Brendan's eyes; a realization of some kind. But then it was gone and he was listening again.

"Around that time, my friends and I were starting to like boys, talk about hair and make-up and the usual things. And I had a really close girlfriend who I was inseparable with. We liked this boy who we thought was way out of our league, so there was no real competition, I thought. Because it wasn't as though either of us had a chance in hell of getting to go out with him.

"But then there was a school dance, and he asked me to dance and didn't ask her. And he spent the whole night talking to me, and didn't pay attention to any other girls and I was over the moon. But my friend ... she was upset and we had a huge fight the next week at school in front of everybody.

And then she told me what everyone knew. Everyone except me.

"That my mother was a slut. And I was a bastard and a slut like my mother; and that I had driven that girl who looked like me out of the school because it made her mother sick to her stomach to have her daughter attend the same school and be in the same class as her husband's bastard."

Tracy swallowed and looked around the room, trying to look anywhere but into Brendan's eyes. She knew how they would look. He would be feeling sorry for her. And that was something she didn't want to see.

"Anyway, you know I had to go right home and ask my mother. And when I did, she turned all pale, and couldn't say anything and so I knew it was true. And I *hated* her. I hated that she let me go to that school without knowing. And after that, things were very different for me there.

"It was like, in saying aloud all the stuff that people had been saying behind my back, my friend ..." Tracy laughed a mirthless laugh. "My *ex*-friend at that point, made it a live, true thing. And so everyone started treating me like a slut. Even that boy I liked, who I thought liked me."

Brendan made a move as though to come to her and Tracy shook her head, so he sat down again.

When she continued he might not want to come to her. It was better that he not touch her now, because it would hurt like hell when she told him the rest, and he let her go.

"So I *became* a slut," she said matter-of-factly. "The first time I had sex, it was with that boy. And then I had sex with other boys, not because I was interested, but because they were other girls' secret crushes, or their boyfriends. I had sex for the first time when I was fifteen, and by the time I graduated, I'd probably had six or seven sex partners. And that's only the ones I had actual intercourse with.

"It was like I had a double-life. I had no friends, so I studied a lot. But I had these secret hook-ups with guys that only they and I knew about. And I felt powerful and spiteful and I hated them and I knew they didn't give a shit about me."

"Tracy, you don't have to ..."

"I know it's tough to listen to," she said, wryly. "It's tougher to have to tell you, believe me."

At that Brendan was quiet and allowed her to go on.

"Occasionally a parent would get wind of a rumor and complain about me, or call my mother. And I lied so convincingly that she believed me, and told me that it was because I was beautiful and they were all jealous.

"In the middle of senior year, I met Malcolm for the first time. I met him as Malcolm at first, not as my father. I found out later that his wife had died and so he was free. So he came to visit my mother openly, and took her out and for a while she was happy. Or seemed to be.

"But his daughters were pissed. The one I knew from school, Charlene? She moved away to be with her sister who was in college, and finished high school there. And Malcolm finally married my mother and she pretended we were this perfect little family. But he cheated on her too, *big* surprise.

"And she wanted me to treat him like my dad, but to me he was just the man who'd made a whore out of my mother. And in some ways, made me a whore, too."

"Tracy, you're not a whore," Brendan said.

"Really?"she asked, her voice lifeless. "What if I told you that I did the same things I did in high school all through college and beyond? That as recently as a year ago, I was still doing those things?"

Brendan said nothing. But his face had changed. It was finally starting to sink in.

"Well I was," she nodded. "I picked up men all the time. I

hardly ever dated. And even when I did, I couldn't connect with anyone. So I picked men up and I'd fuck them and move on. And as long as I followed my rules of being safe—always using protection, getting tested every three months—I felt like I was just someone in charge of her own sexuality.

"I never went for men who chose me. I always chose them. I'd never take them home. It was always someplace other than where I live. And I always made sure someone knew, even in a general way, where I was. In college, Riley found out what I was doing and she was ... I guess you could say, inconsolable?" Tracy stopped and put her face in her hands for a moment, remembering what that had been like, and the tears she had been holding back spilled over onto her cheeks. She couldn't help but notice that Brendan wasn't trying to come to her any longer.

Well, that was about what she expected. She felt numb. There was no point not going on now.

"I mean, I always *understood* that sex and love could be connected, but I never felt that, y'know? I didn't even *like* some of the men I had sex with. And for sure some of them despised me."

"I don't want to hear anymore," Brendan mumbled.

"And that's what you saw that night when Lounge Two-Twelve opened, Brendan. The aftermath of me fucking some stranger who ..."

"Tracy, stop."

"Who thought of me as a whore, and who told me so right to my fa..."

"*Stop*!" Brendan put his head in his hands, his breath audible.

"You want to know who I am?" Tracy said, harshly. "Why I don't let you in? Then you have to be prepared to hear it."

Brendan was shaking his head. "This doesn't make sense.

You were never that easy, Tracy. I cracked on you almost every time I saw you, and ..."

"Because I never let men choose me, Brendan. I told you, I chose them. And besides ..." She stopped.

"What?" he asked leaning in. "Besides ... what were you about to say?"

She looked up, tears still in her eyes.

"I liked you. I always liked you, *so* much, and I didn't want to ruin that and even when you hit on me, you were different somehow. You never disrespected me, or ... you were just different." She shrugged. "And after what happened between us at the Grammys that time, I knew for sure I wouldn't know how to ..."

Brendan's head was still down, his shoulders hunched. Tracy could hear him breathing.

"I didn't know what to do with someone like you, Brendan. Or where to put you in my life. I'm still not sure I do. But I had this great excuse. My mother, even though she eventually married Malcolm, always told me about how men could turn your head—that's what she would say, they can '*turn your head, Tracy*'— if they were charming enough, that if you weren't careful, they would make you lose your way.

"So I told myself you were that man, and that you would make me lose my way. And it made sense because with you I *feel* things. And sex with you is not just fucking, it's something different and I don't know what to do with that, Brendan. I just ... I got *scared*."

He looked up at her again and Tracy saw that there were tears in his eyes too. But she didn't know yet what they meant. Did he cry because she wasn't what he thought she was? Or was he feeling sorry for her?

"And Jason. He looked like a good, safe bet. He didn't move me at all. He didn't make me look at him and want things like what Riley has—a baby and a family. I look at him and I'm stone-cold. And I can handle that. But with you, I feel like I'm out of control and ... there's other women around, and for the first time in my life, I feel jealousy and all of that's new for me. You don't understand how confusing it is.

"Jason looked like the guy my mother said I should want and I told myself it would be stupid to pass up the safe guy in favor of the one who makes me feel like I'm losing control."

Brendan said nothing. He just looked at her. His expression was unreadable, except that there were still tears in his eyes. Tracy knew she asked him not to respond to what she said right away, but she wished she had some indication, something to go on.

Was he disgusted with her now? Would he ever want to touch her again? Would he even want to *know* her?

"Are you sleeping with Jason?" he asked, unexpectedly.

She shook her head, relieved to be able to say no, and have it be the truth.

Brendan's shoulders sagged somewhat, as though in relief. "Anyone else since we'd been together?"

"No," she said looking him in the eye. "You?"

"Meghan," he said after a moment. "But that was only after you said ..."

And that—embarrassingly—was when she *really* started to cry; a messy, sloppy, snotty, loud cry that had her wiping her eyes and nose with the back of her hand. She didn't even hear the rest of his sentence, if there was a rest, because she was crying so loudly.

"Tracy ..."

"No, no." She shook her head and stood to leave. "I get it. I ... I told you I was going to ..."

Brendan stood as well and took a step toward her but she held up both her hands like a traffic cop.

"Nope," she said, trying to interject some humor into her voice. "If you touch me, I won't last a second. I'll be all over you and you'll feel bad, and I don't want it to be about that."

Brendan nodded and kept his distance and Tracy turned to open the door.

Walking away from that hotel room, and away from him felt like the hardest thing she had ever done, but it also didn't escape her notice that Brendan simply let her go.

"PLEASE DON'T TELL me you drank that entire bottle all by yourself," Russell said, taking note of the merlot sitting on Tracy's coffee table, and her relatively full wineglass nearby.

"So what if I did?" Tracy asked, taking another swig from her glass.

"Oh *girl*. This is not a good look. Drinking at noon, alone on a Saturday?"

"Russell, I'll have you know, I drank this over about three weeks, okay? Contrary to what you may have heard, I'm perfectly fine."

"Well you *look* a hot mess," Russell said dryly holding a handful of her hair and dropping it again. "When was the last time you got your hair done?"

"The week Malcolm died."

"A *month* ago, Tracy?" Russell said, incredulous. "Okay, get dressed, we're about to go get waxed, buffed, massaged and tweezed."

Tracy smiled. "That actually sounds pretty good," she admitted.

"It will be. C'mon, let's go get you something to wear."

Russell pulled her up off the sofa and dragged her upstairs.

An hour later, Tracy was groaning on a massage table while

a masseuse worked out the kinks and knots in her lower back. She had spent many more nights than she wanted to admit on her sofa over the past three weeks, and most of those nights were pretty close to sleepless.

The good news was that she had lost the seven or so extra pounds she was worried about, and had clocked some serious time at work. Those three a.m. emails to her boss were paying off. He now believed she was beyond dedicated.

"After this we need to go to Serendipity 3," Russell said from the table next to hers. "You feel like a frozen hot chocolate?"

"Well, you're camp director for the day," Tracy said. "So whatever you say."

"Not sure I know what to do with this new *I-don't-give-a-shit-about-anything* attitude of yours, Tracy."

"I do give a shit," she said, not really knowing whether that was true.

"Sure. But about what? That's the question."

Tracy couldn't disagree with that. Since she left Brendan in that hotel room almost a month ago, she had been on a quest of sorts; a mission to re-order her priorities, clearing the decks, so to speak. Little things like eating regular meals, hair appointments and housecleaning didn't make the cut, but she was a beast at work. And even though she had been dodging his phone calls, Jason Miller had not pulled out his investment, which was a lucky thing since it would have raised some questions around the office. In some ways it would have been better had he decided to go elsewhere, because it seemed wrong somehow that she held on to the Miller account but lost Brendan.

Apart from work, there wasn't much else going on. She hadn't seen Riley or her godson in ages either. Riley was still angry, even though Tracy explained to her that she'd taken her advice and told Brendan everything—the whole unvarnished truth about who Tracy Emerson really was, under all the expensive clothes, expertly applied makeup and cool, calm demeanor.

Brendan now knew the full ugly and not surprisingly, he couldn't deal with it.

And as the weeks wore on, the more she thought about it, the more upset Tracy became. Not that he was shocked by her past—after all who wouldn't be? She was upset because when she told him she might go out with another man, instead of trying to persuade her not to, instead of claiming her as his, he'd thrown his cards in and walked away, but only after screwing her like she was nothing to him, refusing to kiss her ...

It wasn't as though she had never experienced that before, but coming from him it was unimaginably painful. It was almost as though he had sensed something about her that he did not yet consciously know: that she was the kind of woman that men treated like a whore.

"Chocolate, and then we can go do some shopping," Russell said now, as though he'd just made up his mind. "If you don't give a shit, I'll just take over making the decisions from now on."

"Fine by me." Tracy lowered her head again, shutting out her sense of everything except the pressure on her back, working out the tension of the last several weeks.

Thanks to Russell, by early evening she had gotten her hair, nails, waxing and plucking done, was stuffed to the gills with chocolate had several new outfits and was pleasantly exhausted. It didn't feel like the end of the world suddenly. She could almost see herself going out to dinner or something. As she and Russell pulled up in front of her townhouse, she turned to him and suggested it, and watched as his eyes lit up.

"I brought you back to life!" he said, pretending to dab tears of joy from his eyes.

Tracy laughed. "You just might have."

"Who ever said a day at the beauty salon don't solve nothin'?" Russell scoffed.

Because he didn't want to risk her changing her mind, Russell insisted on getting ready at her place for their night out.

Luckily, he bought himself a couple shirts during the shopping trip that afternoon and had something to wear. So they got ready, polished off the remaining half-bottle of merlot Tracy had been working on earlier in the day, and grabbed a car service back into Manhattan.

"Is it too late to drop in on Riley?" Russell asked. "I know she'd love to see you."

"Not ready to see her yet," Tracy admitted.

"She's ready to see you, though," Russell said quietly. "She may be a little annoyed with you, Tracy, but ..."

"I don't want to talk about her! I just want to have fun!"

"Okay, *okay*. Fun it is."

So they ate a sushi dinner and walked the trendy downtown streets, stopping in at clubs and bars and lounges whenever one struck their fancy. Tracy could feel herself reviving; the lights, the music and voices of people enjoying themselves in the cool, fall evening, and the raw energy of the New York City streets all reminding her that no matter what, she would not break. She could bend, *and boy had she*, but she would not break.

Missing Brendan was still a sharp pain for the moment but it would dull over time, and maybe even disappear. Turning her head to look up at Russell's handsome face, as animated and alive as her own, she felt the first pinpricks of happiness beginning to peek through the clouds.

FOURTEEN

"No matter how many times I hear it ..." Brendan said.

"Yup. A heroin addict," Shawn said, slower this time. "Sam Gaston. The artist we put all this stock into. All this time ..."

Brendan covered his face with his hands for a moment and heaved a sigh. "Don't rub it in, Shawn. But here's the thing, how bad of a heroin addict?"

Shawn gave a short laugh. "Are there *degrees* of heroin addiction, B? Because from where I sit ..."

"I know," Brendan said. "I'm just thinking about what the hell we do now."

"Send him to rehab and hope for the best," Shawn said shrugging.

"Why are all the talented ones so fucked up?"

"I was never *that* fucked up," Shawn said.

"And you were never that talented either. Not like Sam Gaston," Brendan said.

"Fuck you, man," Shawn laughed. And then he paused for

a moment. "But you're right. It would be a shame to lose this kid. And to see him lose this opportunity."

"So we'll take care of it," Brendan shrugged.

But shit. Not that he was too surprised. When he'd taken Sam out to California, there had been moments where he could have sworn the kid was a little out of it. But the worst Brendan had imagined was that he was slipping out back with some of the band to burn one. Not this hardcore shit involving needles.

Well, there went his distraction. The last few weeks, Sam Gaston, had been his salvation; the only diversion from almost overwhelming thoughts about Tracy and what she told him back in Atlanta. Grooming this kid to be the next big thing (which was the title they actually decided on for his debut CD) had taken damn near every waking hour of every day, and even some of his thoughts during sleep, and for that he had been grateful. But now this shit.

Selfish as it was, with Sam Gaston in rehab, he would have too much time on his hands, too much space in his head. And that he definitely did not need.

Not that he hadn't been thinking about her at all. He had. Every day, every spare moment of every day. The trick was not to have too many spare moments.

And thanks to Sam Gaston, he hadn't. The kid was twenty-three years old, good-looking enough to sell CDs on that basis alone and a grungy, soulful vocal genius. And now, according to the voice coach Brendan and Shawn hired, also a raging heroin addict.

"You never noticed him nodding out on you or nothin'?" Shawn asked now.

"Shawn, *I* was nodding out. We were traveling ten hours a day and working the other fourteen. How the hell would I know he was snorting or shooting up shit in the bathroom?"

"Sad thing is, if it gets out, it'll probably help you sell more

CDs," Riley said as she walked through the living room, Cullen balanced on her hip.

Shawn and Brendan looked at each other and she stopped.

"Oh my god, I sure hope you two aren't that mercenary," she said, grimacing.

"No baby," Shawn said shaking his head emphatically. "We would never ..."

But when she was safely in the kitchen he and Brendan exchanged a look and then laughed.

"Well," Brendan said, keeping his voice low. "It *would* help move some product."

"You two, no!" Riley called from the next room.

Shawn and Brendan laughed again.

"Well man, look at the bright side. You get to spend some time at home again," Shawn said.

Brendan snorted. "How is that the bright side?"

Shawn said nothing.

Being home was the *last* thing he needed. Now that she was no longer there, Brendan realized one more reason it had been a bad idea letting Tracy stay at his place. It just wasn't the same without her. But he supposed he could put in some more hours at Lounge Two-Twelve. The club had begun to gain itself a good reputation among their target demographic and most evenings was packed to capacity with high-rollers and big-spenders from the recording industry, all hoping to rub shoulders with the likes of K Smooth and Chris Scaife.

But the truth was, while Chris was more than happy to lend his profile to the club, Shawn was very rarely there. He was all about his family these days, and Brendan couldn't say he blamed him. Babies had never been particularly interesting to him, but watching Shawn with his now five-month old son, Brendan could see some of the appeal. Not only did this little person look just like Shawn, he seemed to think his father was the best thing ever.

Every single time Riley walked into a room and held him out for Shawn to take him, Cullen squirmed and squealed, pumping his chubby little legs and arms as though he couldn't get to him fast enough, his squeals turning to wails if his mother didn't manage the hand-off quite as rapidly as he would prefer. And once in Shawn's arms, the crying would magically cease, like someone flipped a switch.

Brendan watched with awe and tiny slivers of something that felt like envy when Cullen settled on Shawn's lap and explored that small area within his reach—no more than a foot or two—with the contentment of someone who had everything they needed in the entire universe. And Shawn was good with him too, handling the baby as though he were an extension of himself, managing to do anything from conference calls, to emailing, to frying an egg while holding Cullen, safe and sound with one arm.

And of course there was Riley.

Brendan had always wondered at the ability of a man—or a woman for that matter—to mate for life. It seemed too implausible, and certainly for Shawn at one time it seemed impossible. But now, there was such synchronicity between them that Brendan couldn't imagine them being anything other than a unit.

The look in Riley's eyes when they came to rest on her husband was almost difficult to take in. Was it even possible that she loved him *more* than those crazy days when even Brendan—his best friend—had wondered if Shawn deserved that much love? So yeah, it made sense that Lounge Two-Twelve was a sorry substitute for what Shawn had going on right here. For Brendan though, the club was the *best* thing he had going.

He stopped in at least one hour each night, just to make himself known and seen by the staff. The manager, a young woman they'd hired only recently, named Gabrielle, had been a find. She was organized, communicated well with line staff and was a pretty, bubbly personality that the patrons loved to spend time with. For a hot second, Brendan had considered sleeping with her. She was slender as a reed with a long elegant dancer's body, and a laugh that sounded like tiny bells ringing. She would make him smile for a little while, that was for sure. But it would only be for a little while. His thoughts and hell, his heart, were someplace else entirely. So why bother?

"I'm about to bounce," Brendan said now. "Get some sleep. Think about what to do about this Sam Gaston problem. We'll talk in the morning, man."

Riley emerged from the kitchen.

"You don't want to eat, Brendan?"

"Nah. I'll grab something on the way home," he said leaning in to kiss Cullen on top of his curly-haired head.

He stopped at Dean & DeLuca before heading home and grabbed some brioche, cheese and some of that expensive, imported ham that Tracy favored. And as an afterthought, got a six-pack of imported beer as well.

The apartment seemed cavernous lately, and quiet. Sometimes he left the television on when he was leaving, so he could hear it when he got back. Today he'd forgotten, so it was dark and quiet when he opened the door.

Brendan headed straight up to the kitchen and made himself a sandwich, but he'd forgotten that spicy chipotle mayo that he liked, so it was dry and unsatisfying. He only ate a half of it before dumping the rest in the trash and deciding instead to focus on polishing off the beer. He opened one and stashed the rest in the fridge, then thinking better of it, opened a second one and took both with him to the bedroom.

He was done with the first before he even had a chance to kick off his shoes in his dressing room, and had almost done with the second when he undressed for a shower. Number three was done less than a half hour later, and by then he was a little fuzzy-headed, from drinking them fast, and having eaten very little all day except for the dry half-sandwich. By the time he'd consumed numbers four and five, he'd made up his mind.

It was stupid. He missed her so much he fucking ached. Why shouldn't he call her? He might say exactly the right thing, or he might mess up, but at least he would hear her voice. She hadn't said as much, but he was certain she felt something for him, something deep enough to make her come to his hotel room and confess all those dark, ugly things about her past that he hadn't even had the emotional stamina to begin to think about yet.

But why *did* he have to think about them? He could stuff them down, put them way back in a drawer in the back of his mind and just move forward. He still wanted her, no matter what had happened back then. He even missed those crazy jealous rages of hers.

Brendan picked up the phone and dialed the number, waiting through the first few rings, wondering why she wasn't picking up right away. It was only just ten p.m. Where the fuck could she ...

"Brendan?"

The sound of her voice made him wish he could crawl through the phone line and just grab her. When had it happened that he began thinking of her as small and fragile instead of hard and unyielding? Ages ago, he now realized. Tracy had never been hard and unyielding with him; not really.

"Yeah," he said. "It's me."

"Hi."

Her voice sounded small, but full of wonder, happy for sure, and for that he was relieved.

"Hi," he said back to her.

And for a while there was silence between them. *What now?* He didn't really have anything to say. Didn't even know how to begin to talk about the huge elephant in the room.

"You there?" she asked.

"Yeah, I'm here. So I was thinking ..." he began, not knowing what he was going to say next. "That you and I got off on the wrong foot."

Tracy laughed softly.

"No seriously," he said, gaining confidence from her laughter. "Things got a little intense real quickly. So I wondered whether we could maybe just go out to dinner sometime. Y'know, like I could ..."

"Like a date?" she asked.

"Yeah. I'd come pick you up, we'd get something to eat."

"Another trip on the subway to Gray's Papaya?" Tracy asked, but there was amusement in her voice, affection even.

"No," Brendan said. "Someplace nice."

"Brendan, I loved our date to Gray's Papaya," she said. "I was only teasing. And I would love to go to dinner with you."

"You would?"

"I would." And then after a pause, "have you been drinking?"

"Maybe a few beers."

"Do me a favor?"

"What's that?"

"Call me tomorrow and ask me again?"

Brendan squinted, trying to understand her point.

"Brendan, I miss you," she said simply. "But I want to make sure when you call me, you're ready to call me. Not because it's late, or you're lonely, or you're drunk."

"I'm not dr..."

"But are you ready?" she asked, her voice a little sad now.

Brendan said nothing.

"I mean, do you remember what I said in your hotel room that night? I want you to think about the things I told ..."

"And I can't do that with you? We have to not see each other for that to work?" Brendan asked, his voice insistent. "What does that accomplish except make us—or maybe I should speak for myself–make *me* miserable?"

"You're miserable?" Tracy asked, clearly not even trying to conceal how pleased that made her.

"Will you let me take you out or not?"

"Call me tomorrow, Brendan," she said, her voice firm this time. "Okay? Goodnight."

When she hung up, Brendan cursed under his breath and turned over in bed, tossing the phone aside and almost immediately falling asleep.

STANDING OUTSIDE TRACY'S TOWNHOUSE, finger poised over the bell, Brendan took a deep breath and pressed the button. He waited and called to ask her out again just as she told him to. *It's tomorrow*, he'd said, barely awake himself. *So can I take you out to dinner or what?* And she said 'yes' right away even though it was six a.m. and she was half-asleep.

It was a Thursday night so they would get something to eat and he'd bring her right back home, that was his plan. After having been apart for so long, that was probably all they could manage right now, so he was going to take it really, really slow.

Tracy opened the door and it was impossible not to smile when he saw her. She was wearing a brown mini-dress and underneath it black tights with ankle boots. She had lost weight since he'd seen her last, which he now realized was about two months ago. The plan was to play it cool but when she smiled back at him, giving him the sweet-Tracy smile, he leaned in slightly and she pulled him down the rest of the way for a kiss. When Brendan raised his head, Tracy's lips followed his until she had to stand on her toes.

"We have reservations," he laughed, pulling back until she could no longer reach him. "Where's your jacket?"

Tracy took a light jacket down from her coat-tree and turned to lock her doors.

"Where are we going?" she asked.

"Spice Coast," Brendan said.

"Nice."

They didn't talk much during the drive, just made polite conversation that felt forced at times. It was difficult keeping both hands on the steering wheel with her sitting next to him. Brendan recalled when he used to drive with one hand resting on her inner thigh, and if he didn't put it there almost immediately, she would reach over and do it for him.

"You look good," he told her. "How've you been?"

"About as you would expect," she said.

"Which is how?"

"Not so great and then better," she said.

Brendan glanced over at her, surprised by her candor. She seemed different. Calmer.

"You could have called me," he said.

"No, Brendan. I couldn't have," she said, shaking her head, and he knew what she meant.

It had been his move to make. After everything she told him, it was his move, and now that she was sitting here in the car next to him, he couldn't even think of why it had taken him so long to make it.

At Spice Coast, they ordered the best house specials and

Brendan chose one of their most expensive Chilean wines to pair with their dinner. While they ate, they talked about Lounge Two-Twelve and Tracy's work. Brendan told her about the new hours at the club and Tracy told him about a conference in Paris later in the winter that her boss was sending her to.

It was pleasant.

And he hated it, because it was nothing like the way they used to be with each other.

After the meal was done and he paid the tab, they walked out into the cool evening and Brendan felt the urge to hold her hand. But Tracy had stuffed them into the pockets of her jacket and was walking next to him, but not very close. Despite their warm greeting at her front door, a new distance had sprung up between them and as he drove her back home, Brendan felt his optimism about the future begin to fade.

Maybe he had stayed away too long, and she just wasn't feeling it anymore. Maybe it was for the best.

Outside her townhouse, he found parking not too far away and was able to walk her up the steps to her door, waiting while she pulled out her keys.

Finding them, Tracy unlocked the doors and turned to face him.

"Well," she said, "that was ... just awful."

And they both started laughing at the same time.

"Yeah," Brendan said. "It kind of was."

"Come in?" she asked.

"Ahm, I don't know," he said, not sure she really wanted him to. Who invited the guy in after an 'awful' date?

Tracy grabbed one of his belt loops and yanked him inside, shutting and locking the doors behind him.

"Brendan," she said, her voice reassuring. "It was awful

because it's not your kind of date. It's not *our* kind of date. That's all."

"You think so?" he asked.

Tracy nodded. "You should have taken me for hot dogs, or to 34th Street for some street food. *That's* our kind of date."

He smiled. "I thought you hated when I took you on dates like that."

"I only pretended to. I'd have gone anywhere you wanted to take me. I still would."

He leaned in to kiss her and as if she couldn't wait, she pulled him down to her. Their lips met again, this time in a slow, exploratory kiss. A kiss of re-acquaintance.

When Brendan made it deeper, Tracy moaned. She actually moaned. Brendan felt a twitch in his pants, the start of his arousal and his cue to go home. But when he tried to pull back, Tracy put a hand up and at the back of his neck, holding him to her, kissing him with even more eagerness.

"Stay with me," she said into his neck.

"Shouldn't we take it slow?" Brendan asked.

"No," she said. "We shouldn't."

Tracy took his hand, and turning, led him up the stairs and into her bedroom. She turned to face him and shrugged her dress over her head so she was standing before him in her tights and boots, and a bra.

"I missed you touching me," she said, looking up at him.

And that was all he needed to hear.

THE SOUND of a garbage truck in the street below was what woke him.

Brendan opened his eyes and saw that he was alone in bed among Tracy's sheets that smelled of spring. He could vaguely hear movement and activity downstairs in the kitchen, and smell something cooking. She was making him breakfast. Out of nowhere, an image flashed in his mind, of Kelvin, in this very bed, as naked as he was now.

Thinking of last night, how Tracy looked, sounded, how she tasted was marred by thoughts of Kelvin experiencing the same. Kelvin, and countless other dudes. Well, not *countless*, he told himself. There had to be a finite number. And that quickly, he was obsessed with knowing exactly what that number was.

Getting out of bed, Brendan went into the bathroom and washed his face and brushed his teeth with Tracy's toothbrush. She used his all the time back at his place—or used to—so that was hardly taboo for them, but everything felt different here, at the scene of the crime so to speak. He couldn't stand thinking of any man, let alone a man like Kelvin, in his woman's space, much less in her body.

His woman. She wasn't yet. Not officially. But he was about to clear that up right now.

Tracy was wearing only a t-shirt and looked up when he came in, dressed only in boxers. She was standing at the stove and transferring an omelet to a plate.

"Perfect timing," she said sliding the plate toward him.

"Thanks." Brendan took the plate and found a drawer with eating utensils. He didn't know where things were here, because they had always stayed at his place.

That was something else he was going to change. He would stay here more, and he would bring and leave all kinds of shit. When he was done, no one who might come here would be under the impression that Tracy was in any way whatsoever available.

"You going to work?" he asked curiously. "You don't look like you're in too much of a hurry."

"I thought I might call in sick," she said, without looking him in the eye. "And that maybe you'd want to do the same."

"I don't have to call anyone. I just won't go in."

Tracy looked up at him and smiled. "So we'll hang out today?"

"Uh huh," Brendan started eating.

The omelet was good, so he ate with increased enthusiasm. Noting this, Tracy slid him the second one as well when it was done and cracked more eggs to make her own.

"So what should we do today?" she asked.

"Take some of your stuff over to my place. Take some of my stuff here," he said without hesitation.

Tracy stared at him for a moment and he knew he wasn't misinterpreting the look on her face; it was elation.

"Okay," she nodded. "We can get you a key made for here. Is my key to the apartment ..?"

"Is it what?"

"Still good."

"Of course it's still good. Why wouldn't it ..?" Brendan put down his fork and went around the kitchen island to wrap his arms around her from behind. "You think I would have changed the locks?"

She shrugged.

"Baby, no. Every day I *wished* you'd use that key. I'd never lock you out."

BRENDAN HAD EVEN AGREED to the placemats. Tracy walked through the familiar space of his kitchen, putting away the food they'd bought, stashing away a few things here and there that they picked up in Target, including brand new white placemats that were impractical as hell. But they were the only ones Brendan liked, so she'd given in, still amazed at how changed her life was in the less than 72 hours since he'd called.

Just as she was beginning to believe she might be able to get on with it, that maybe she could do this, her cell phone rang and the barking dog ringtone had just about stopped her heart. That reminded her—she would have to change that ringtone. Nothing about it had anything to do with who Brendan was. And as of today, who he was—officially, no playing around—was her man.

After last night—when she decided that she wanted him, no matter the aftermath, even if he left the next morning and never called her again—she was prepared for him to get skittish and weird on her, but instead he came downstairs and readily agreed to take the day off. Then he announced that they would be spending it moving into each other's places. And if that were still too ambiguous, on the drive into Manhattan he grabbed her thigh, running a hand back and forth on it.

There can't be anyone else, he said. *No one between us.*

The relief was overwhelming. That was the only remaining thing she had been worried about. Whether he would think she still wanted to play the field, whether he would want to resume that crazy, wrongheaded arrangement they had before. But his words put that to rest and she had been fine since then.

If Brendan said it, he meant it. She knew that without the ambiguity that had existed before, she would get a handle on her possessiveness, and feel more confident about dealing with the women who approached him.

Her only remaining worry, which was not a worry so much as a chore, would be telling Dr. Greer. Dr. Greer had been Russell's idea. She was someone he said he'd spoken to when he was "going through changes" and he credited her with helping him love his life, love himself even. The idea of loving herself sounded so foreign a concept that Tracy was intrigued.

She loved *many* things about herself for sure—the way she looked primarily. The kind of friend she was, the kind of godmother (though not lately) and the kind of employee. But she couldn't honestly say she loved who she *was* at her core. And how could she? After all she'd done? The men ... all of that was basically self-abuse she now realized. Not the actions of someone who had self-love.

So she'd gone to see Dr. Greer and found to her surprise that it helped to talk things through, to take responsibility for her actions. To own them and to forgive herself for them. Another of the reasons she'd gone to see the doctor was that she secretly hoped that it would make her see somehow that her persistent feelings for Brendan weren't what they appeared to be. Yup, she'd been hoping for a Brendan Cure.

But there was no cure to be found, at least not in her sessions with Dr. Greer. If anything, they made her love him more, because it brought into sharp focus how much he had valued her even when she hadn't valued herself.

Still, she was concerned because during one session when she admitted to having no interest whatsoever in men, Dr. Greer had shrugged, explaining that Tracy didn't quite trust them yet, and would have to reconfigure her idea of what men were, and that that would take time.

In any event, I don't see that it would be advisable for you to be in a dating situation just yet, Dr. Greer said. *So we have time to work on it.*

And now she wasn't just in a "dating situation" she was practically overnight in a full-blown, committed relationship. Still, "not advisable" didn't mean forbidden or anything. And she was happy, happier than she had been in longer than she could remember, so that had to count for something.

Didn't it?

FIFTEEN

ALWAYS, IT HAPPENED WHEN HE LEAST EXPECTED IT. THEY didn't even have to be around other men. Tracy could be standing at the stove making dinner for them, or digging through the dresser looking for one of her nightshirts, or just talking on the phone. And suddenly Brendan would be awash with anger, thinking about the men—the nameless men who she had allowed to put their hands on her, their mouths ... who she had touched, on whom she had put *her* mouth. That last part, that was the worst.

Well, almost the worst. He also wondered whether there were things she did with these men that she hadn't done with him, illicit things, and deeply intimate things. That was the one very specific question that preoccupied him no matter how many times he tried to drive it away. He knew he wasn't going to be able to let it go until he asked, but he didn't know how to ask either.

And it wasn't exactly true to say that the anger came only when he least expected it. It came at other times, too. Like when they went to Lounge Two-Twelve. Tracy came with him more often than not now, even if all she did was hang out in his office in the back, away from the noise and music. But when she stayed out front in the main club, he found it hard to concentrate on anything other than where she was and who she was speaking to. And that by itself was a full-time job because dudes were always trying to talk to her.

It used to be that he didn't sweat any of that, because he knew she was with him, however incomplete their understanding of what they were to each other. It was ironic that now that he had her full and unambiguous attention, he would be plagued by uncertainty like this.

Funny thing was, she didn't court male attention at all, but that only seemed to make it worse. Men tried harder to get her because of it. If he had a dime for the number of times men sent over drinks while she sat at the bar, just making conversation with Gabrielle, or the occasions when he had to make his presence and claim over her known, because some persistent dude wanted to dance or engage her in unwelcome conversation.

So now, just as he was walking into the apartment, feeling himself grow more and more tense at the thought of the Friday night crush in the club, Brendan made up his mind. She couldn't come to the Lounge anymore. It was too stressful. All that remained was breaking the news to her. Friday nights at Two-Twelve had become kind of a ritual for them. She expected to go and right now was probably in the bedroom, getting a post-work nap, resting up for the night that usually ended only when they returned home around four a.m.

She wasn't sleeping, but was sprawled across the bed wearing one of his shirts again, her long shapely legs exposed, only two buttons fastened so he could see the curve of her breasts, glimpse a dark plum-colored nipple. When you were a jealous man, your woman's beauty felt like a personal affront.

"Hey there." She looked up from the magazine she was flipping through. "How was your day?"

"Good," he said sliding off his shoes. "You?"

"So-so. Want me to make you a sandwich or something?"

"Nah," he said, sitting on the edge of the bed. "Maybe a little later."

He shed his shirt and pants, draping them across a chair and crawled up next to her. He reached for the television remote and switched the tv on, not caring much what he watched.

"You know you don't have to come to the club *every* Friday, right?" he said, trying to keep his tone measured.

"I don't mind," she said, without looking up.

He waited a couple of beats. "You don't seem to have that much of a good time when you go."

"I like watching you work," she said, shrugging. "So it's fine."

"No. It's not," Brendan said finally.

At this, Tracy put down her magazine and gave him her full attention. She said nothing, but searched his face, trying to read him.

"I don't have time to ... be with you all night," he said clumsily. He almost said "to *watch* you."

But it didn't matter what word he chose. She understood completely.

"Why do you think you have to?" she asked slowly.

"You know why."

She shook her head. "No. I don't."

Fuck. Was he going to have to spell it out?

"Do you not trust me or something, Brendan?" she asked quietly.

He thought about it for a moment. No, that wasn't it. He did trust her. Some people would say it was dumb of him, but he did. So it begged the question: what *exactly* was his fucking problem?

"I do trust you," he said finally.

"But you don't want me to come to the Lounge because ..."

"I don't like dudes pushing up on you, okay? I don't like seeing it, I don't like knowing it's happening, I don't even like you being around them. *Is that clear enough for you?*"

Tracy looked taken aback, but only slightly.

He knew she noticed the change in him, the new hyper-vigilance he had where she was concerned. The same hyper-vigilance she no longer had with him being around other women. While she found a new sense of security in their relationship, he developed the opposite.

"Yes," she said after a moment, her voice quiet. "That's clear."

"So you'll stay here tonight then?"

She nodded, but her brows were furrowed, troubled.

"Good," he said, sighing.

"Tonight?" she said. "Or every night?"

He should have known it was too easy. Tracy was too smart to have missed the underlying significance of his request. But he'd been hoping that he could just get past this one Friday and tackle the next one when it came, and the next, and the next.

"Let's just ... tonight, okay?" he lied. "Just tonight. Shawn's there tonight anyway so it's going to be hectic."

"Okay," she said.

She picked up her magazine again but it was clear she didn't buy it, and was placating him. The enormous pink elephant sauntered into the room and sat at the foot of the bed, but they both—for the moment—decided to ignore it.

"WHERE'S YOUR WOMAN AT?" Shawn asked.

The Lounge was packed because they had advertised Shawn's appearance to boost patronage. People didn't go out as much once the temperature dropped, so they were planning something for every week now, some kind of star attraction; and as a kick-off, it was easy enough for Shawn to haul himself away from the condo for a few hours to smile and take pictures.

"Home."

"Good for you," Shawn said. "You sure you can stand it? The separation for six whole hours?"

Brendan shook his head, saying nothing.

"You know I had to, right?" Shawn grinned. "The way you used to ride me about my shit."

Yup. He remembered. Shawn's singular obsession at one time had been whether or not his wife was noticed, admired, wanted, talked to, touched by some man other than him. It seemed to Brendan at the time like a unique kind of madness. And in Shawn's case, it had been madness, he told himself now. Because Riley had never done some of the shit Tracy admitted she'd done. Riley had never been a ...

Brendan raised his hand, summoning one of the bartenders, doubling up on his drink, driving away the ugly word that for one moment had sprung to mind to describe the woman he loved.

TRACY FELT his weight on the bed next to her in the dark first, and then she smelled him. *Whoa.* He had the strong odor of a distillery. The smell of alcohol probably seemed much worse, she told herself, because she hadn't been in the club tonight.

Brendan reached for her, fumbling in the pitch blackness of the room and Tracy slid back toward him pulling his arm about her waist.

"You awake?" he slurred.

Yup. Her first impression had been correct. He stunk of alcohol and was shit-faced. Shawn's presence probably hadn't helped matters much tonight. It was rare now that Shawn went out, and so they'd probably made a boys' night of it.

"Yeah," she said. "You *reek*, Brendan.

He laughed, a little too loudly, and without real mirth.

"Because I'm fucked up," he said. "I am. Really. Really. Fucked. *Up*."

"You want to take a shower?" she suggested. "It might make you ..."

"Only if you take it with me," he said, sitting up.

Tracy considered. She was exhausted and tomorrow Riley was going to yoga with her; one of their very first real overtures to being close again. But she knew that the quickest way to get Brendan clean and smelling like himself again was to get this shower out of the way.

"Okay," she yawned. "Let's go."

As he stood under the water, Brendan swayed and Tracy put a hand on his arm to steady him, standing out of the stream of water herself, struggling to keep her eyes open and failing. When she opened them again, Brendan was watching her. His eyes were red and unfocused, and he was allowing the water to run in rivulets over his face. Just standing there and watching.

After a moment he reached out and with just the tips of two fingers, ran his hand down the side of her face, over a breast, down her stomach and between her legs. Once there, he parted her with his fingers in a scissoring motion. Tracy closed her eyes, still loving the feeling of his touch, no matter how tired she was, or how drunk he was.

"You're so beautiful," he said, but his voice was almost sad. "*So* beautiful."

Tracy leaned slightly against his fingers, closing her eyes again.

"How many, Tracy?"

Her eyes flew open.

Immediately. She knew *immediately* what he was referring to. Her heartbeat, already accelerated from the excitement of him touching her began to gallop.

"Brendan ..."

He removed his fingers. "How many?" he said again, his voice flat.

"Brendan, I don't ..."

"*Don't tell me you don't know!*" he said, his voice unexpectedly loud, causing her to jump. "Ballpark it. What're we talking about? Ten? Twenty? *Thirty*? Fifty? One hundred and five? How *many*?"

Tracy turned away from him and opened the shower door, stepping out and grabbing a towel, wrapping it about herself and walking out into the dark bedroom. Brendan followed, leaving the water on and the shower door open.

"So ten was just high school for you, we know that, so after that how many?" he demanded, following her. "Okay, so how many per *year?*"

Tracy flipped on the bedside lamp, sitting on the edge of the bed. Brendan was naked, wet and standing a few feet away looking down at her.

"I don't know," she said.

"What did you do with them?"

"Almost everything."

She felt numb. Looking at him was like looking into the eyes of a stranger. He was like a man possessed, as though Brendan, her Brendan wasn't even in there. And he wasn't even being mean, just insistent. Like he *needed* to know. So she decided to answer him. Whatever he asked, she would answer.

"Everything like what?"

"*Everything.*"

"Things *we* haven't done?" Brendan asked, his face looking pained.

Their eyes locked and she knew specifically which act he was referring to. Her face darkened in shame.

"Things you've never asked me to do," Tracy said, wearily.

She shouldn't be surprised. They had never had this conversation. When they got back together it had been wonderful and romantic and almost effortless and that had gone on for a month now, but she should have known that that was not real life. Now, it was time to face reality. And in real life, men did not easily forget that their girlfriend had fucked maybe dozens of guys before him.

"And what if I asked you to ... do those things?" he said.

"I would do them," she said without hesitation.

"And the things you didn't do with them, if I asked you to do those things ..."

She nodded. "If you wanted me to."

Though that should have made him feel better, she could tell it didn't. It might even have hurt him more.

"Why?"

She said nothing.

It was written all over his face. He was wondering if it was because she had no self-respect, if she would do anything that anyone asked her. If she could speak at length without crying she would explain. She would tell him what she'd learned from going to Dr. Greer. With all those men, she hadn't been doing things *for* them she was doing things *to* herself.

"*Why*?" he asked again.

"Because I love you," she said.

Brendan looked at her, and she could see the heartbreak in his eyes. "That's not how I need you to love me, Tracy."

She knew that. If there was one thing she knew more so than most people, it was that specific sex acts didn't equal love, and she knew that Brendan didn't need her to prove anything in that way. But after giving so much of herself away to men who didn't matter, she also knew that if there was something, some part of her he wanted that she'd given to no other man, she would not refuse him. Hell, she never said she wasn't still a little fucked up in the head.

"You have to forgive me," she said, finally.

Brendan sat on the edge of the bed, far away from her. He looked defeated.

"I've forgiven myself, Brendan," she said. "Or I'm starting to. But if *you* can't forgive me, we aren't going to work."

IN THE MORNING when Tracy got up, Brendan was in the kitchen dressed for the gym or basketball. When he looked up and saw her, he sat on one of the stools and called her over to him. She went to stand in front of him, between his legs.

"I'm sorry," he said. "Last night I was out of control. Some of things I asked you, I don't even know where that came from."

"You want to know what you've gotten yourself into with me." She shrugged. "I get it."

"*Do* you get it?" he asked.

"Yes," she nodded, feeling tired and resigned, almost indifferent. "It's a lot to ask any man to accept."

"I love you, Tracy ..."

She nodded, hurrying him along to what she knew was coming next.

"No. Look at me," Brendan said, emphatically, forcing her

to meet his gaze. "I *love* you. And I'll do whatever we need to do to work through this."

Tracy sighed. "But I'm tired," she said. "I'm trying to work through it for myself, and I don't think I have the stamina to work through it for anyone else on top of that."

"What're you saying?" Brendan asked, taking her face in his hands.

"I'm saying that ... I have that trip to Paris the day after tomorrow. I'll be gone a week. And when I come back, I'm going to Brooklyn." Brendan opened his mouth to protest but she held up a hand to stop him. "And I'll stay there until and unless you come and say you're ready for me, Brendan. And if you do that, we have to close the door on this for good.

"For the first time in *years*, I can look in the mirror and not be disgusted with myself. I can't get that far only to look across the breakfast table and see that disgust in someone else's eyes."

"Tracy. I would never be disgusted with you. No matter what your past."

"Okay, well last night, the guy who came home stinking drunk seemed a little put out by my past, so ..."

"How can I not be *put out* by it? Other men touched you like I touch you, some of them in ways that I *haven't* touched you. They were ..." He broke off and shook his head. "You know what that feels like?"

"No. So that's why you have to be the one to decide whether you can deal. And if not, I'm sure we'll handle it. We'll always be frien..."

"I don't want to be your fucking *friend*! This is more than that. And it always has been. You know it and I know it."

Tracy nodded. "I do know it. But it doesn't make any difference if we can't hold it together."

"So now what?" It was his turn to sound resigned.

"Now I go to Brooklyn and pack for my trip to Paris. I'll probably stay there tonight and tomorrow night, just to get ready and stuff."

Brendan's arms fell to his sides and he let her go.

SIXTEEN

While cross-legged on the floor, Tracy held Cullen so he was balanced on her knees as though standing, reveling, and delighting in the sight of him. She pressed her nose into his soft curls and inhaled. Cullen drooled on her blouse but she didn't care. He tugged a lock of her hair, pulling it out of place and she didn't care about that either.

"I know it doesn't seem like it," Riley said. "But it's really better this way, Tracy."

She'd stopped by on her way to Brooklyn see Riley and her godson, delaying the inevitable return to her empty house. Even with the issue they were having, she still wanted to be with Brendan. Sleeping without him next to her remained the less attractive option, but it was necessary.

"Yeah?" Tracy took another sniff of her godson.

"You did the right thing. You can't work his shit out for him, that's the bottom line. And make no mistake about it. This is *his* shit, not yours."

"He wasn't the one who slept with all those people."

"But you're dealing with whatever led to that with Dr.

Greer. Now Brendan has to deal with his feelings about what you did."

"But I don't want to lose him," Tracy said, shrugging.

"If he doesn't figure out how to deal, you'll lose him anyway," Riley said.

"Thanks for the sunny outlook," Tracy said dryly.

"So how's it been otherwise?"

"There is no 'otherwise'," Tracy said. "It was great and then he asked me how many men I've had sex with and what I did with them. That's the whole story."

"Shawn said he's been a mess lately," Riley offered.

Tracy looked up.

"See that's the thing. I don't *want* him to be a mess," she said. "I want him happy. I want him to be happy with *me*. Not wake up every morning wondering why he had to go fall in love with a slut."

Riley recoiled at the use of the word. "Tracy!"

"That's the bottom line, Riley. I know Brendan loves me. That's the killing part. He just doesn't want to love me. I'm like a *disease* he has."

"*Jesus*, should we get Dr. Greer on the line? Why do you talk about yourself that way?"

"Because it's true." Tracy shrugged.

"It is *not* true," Riley said, looking as though she might cry. "Tracy you are . . ." Her voice broke. "The most generous, caring, honest and loyal person I know. When I was going through everything with Shawn you were there for me, even when my own mother wasn't.

"Every dumb thing I ever did since I was eighteen, you have been there. Brendan is as lucky to have you as you are to have him. And if he doesn't realize that soon, then fuck him. I mean it, *fuck him*."

And then they were both crying, and Cullen, confused by

all the fuss joined in as well.

Shawn walked through the living room and seeing them weeping asked no questions but rolled his eyes and took his son from Tracy's arms, heading into the den. Riley looked at her and they both laughed.

"Come over here," Riley said.

Tracy went to her, and they hugged.

"I'm sorry," Riley said. "For being so caught up in my own stuff that I didn't realize how important he is to you. I doubted your motives and I shouldn't have."

"It's okay," Tracy said. "For the longest time *I* didn't even know what my motives were."

"So what now?"

"I go to Paris for that conference and maybe I'll come back and he'll have cleared his head a little bit, figured out what he wants."

GOING BACK to her place in Brooklyn didn't exactly give her distance from Brendan either, if that's what she had been hoping to accomplish. His shirts were in the closet, boots in the mud room, and remnants of a cheese he liked but she hated were in the refrigerator.

Tracy packed with swift efficiency and contemplated the remaining expanse of her weekend laid out before her. She could call Russell and they might go into the city for drinks and dinner, or to a movie. She hadn't seen him since she and Brendan got back together and his loud upbeat mood might be just what she needed right now. But something about being alone was okay too. It was scary, but it was okay.

What she said to Brendan that morning she meant. She'd had enough of dirty little secrets to last a lifetime, and she wasn't going to be his. The things she'd done, she had done. They were past and gone, and no trace of those men remained with her, except in her psyche if she let them.

She wanted to replace every single one of those bad memories with all the good things Brendan gave her—his smiles, the way he held her, the way he told her she was beautiful, the way he made love to her, the way he called her "sweetheart" and meant it. And even if he couldn't get past everything, she would always love him for that. He helped her dare to believe—no, to *expect*—that she would have a life like that. God, she hoped, she *prayed* that when she got back home from Paris he would come to her because it was almost impossible to believe there might be another one like him out there.

For the rest of the afternoon, Tracy did a cathartic housecleaning, doing all the laundry, including some of Brendan's, tossing out old food in the refrigerator, and even polishing the wood furniture. By nightfall, she had a pleasant achy exhaustion and was looking forward to bed.

Tomorrow, she would go to the neighborhood coffee shop that she used to frequent but hadn't visited in a dog's age, and catch up with some of her neighbors. And there was always one of the perpetual *Law & Order* marathons that she and Brendan watched together on Sundays. And then on Monday she would be on her way to a beautiful city she had never visited before.

Rather than dirty the dishes she painstakingly washed, dried and put away in cabinets earlier, Tracy ordered Chinese take-out and watched a design show on the television in her bedroom as she ate. It felt good to be alone but not lonely. She wondered what had changed because she undoubtedly missed Brendan, but still, she felt centered in a way she hadn't in a long time, or perhaps ever.

Last week she had spoken to her mother who was still having a surprisingly hard time with Malcolm's death. As

Tracy listened to her recital of all the ways she'd been wronged by the man when he was alive, she felt a wave of sympathy for her mother. And the wave had remained even when she listened to her describe all the ways Tracy was ruining her life by being with a man like Brendan Cole.

She listened and she said nothing, but in her mind and in her heart, she was saying, *Mom, I only wish you had someone like him. Your life and mine might have been so different if you had.*

It was well after midnight when Tracy heard the barest hint of a sound downstairs. She was immediately alert because sleeping in the house alone had become unfamiliar to her. She listened until she heard the keys in the lock and the quiet slipping of the bolt back into place from the inside. She exhaled, relaxing as she heard his quiet tread as he ascended the stairs, and she turned onto her back just in time to see him silhouetted in the bedroom door.

Her sigh of relief was audible, so he must have known she was awake, but he didn't speak, so neither did she. She watched as he shed his clothes and then he was coming toward her and getting under the covers. Tracy turned to face him, and his lips were immediately on hers, his hands under her nightdress. She willingly raised her arms above her head to allow him to remove it, and cradled his head against her chest when he lowered it to take the tip of one breast in his mouth, and then another.

When he moved down her body, she parted her legs for him and gasped at the warm feeling of his breath against the most sensitive part of her. His fingers parted her and all she could do after that was feel—his tongue, his lips, his breath and light nips from his teeth. She reached for him but he resisted, bringing her twice to completion before moving up to rest his head on her stomach. Tracy stroked the side of his face, waiting for him to speak, thinking that surely he must intend to say *something*. But he didn't.

Instead he kissed her stomach, her hips, the crook of her elbows, her fingers, thighs, and behind her knees. Then he kissed her mouth, and even though she could feel his excitement, he was slow and sweet and gentle, loving her, cherishing her, making her feel as though there was nothing more precious to him.

That was when she stopped wishing he would speak. He *was* speaking to her, telling her everything she needed to know with his body, with the most secret part of himself in the most secret part of her. He moved inside her so slowly it was almost torturous but it was beautiful as well, and Tracy trembled and quivered uncontrollably, all her nerve endings set on fire.

Finally, he grew tense and raised his upper body, his elbows holding its weight on either side of her head, and he was breathing her name rather than saying it, his breath stirring the hair at her temples. So she said his name back to him, telling him she loved him, hearing him say the same to her. When he climaxed, she could feel him deep inside her, jerking and convulsing even as the rest of his body went slack.

Afterwards Brendan seemed not to want to part with her and simply rolled over so she was lying on top of and astride him. Beneath her left ear, Tracy could hear the rapid rhythm of his heart, which was also her heart. She was soon asleep and when she woke up on Sunday he was gone.

THE SILENCE WAS the worst part. It was almost as though she had dropped off the face of the earth. The night when he'd crept into her bed, he wasn't sure whether he meant their love-making as an apology or a goodbye, and so he didn't stay. Because he knew Tracy didn't like to be left, he almost expected that she would call him on Sunday, but she didn't.

Brendan spent the day playing basketball and then went to Shawn's to spend some time with his godson. Riley watched him like a hawk as if trying to decipher his facial expressions and read it for things he did not say. He left at Cullen's bedtime and was himself asleep before ten.

On the second day, the day she left for Paris, Brendan went back to Brooklyn and found that Tracy had made the bed and cleaned the bedroom before she left. The rest of the townhouse was spotless as well, like a model unit where no one actually lived. The only reassuring thing was that she had washed and folded the clothes that he kept there and put them back in the drawer.

One entire side of the dresser, he recalled her saying when he first brought his clothes over. *You have no idea what a concession that is for a woman to make.*

That day they were playful, and she was sexy in faded jeans and tank top with no bra, her hair in a ponytail, her face devoid of make-up. Without make-up she looked so young, like a college girl. Even now, it was hard to reconcile that image with the one she'd painted for him, or her trolling bars, going home with men she barely knew, or didn't know at all.

He wanted to do what she asked him to do, put everything in the past and close the door, but how the hell was he supposed to promise that he could stop the tape playing in his head of her, naked and open, her body covered by someone else's?

By the third day, try as he might, there was also no escaping the fact that he didn't know yet what he was going to do. Still, one choice was clearly far more painful than the other—letting her go would mean taking the chance that one day he might arrive at Shawn's house in New Jersey, and Tracy would be with someone who had been man enough to face down her demons and claim her for himself. Someone who might marry her, maybe even start a family; someone who would close Tracy off from him for good. The possibility of her having that future —marriage, kids and family—without him was at least as painful, if not more so, than his recurring thoughts about her past.

On the day she was scheduled to return home, Brendan found himself unable to concentrate. Thoughts entered his mind and flitted away moments later. All he could focus on was the clock. She was landing at four. It would take her another two to three hours to get home. She would for sure be home by eight, more likely by seven.

At six he was at Shawn's condo, sitting with him in the den, listening to some of Sam Gaston's stuff. They were thinking of releasing the CD anyway, even without Sam around to help promote it. It would be risky, but they were banking on the music selling itself. A few people they had listen to it believed it was that good, and worth the risk.

Brendan glanced at the time. Six-seventeen now. Almost certainly she was home. She had driven her car to the airport, he knew, because he hadn't seen it parked on the street when he went by earlier in the week.

"What d'you think man?" Shawn asked.

Brendan looked at him blankly, having missed entirely whatever it was Shawn had asked him.

Shawn shook his head. "What's going on?" he asked finally.

"Nothing. Stuff with Tracy."

Shawn nodded. "She's a handful, isn't she?"

Brendan laughed. "You could say that."

"Thinking about quittin' that?" Shawn asked.

Brendan shrugged.

"You know how many times I thought about leaving Riley?" Shawn asked.

Brendan shook his head. "You never thought about leaving Riley," he scoffed.

"You kidding me?" Shawn said. "In the second year, I thought about it *constantly.*"

"The second year?" Brendan asked, skeptically. "By then she owned your ass. You ain't forget I was there, right? I saw how you felt about her."

"Exactly," Shawn said. "It was like a ... fight or flight response. There was no fighting how I felt about her, so flight was all that was left. I mean, I knew that this woman *had* me, man. Like I mean, *for life* had me. That's some scary shit. I had escape fantasies."

"I asked you about that just this year and you said permanent didn't scare you at all."

"Not now it doesn't. And even back then when I wanted to run, the funny thing was, I was more afraid she would let me go." Shawn shrugged. "Now I'm not sure whether that has shit-all to do with what you and Tracy are going through but I just thought I'd share."

Brendan laughed. "Thanks for the thought."

TRACY FELL backward onto her bed and flapped her arms and legs like someone making a snow angel. The beds in Paris had left much to be desired. In her hotel room at least, the mattress had been lumpy and uncomfortable. A quick relocation request hadn't made much of a difference. But in all other respects, the trip had been amazing. Even the conference was just short of boring.

In the afternoons, she had walked along the Seine and shopped in boutiques that in the States were just names on labels affixed to pricey clothing. She even splurged on a seven-hundred-dollar purse because the sales clerk convinced her that it was practically an investment. Shamefully, she hadn't been to a single museum though, and had confined her tourist time to shopping. Maybe next time she would check out the culture. She already knew there would be a next time because lumpy mattress notwithstanding, Paris had been beautiful and amazing.

Somehow the world seemed so much larger after a trip like that, and Tracy was beginning to wonder whether she might not think about doing a full European tour in the spring.

Still, by the time she landed at JFK, her thoughts were dominated by Brendan. She wanted to tell him everything, describe every incredible meal, each tiny gem of a boutique she "discovered" and every little trinket she bought. But in all honesty, she wasn't surprised to find the townhouse quiet and undisturbed when she got there.

For the past five nights, she had turned it over and over in her mind and decided that it was better to prepare herself for the worst. She wasn't prepared of course. It still hurt.

Tracy turned over and snuggled against her pillow, holding it close to her chest. Back to hugging pillows for a while. At the foot of the bed, there was one extra suitcase filled with the spoils of her Paris adventures, gifts for Riley, Russell, Cullen, Brendan and even something for Shawn. Something for each member of her little family of choice.

She sat up and contemplated unpacking, but decided to shower first, since she might want to try on some of her new stuff.

Alone in the shower, her thoughts shifted to Brendan again and she permitted herself a few minutes of self-pity before washing up. She stayed in only as long as it took her to get passably clean, because she was still a little tired. The warm water was soothing and made her even sleepier, so that when she was done, all she had energy to do was towel dry, shut off the lights, curl up on her side and go to sleep.

When she opened her eyes again it was morning and Tracy thought for a moment that she was dreaming. An arm was draped across her abdomen, and she was snugly wedged against a warm body. The pillow she went to sleep with had been tossed aside and her butt was pressed against a very familiar groin.

Still not sure she should believe, Tracy turned so she was facing him. He was there alright—her man. She studied his face as he slept; his lashes casting feathery shadows on his cheeks, the smooth line of hair on his jaw, his dimple visible even now. And the mouth that always looked as though it had, or was just about to smile.

Unable to help herself, she reached out and touched the side of his face. Brendan opened his eyes.

Tracy smiled at him and he smiled back, more with his eyes than his lips.

"Hi," she said.

"Hi," he returned, his voice hoarse. Brendan swallowed and cleared his throat. "You told me only to come if I was sure I was ready for you. Well, I'm here," he said. "And I'm ready."

Later, when they were both fully awake, they would talk and the conversation would be difficult. Or it would be easy. Maybe he found a way to put her past behind them and leave it there. Maybe he was still working on it.

Maybe he had decided that whatever she'd done before wasn't nearly as important as all the things they wanted to, and would do in the future. She hoped so, but Tracy had no way of knowing. Just as she had no way of knowing what the path ahead for their relationship would be like.

But he was here, and he said he was ready. And for now, that was enough. She moved closer, shut her eyes when he put his arms around her, and held on tight.

ABOUT THE AUTHOR

Nia Forrester lives and writes in Philadelphia, Pennsylvania where, by day, she is an attorney working on public policy, and by night, she crafts woman-centered fiction that examines the complexities of life, love, and the human condition.

Subscribe to Nia Forrester's Newsletter for free reads, exclusive samples, short stories, giveaways and more: https://bit.ly/2UorIXl

Reach her at: authorniaforrester@gmail.com

ALSO BY NIA FORRESTER

The 'Commitment' Novels

Commitment (The 'Commitment' Series Book 1)

Unsuitable Men (The 'Commitment' Series Book 2)

Maybe Never (A 'Commitment' Novella)

The Fall (A 'Commitment' Novel)

Four: Stories of Marriage (The 'Commitment' Series Finale)

The 'Afterwards' Novels

Afterwards (The Afterwards Series Book 1)

Afterburn (The Afterwards Series Book 2)

The Come Up (An Afterwards Novel)

The Takedown (An Afterwards Novel)

Young, Rich & Black (An Afterwards Novel)

Snowflake (An Afterwards Novel)

Rhyme & Reason (An Afterwards Novel)

Courtship (A Snowflake Novel)

The 'Mistress' Novels

Mistress (The 'Mistress' Trilogy Book 1)

Wife (The 'Mistress' Trilogy Book 2)

Mother (The 'Mistress' Trilogy Book 3)

The 'Acostas' Novels

The Seduction of Dylan Acosta (The Acostas Book 1)

The Education of Miri Acosta (The Acostas Book 2)

The 'Secret' Series

Secret (The 'Secret' Series Book 1)

The Art of Endings (The 'Secret' Series Book 1)

Lifted (The 'Secret' Series Book 3)

The 'Shorts'

Still—The 'Shorts' Book 1

The Coffee Date—The 'Shorts' Book 2

Just Lunch—The 'Shorts' Book 3

Table for Two—The 'Shorts' Book 4

The Wanderer—The 'Shorts' Book 5

À la Carte: A 'Coffee Date' Novella—The 'Shorts' Book 6

Silent Nights—The 'Shorts' Book 7

Not That Kind of Girl—The 'Shorts' Book 8

Resistance: A Love Story—The 'Shorts' Book 9

After the Fire—The 'Shorts' Book 10

À la Carte: The Complete 'Coffee Date' Novellas

Standalone Novels

Ivy's League

The Lover

Acceptable Losses

Paid Companion

The Makeover